Her arms encircled his neck, and she allowed herself to be engulfed by his passion. His erection pressed against her belly; she wanted him inside her.

"Baby, join me," he said, leading her to the tub and helping her into the water. She settled next to him and let her body relax.

He wanted to savor the moment. If, in all his dreams, he could have believed that one day she would be his and accept the love that had burned for her all these years, he would have saved himself a lot of misery.

Shelia sat still as Charles began to rub bath-oil over her body, starting with her shoulders and neck and then moving to her back. He sponged down her arms and hands. Facing her and looking into her eyes, he dribbled water over her collarbone and breasts. Shelia couldn't hide the blush that crept up to her eyes. Not even in her wildest dreams had she thought a man could cherish her this much. Layer after layer of self-consciousness slowly fell way, and she allowed herself to enjoy this pampering.

"Stand, Shelia."

Doing as she was told, she let Charles wash her from the hips down. The attention overwhelmed her. Her body shook with excitement and the anticipation of what was to come.

ONE OF THESE DAYS

MICHELE SUDLER

Genesis Press, Inc.

Indigo

An imprint of Genesis Press, Inc.
Publishing Company

Genesis Press, Inc.
P.O. Box 101
Columbus, MS 39703

ISBN-13: 978-1-58571-249-6
ISBN-10: 1-58571-249-3
Manufactured in the United States of America

First Edition

Visit us at www.genesis-press.com
or call at 1-888-Indigo-1

DEDICATION

There are so many women waiting for One of These Days to come their way.
So many women waiting for the man of their dreams,
Their knight in shining armor,
Who will help them to exhale.
Sometimes the wait is longer than expected,
Sometimes you have to get the wrong man out of your life
Before God brings the right man in.
That man has a goal and is on a mission.
He may not be a millionaire, or he might,
He may not be a movie star, or he might,
But what he is will give you the encouragement and support you need,
The happiness and joy you deserve,
And all the love and ecstasy you crave.
To Marvin "T-Bone" Thomas
Baltimore, Maryland

ACKNOWLEDGMENTS

To everyone who has supported me this past year in everything that I've been going through. I want to thank you.

To my children, Gregory, Takira, and Kanika Lambert who put up with me because, basically, they have no choice. Kisses.

To my daughter Tanisha Lambert, who is growing into a beautiful young lady. Love ya.

To my girls, always there through thick and thin: Cecilia Brokenbrough, Townsend, Delaware, and Cynthia D. Ford, Dover, Delaware. I love ya'll with everything. Dang, we go soooo far back. Remember the really fun times.

To my baby brothers, who I used to beat up on (literally) back in the day: Darryl "Butchie" Sudler and Marion "Jay" Sudler, both of Smyrna, Delaware. Ya'll are my hearts.

To my parents, Larry and Vondra Brokenbrough, of Dover, Delaware, who continue to give me support and encouragement and help with the kids. THANK YOU!!!

To my crazy aunt, Brenda L. Henry (Aunt Bea) of Smyrna, Delaware. Thank you for keeping me strong and going on with laughs, laughs, and more laughs. I love you too much.

And her crazier kids, Michael, Tiana, Annie, and my godson Josh Henry (thank God he's 21 now). Hugs and Kisses.

To her husband, Uncle Mike. Although we argue like we can't stand each other, you're always looking out for me. Love ya.

To Durand Arness Jones of Bear, Delaware, my boy of boys, who has helped me in so many ways and came into my life when, God knows, I needed him. Much love.

To the *In the Company of Sisters Book Club* of Dover, Delaware, whose members have held me down. Thank you.

To David "Pop" Williams and Darin "Cool" Williams, originally of Smyrna, Delaware and both serving in the US Army during these troubled times. God Bless.

To Yvonne "Bubbles" Henry-Whaley of Smyrna, Delaware, who is the best cousin a girl could ever have. Thanks for reading.

To Rickey "Pretty Rickey is what they call him" Harris of Baltimore, Maryland, my adopted older brother. Keep looking out. Peace.

PROLOGUE

Fourteen-year-old Shelia Daniels sat on the floor in the family den with her best friend Elizabeth, a bowl of popcorn between them. Her dog, Butter, a golden Labrador retriever, lay nearby. She and Liz spent most of their free time together. They loved watching old romance movies, looking at fashion magazines, and talking on the phone. They attended most school sporting events, especially football and basketball games—Shelia's brother played both sports—and all of the honor-society functions, but none of the really fun stuff. School dances and after-school socials were off-limits. On weekends, they took turns sleeping over at each other's house. That was her life and she was bored to death with it.

Leaning against the sofa's multicolored throw pillows that they had positioned on the floor, the two friends were about to watch a movie when they heard voices coming from the kitchen.

Shelia recognized one voice as that of her brother, Jeff. One of the voices she heard made her pulse jump.

A rush of color came to her cheeks, and she became keenly aware of her appearance, fussing with her shoulder-length, golden-brown ponytail and straightening her long-sleeved tan and blue peasant shirt over her new khaki-colored jeans.

Shelia wasn't going to win a popularity contest at Forest Oak High School, but she was seen as one of the best-dressed and prettiest girls in the ninth grade. Being popular was not a big deal to her. She had a 4.0 grade point average and excelled in science. She had bigger goals because all her accomplishments and dreams pointed to one thing— becoming a doctor. Having skipped the eighth grade, Shelia was some-what overwhelmed by the high-school experience. Elizabeth, who is a year older, was a big help in getting her acclimated to her new surroundings.

Jeff ambled into the den with two of his friends, Charles Avery and his cousin, Chauncey. Jeff and Charles were both eighteen and seniors in high school. They were the best of friends. Chauncey, two years older, had just recently started hanging out with them. Since the death of Brian, Shelia's oldest brother, the year before, he had begun to bring Jeff under his wing. Chauncey had been tagged as a tough guy around the neighborhood, but Shelia liked him.

"Ow," Shelia groaned when Jeff playfully tapped her across her forehead, something he did all the time. He called it his brotherly touch. She didn't complain about it anymore because she knew it was his way of expressing his love for her. Since Brian's death, he had become a lot more protective of her. And, unwittingly, the source of her problems.

"What's up, squirt?" he asked.

"Nothing. Liz and I are about to watch an old movie. Want to join us?" She reverently hoped that he would say yes, but she already knew his answer. When he left, his friends would leave, too. She didn't want Charles to leave.

Charles and Chauncey sat on the sofa, waiting for Jeff.

He doesn't even know I'm alive, she thought to herself, pretending to look at the opening credits of the movie in which she had lost interest.

"No, we're going to play some ball before the dance tonight," he answered casually, unknowingly dashing her hopes.

"Hey Shelia," Charles said, "pass the popcorn. Why are you hogging it?"

He didn't have anything better to do than to start picking on me, too, she thought. He did it every chance he got, unaware that she had a huge crush on him.

She handed Charles the popcorn, sneaking a look at him in the process. He was gorgeous—dark-brown skin, lean, muscular body. His eyes were light-honey brown set off by thick black lashes. A dimple appeared in his left cheek when he smiled. Over six feet tall, but not as tall as Jeff and Chauncey, Charles was the high-school heartbreaker. He was the guy who dated cheerleaders, female athletes, and the preppie girls.

Shelia, briefly losing herself in those eyes, was startled when he winked at her. She almost dropped the bowl of popcorn, but Charles caught it just in time, laughing.

Jeff and Chauncey also laughed at her. Shelia was embarrassed for having been caught with her heart on her sleeve, especially since it had not been lost on Charles.

Time to leave, Charles thought. "Come on, Jeff; the sun's leaving." Having looked at her really hard a few times, he thought she was cute, and was even interested in her, but she was his best friend's sister. Not that it should matter, because Jeff was going with his sister, Tia. But Tia was seventeen, and Shelia was only fourteen. Besides, he was beginning to get into things that she was too young for.

"All right. Shelia, you and Liz be good for Mom tonight. Dad's still out of town, and she doesn't need any hassles." Their dad worked for the state of Illinois as a social services director. Occasionally, he had to travel to the various state offices for conferences and training.

"Jeff, I'm fourteen years old. Stop treating me like a baby." Shelia slammed her palm against the coffee table for emphasis.

"Yeah, Jeff," Liz said, sticking up for her best friend. "Haven't you noticed your sister's growing up and filling out?" she asked, using her hands to demonstrate and hoping to help her friend get Charles' attention. "Pretty soon she'll have more dates than you can handle."

"Yeah, right. Shelia won't be dating anyone for a long, long time. Ain't nobody around here worth dating, anyway. Right, Shelia?"

"Jeff, I'd be dating right now if it weren't for you telling Daddy that I needed to be at least sixteen. I should be going to that school dance tonight. Guys do notice me, you know."

"Who notices you?" Jeff walked over and stared down at Shelia and Elizabeth. "Has somebody been trying to talk to you?" When she and Liz started giggling, Jeff got mad. "*Who*, Shelia?" Squaring his shoulders, he said, "You must be putting me on. You're only fourteen. Who would give you a second look except another fourteen year old?" He laughed as he moved away from them.

Charles put his head down and feigned interest in the basketball he was holding. He himself had taken more than a second look.

Chauncey, seeing his cousin's dilemma, defended Shelia. "Jeff, lay off her, man. Not that I'm interested or anything, mind you, but your sister is a cute girl. When she gets older, you probably will have your hands full. Come on, let's go."

"I don't know what you're talking about, Chauncey. I won't have my hands full because she's not going to have any boyfriends. I'll make that fact clear to everybody myself."

"Man," Chauncey replied, "you're not being reasonable. I said the same thing about my sisters. So did Charles, and you go with one of his sisters."

"That's different."

Charles sat back, not joining in the semi-serious exchange. Afraid of exposing himself, he wanted no part of the conversation.

"Well, what if Charles started dating Shelia?" Chauncey asked.

Charles stared incredulously at his cousin.

Shelia held her breath waiting for Jeff's reply.

"Charles? Yeah, right. Imagine that," Jeff said, laughing again.

"Yeah, imagine that." Chauncey had received a warning look from Charles but would not let the topic rest.

"Charles, would you be interested in my sister?"

"Whoa," Charles said. "Don't get me in the middle of this conversation. I'm just sitting here eating my popcorn."

"No, it's my popcorn," Shelia said, snatching the bowl from him, disgusted that he thought so little of her he couldn't be bothered with an answer to the question.

Charles looked at her apologetically. She had no clue. He did have feelings for her. And he definitely had to keep her brother in the dark about them. But Chauncey knew because he had caught Charles staring at her one day and had bugged him about it until he confessed.

"Look, man, let's go." Charles got up from the sofa, mad at both his cousin and Jeff for making Shelia mad at him. "I'll meet y'all outside."

Jeff watched him leave, curious about his sudden change in attitude. They were just joking with him.

After the guys left, Shelia turned back to the television, a defeated expression her face.

"He knows," Liz said, trying to boost her friend's self-esteem.

"He does not." She refused to allow herself to even imagine that possibility.

"Shelia, he winked at you, and I saw him peeking at you when Jeff went into the other room. And he got so mad at those guys for teasing you."

"Liz, you're imagining things. He doesn't even know I'm alive. He's about to graduate and go off to college or to sing somewhere. Every girl in school is after him because of his voice and his looks. He probably thinks I'm just a kid."

"Mark my words, Shelia Daniels, he notices you. You just wait. One of these days…"

CHAPTER 1

It had been too long. Charles could feel his excitement intensifying. His palms were sweating, his breathing uneven. Drawing a deep breath, he tried to suppress this familiar reaction. This is how it had been for as long as he could remember. But now, the situation had taken on a new urgency. This time, Charles was determined to reveal his feelings. If nothing came of it, so be it. He had nothing to lose by at least trying.

For nine years, he had patiently waited in the background for this flower to blossom. And blossom she did, having grown into the most beautiful woman he had ever seen. Charles remembered her voluptuous frame and long limbs from the last time they met. He had always stayed just within striking distance, or so he thought, trying to make sure that another man didn't come along and capture her love and attention. So far, no one had. But he couldn't believe it wouldn't happen sooner or later.

When he was away, he would ask his brother Troy about her. She was always away at school. But today she was here. If he was going to make any kind of move, Charles knew that it would have to be soon. Today. All he had to do was get up the courage, something easier said than done.

Charles wasn't used to being afraid. He usually just went after whatever he wanted. But with her, it was different, very different. He didn't know how to begin to approach her. He didn't want to admit it, but he knew he was just plain scared. He wanted her too badly.

Charles was aware of the little crush she had on him back in high school; a lot of younger girls had. It was probably because of his voice or his popularity. But no one knew how much in love with her Charles had been. Charles had kept that his deep, dark secret. After all, she was supposed to be like a little sister to him. Watching her now, he knew that his love had only grown stronger.

Having been a teenager then himself, Charles had done what teenagers do to suppress their unfulfilled yearnings. He had dated as many girls as he possibly could. When he finally settled on one steady girl, his strong desire for his true love was repressed for a short time. He never had any romantic interest in any of girls he had dated. None of them could to live up to her. None of them had made him feel the way she had. No one had given him goose bumps or had rattled his nerves. No one except Shelia.

Charles visited their house often in his youth, but his interaction with her was very limited. He needed it to be that way. Every so often while he waited for Jeff, he and Shelia would have small talk and joke around a little, but he never would allow himself to take it any further.

Beautiful, absolutely beautiful, thought Charles as he watched Shelia walk down the church's center aisle on the arm of his brother, Troy. He hadn't seen her since his parents' thirty-sixth wedding anniversary party two years ago. In between, he had visited home as often as he could, but they always missed each other.

It was Troy who kept Charles up on home news when he was away. Based on the many questions his brother had asked about Shelia, Troy had figured out for himself how Charles felt about her. They were as close as two brothers could be, and Charles couldn't have hidden his feelings from him if he had tried. A smile on his face, he watched his younger brother's reaction to seeing this beauty again. When he took his place next to Charles at the front of the church, Troy nudged him to bring his attention back to the ceremony.

The nudge wasn't much help. He did take his eyes off her, but only briefly. His eyes were soon back on her. Watching her made Charles think about how lonely he had been lately. Something was seriously lacking in his life. In his heart, he knew it was Shelia.

Yes, he was a huge success, and yes, he had tons of money. People loved his music, and he had many adoring fans. He had a loving family and good friends. And he had every reason to be happy, really happy. But he was lonely, very lonely. He had to fix that.

Determination sparred with fear as Charles debated going after what he wanted. He didn't want to be lonely for the rest of his life, and no one had done for him what he thought Shelia could. The mere thought of her lifted his spirits and made him smile.

A soft smile played on her face as she watched the rest of the wedding party come down the aisle. When she looked at him, he thought his heart was going to explode. That's what was missing; that's what he craved. He barely noticed the rest of the procession because he couldn't stop looking at her.

She stood, graceful and serene, across the aisle, her back straight and a sensual smile on her lips. It wasn't a fake smile; nothing about her was. The soft skin of her chestnut-brown shoulders, bared by the spaghetti straps of her flowing lavender bridesmaid dress, gleamed brightly in the subdued lighting.

Today was a very special day for his family, and Charles was going to make it a special day for himself, too. He would just be patient and wait for his opportunity. Then he would seize it and pray that his dreams become reality.

When he finally tore his eyes away, his sister Tia and her best friend, Denise, were being walked down the aisle by his father. Charles was the best man for Jeff and Chauncey.

Jeff was finally marrying Tia, and Chauncey was marrying Denise. Both weddings had been a long time coming, and the church was filled with overjoyed friends and family members, there to witness the two unions.

Charles felt honored when Jeff and Chauncey had asked him to be their best man. The two had been his boys since forever, keeping him out of trouble and being his biggest boosters.

He and Jeff had been friends since his family first moved from the projects into the new neighborhood. Jeff befriended him without judgment when others wouldn't, and their bond had grown stronger over the years. Chauncey's family moved out of the projects almost seven years later. By his teenage years, he had already been labeled the bad apple in the family, but he had struck up an unlikely friendship with Jeff's brother, Brian. When Brian was killed in an automobile accident his second year of college, Chauncey felt duty-bound to look after Jeff. He believed he owed it to his best friend. From then on, they were a threesome.

This was one appearance Charles couldn't miss. He had doubled several recording sessions and rescheduled two interviews to carve out two weeks of vacation. In any case, a break from his hectic schedule was desperately needed. The last two years had been jam-packed with career-related obligations.

His career as a recording artist seemed to have taken off almost overnight. It was easy to think that way now that he was where he wanted to be. But he did have a few hard years in the beginning that he would sooner forget.

After touring as a backup singer for four years, he signed his own record deal. His first CD was released soon after. The record exceeded expectations by going to number two on the music charts and selling over two million copies. After a short concert and promotional tour, Charles had gone back to the studio to work on his second album. He currently had singles at the number two and five spots, both of which were steadily climbing the charts. He sang mostly rhythm and blues and slow tunes, and both adults and teenagers loved his music and both groups attended his concerts.

Charles couldn't remember a time when he didn't want to sing. He used to sing everywhere when he was younger—in church, at talent shows, and for private parties. In fact, that was how he earned most of his money while still in high school. Unlike other kids his age, Charles had been smart enough to make business cards and flyers advertising his availability for weddings, conventions and other events. He had been very successful once word spread about his talents. He still missed those days. That was why coming home was important to him.

His family was very proud of him, but when he came home, he was just Charles. He loved them all the more for that. They joked with him, made fun of him, and did not make too much of his star status, something he sometimes needed to forget.

Shelia couldn't believe he was really there. Charles, her Charles, was standing in front of the altar, as handsome as ever. She was suddenly struck with an irrational urge to check her hair and makeup. She had to fight the impulse to smooth her hair. Could she stop halfway down the aisle and run to the bathroom to freshen up? *That's ridiculous*, she thought. Still, if she could have gotten away with it, she might have tried.

Shelia knew he was expected, but he had missed the rehearsal and dinner the night before, and she didn't think he would be at the wedding. Nobody had told her he had arrived. Understandable, since she had kept her feelings for Charles very well hidden over the years.

Liz had been her only confidante. Shelia couldn't count the number of times she had called her friend in the middle of the night complaining because Charles was dating another cheerleader or she had seen him at the mall or the movies with this or that girl. And she acted even crazier when he showed her a little attention. She knew that Liz had endured a lot over the years listening to her frustrations, but that's what true-blue friends did for one another.

Shelia focused on the present—and on Charles. As if having a mind of their own, her hands began to shake, and she involuntarily tightened her hold on Troy's arm. Trying to compose herself, she looked away, only to sneak another peek at him a second later.

Troy patted her hand, giving her an encouraging wink. She liked him; he always seemed to sense when something was wrong. Good thing he didn't actually know, though. She wouldn't be able to face him if she thought he did. In fact, if anyone had guessed what she was thinking, her embarrassment would be unbearable.

She had loved Charles for as long as she could remember. But now he was a big-time recording artist. No way would he want someone like her. He was probably dating a model or actress in California. There was no reason for her to get her hopes up. He was here to support his sister and friends, not to see her.

The wedding reception was held at Chauncey's self-named night-club. On the way there, the new brides and grooms rode in one limousine; other members of the wedding party rode in another. Charles unsuccessfully tried to sit next to Shelia, wanting to talk. So far, he had only managed a quick hello. His eyes kept going to her face, and he was only half listening to the chattering wedding attendants. He had been so focused on her at the church he could barely recall details of the ceremony. She had to have seen him sneaking peeks at her. Troy had elbowed him at least twice during the ceremony. He was sure that everyone in the church had noticed his inattention during the wedding.

"Penny for your thoughts, lil' brother," his sister Kristal prodded.

"Oh, just thinking. Nothing important," he replied.

"Could have fooled me. You seem so preoccupied today. It can't be that bad. How's life been as a multimillion-dollar recording artist, anyway?"

"I wouldn't exactly call it that, but it can get pretty lonely. I really miss you guys." Knowing how alert this sister could be, Charles tried to change the subject. Out of his five sisters, Kristal was the most perceptive. She could read emotions, body language, and voice patterns. The woman noticed everything. That's what has made her a successful businesswoman.

"We miss you, too." Kristal added knowingly, "All of us."

"Uh-oh," somebody said. "Will you look at this?" As the limousine turned the final corner on its approach to *Chauncey's*, a crowd that had been standing on the sidewalk began making its way to the curbside.

"See, this is the last thing I wanted," Charles said under his breath, a frown creasing his handsome features.

The mob consisted of women of all ages, shapes, and colors. They screamed and held signs bearing his pictures, blocking the front door to the club. "WE LOVE YOU, CHARLES!" they chanted.

Walking over to their limo, Chauncey signaled for his security to call for reinforcements. "Well, folks, seems like news travels fast," he joked.

"I'm really sorry about this, man," Charles apologized, looking helpless and frustrated.

"No sweat. Everybody else get out first. My security will get you through the crowd."

"Thanks, man." Charles didn't like the intrusion thrust upon his family. He was used to it and could handle it, but to have his family exposed to this was unacceptable.

"Hey, it's the price you pay for being related to a celebrity, right?" Chauncey gave him a pat on his knee, trying to ease his discomfort. Everybody in the limo laughed—except for Charles. He really had just wanted a quiet vacation. And it bothered him that he was being denied. Occasionally, over the past year, he had wondered if it was worth it. Was the fame and fortune worth his privacy?

Shelia saw that his disappointment was real and wished she could get out of the limo and tell these obsessed women to get a life. Security pushed at the crowd until Charles was safely inside the building. But on his way in, he did sign a few autographs, not wanting to disappoint his fans.

Posing as guests, one or two fans managed to get into the reception. Security quickly removed anyone they didn't know or who did not have an invitation.

The reception finally got under way, but Charles kept to the wedding table. He came home to be a part of an important family event, not to be in the spotlight. This was a day for his sister and friends, and he wasn't about to detract from that. This was their celebration, their time to shine.

At Tia's request, Charles sang a song to the newlyweds after the food had been served. Then, before the traditional wedding rituals started, he stood and toasted them. Everyone was having a good time eating, drinking, and socializing.

"Excuse me, everyone, may I have your attention, please," the wedding coordinator said cheerfully into the microphone in the center of *Chauncey's* small stage. "I need all of the single ladies on the dance floor, please. All single ladies to the dance floor. We are about to have the throwing of the wedding bouquets. Ladies, gather around the floor, and no fighting, please. You have two chances at luck today."

The eligible women quickly began moving onto the floor. Shelia decided to stay in her seat. She wasn't about to go out there and make a fool of herself. She was almost a doctor, for goodness sake. But there were doctors, friends of the family and single, already out on the dance floor. So that wasn't a good excuse. She just didn't want to be the center of anyone's attention. Well, maybe one someone, but that was different.

"Wait a minute," Shelia heard Jeff say. "My sister." Smiling, he pulled out her seat.

No, he didn't, she thought, putting her head down.

"Shelia, come on and get on out there, squirt." She didn't move, and neither did he. If she didn't make a move soon, even more people would start looking at them, and she did not relish such attention. Now was not the time to stand up to her brother.

Giving him a murderous look, Shelia reluctantly allowed Jeff to pull her from her seat. She then made her way to the back of the dance floor.

Denise threw her wedding bouquet first, and Devin, Charles and Tia's youngest sister, claimed it after a short struggle with one of their friends from high school. The crowd shouted its approval, but Shelia just moved even further back, trying to remain unnoticed.

"Okay, ready?" Tia looked around the room slowly. She waited for the women to return to their original positions. Tia got a good look at where her intended target was standing and prayed that her aim was still sharp. If she had been facing front, she would have aimed right for Shelia's head. *Who were they fooling? Everybody in the room could see how hard they were trying not to look at each other, which only made it all the more obvious.* Her determination to hit her target mounted.

As Tia got set to throw, Shelia moved back even further, but her worst nightmare came true when the bouquet landed right in front of her. It flew high across the room aimed right at her face. She had to grab it before it hit her. Shelia hadn't wanted to catch the darn thing. It was such a silly tradition, with a very silly dream attached to it.

Who would even want to be the next to marry? Why even build false hope on such silliness? But as soon as she had the bouquet in her hands, she felt unexpected excitement. While she stood there smiling, Tia came over and gave her a quick hug.

"Thought you could get away from me, didn't you?" Tia laughed. "Don't you remember? I was the starting pitcher on the softball team all four years I was in school."

"I guess I shouldn't have forgotten," Shelia answered.

The men sheepishly started gathering for their turns at being big fools.

Tia and Denise took their places in the chairs at the front of the room and allowed their new husbands to remove their garters. The crowd cheered as Jeff and Chauncey each took his very slow time removing his wife's garter. Chauncey used his mouth, and Jeff his hands, but they both seemed to stay under the gowns an awfully long time. When the two grooms finally emerged with the garters, Chauncey threw his first. Chris, Devin's fiancé, caught it with a flying leap from out of nowhere. Jeff threw his, and nobody tried to catch it. It went right to Charles. He didn't have to jump or leap. Nobody tried to snatch it from him. They all kind of stepped back. When he looked up at Jeff and Chauncey, they were both grinning at him.

"Why do I feel like I was just set up?" he asked, walking toward them.

"I'm not going to say whether you were or weren't," said Jeff.

Chauncey patted him on the back and said, "Just enjoy it."

Hesitantly, Charles looked at Jeff. He wasn't quite sure if he was seeking permission. Heck, why did he even feel he needed it? He and Shelia were both adults. But for some crazy reason, he wanted some kind of approval from his friend. So he waited for an okay. When he finally got the nod, before walking off, he said, "Don't worry, I will."

Chauncey winked at Jeff. "He looks just like a kid at Christmas."

"Well, he's been waiting a long time for this opportunity. I just hope it all goes well."

"So you knew how he felt?" Chauncey asked.

"I'm not blind," Jeff said, winking back at his new cousin-in-law. "He's been looking at her since she was about fifteen years old. At first I didn't like it; then I tried to ignore it. But it never went away. I finally realized that it wasn't going to. Hell, then I saw that she was looking right back at him. It doesn't take a genius. It just shows how much of a man he is to have waited this long."

"It also shows how much of a friend to you he is. Hell, any other man would have tried to date her anyway. Not that I ever really noticed, but Shelia is a fox, man. If you weren't so built and had even bigger friends, a lot more guys would have gone after her. They were just afraid to try."

"Believe me, I know," Jeff laughed. "I'm just glad I didn't have to go through it. I had enough dealing with the little nerds and knuckle-heads that wouldn't go away. But I could tell that she wasn't interested in them. Now, if Charles would have just said 'Boo' to her back then,

I would have been in real trouble. I know my sister. If she had known he was even the least bit interested, she would have gone after him full force."

"Oh, yeah? Well it's a good thing she didn't know because he was looking at her way before she turned fifteen."

"Ha. Don't tell her that. Her head is big enough as it is." Laughing, they went looking for their wives.

Putting the garter on Shelia's leg had been hard for Charles. His hands were shaking, and he could feel beads of sweat on his forehead. All thoughts were of his hands moving further up. He knew it would be wrong of him, but if she smiled that smile of hers at him one more time, he was going to risk it. It was that smile that told him she was aware of his dilemma and was willing to help him out. At least that's what he wanted it to say. In the end, Charles did what was expected of him; he acted like a complete gentleman. But how he wished that he hadn't.

Chris had no problem showing off for Devin. Charles didn't like seeing his little sister being kissed up her leg, but she was all grown up now. Besides, she was Chris' fiancée and the mother of his twin daughters. He had to keep reminding himself of that.

Right now, Charles was trying to also remember that Shelia was someone's baby sister. But unwelcome thoughts kept coming to the forefront, and he was unsuccessfully dealing with his own grown-up urges.

Shelia went back to the table and sat down. She had to get herself together. Her leg was still burning along the path his hand had taken to put on the garter. Her feelings for this man were clearly still very strong. But what was she going to do about it? What could she do?

Before she could organize her thoughts, the wedding party was called to the dance floor. Troy came over and took her by the hand to join the rest of the wedding party in a slow dance.

"Are you feeling all right?" His concern was strictly medical. "You look a little flustered."

"Must be from all this excitement," she quickly answered.

Knowing the real reason, he decided to change the subject for her benefit. "I've been meaning to ask you how your studies were going, but I'm sure you're not having any problems. And I want you to be sure to let me know when you're ready to do a full residency at the hospital."

"No. No problems. Everything is going just fine. Howard University is great. And I'm way ahead of my curriculum. I should be—" Shelia didn't get to finish her sentence.

"Excuse me, brother. May I cut in? Kristal said she wanted to talk to you."

Shelia tensed up at the sound of his harmonious voice.

"Of course, man," Troy smiled. With a wink to Charles, he left to find Kristal and give her thumbs up for sending Charles over.

"Finally, Shelia Daniels," Charles said, as he put his large hands around her narrow waist. "I have you all to myself." Putting on what he hoped was his best smile, Charles looked directly into her eyes. He wondered if she could feel his heart beating out of rhythm.

Shelia had to struggle to find her voice. She wanted to at least give the appearance of being under control. "Seems like you do," she barely managed to get out. She stared at his neck as she worked on settling her nerves. She could feel the muscular outline of his body. Charles had always been good-looking. His hazel eyes and strongly defined face made women daydream about an evening with him. In a family of extremely handsome men, he was easily the best-looking. But she probably was biased.

"Can I ask you a question?" Charles flexed his fingers as he pulled her closer.

"Sure." Shelia loved the feel of his hand resting possessively on her back.

"Now don't dog me too much after this. But at the risk of sounding like an old movie, where have you been all of my life?" They both burst into laughter.

Shelia allowed herself to flirt with him just a little. She was still a nervous wreck. "Well, you know how I love my old movies, Charles. So I'm going to let that slide, but you could have done better than that. You're just trying to embarrass me. All of my life I've been right under your nose, and you haven't noticed me one bit."

Looking deep into her eyes, Charles disagreed, "I noticed you, Shelia. Ever since you were fourteen years old, I've been noticing you."

Shelia couldn't believe what she was hearing. It couldn't be true. "Oh, well, if you noticed me, then why did you wait until I was twenty-three to approach me?"

"Well, at first you were too young," he laughed. "Then I was too busy. Besides, now you're at Howard University, and I'm living in California. I guess our timing has always been off. Listen, I'm home on vacation for two weeks, and you're on summer break. Do you think we could get together some time before I leave?" His hands tightened around her waist.

Shelia listened to the music, but she still heard everything he had just said. It was definitely not something she had expected when she rolled out of bed this morning. Her day was looking better with each passing moment. But, she warned herself to be cautious and play it cool.

"Are you serious?" She looked into his eyes, searching for an answer. He was serious. "Charles, wait a minute. This is going too fast. You know I've had a crush on you for darn near my whole life. The last time we saw each other was two years ago. We had a good time together that night, dancing and drinking. But you never called after that. I know you were busy with your career. I probably just disappeared from your mind." Shelia was starting to ramble, but she had to make her point. "I just don't want to be sitting around waiting for you to call or wondering where you are or who you're with." There, she thought, cool or not, she got it all out.

"Shelia, I would never do you like that." Taking a step back, Charles looked at her disbelievingly, almost belligerently. "Do you realize how long I've waited to be able to come and talk to you like this? I mean, I know you had a crush on me when you were in school, but a lot of the younger girls did. I thought you just had a passing fancy for me. I liked you back then. I wanted to talk to you, but I knew it wasn't right. Besides, Jeff would have had a fit. If I had known it was more than a crush, I would have talked to you about it."

"Well, it was a lot more than a crush." They had stopped dancing and were standing in the middle of the floor, unaware that they were attracting attention. "Look Charles, I just don't think I'm what you're looking for to fill in the space between Miss March and Miss June. I'm not a one-night fling sort of girl. I don't want to get hurt."

"First of all," he said, glaring down at her, "you are exactly what I've been looking for, waiting for. I don't know anything about Miss March and Miss June. You know you really do know how to hurt a fellow, Shelia," he took her arm and rubbed it gently. "Do you feel that? Don't you want to find out what it could mean?"

The current sparked by his touch spread throughout her body. She couldn't deny what had been there for so long.

"Yeah, I feel it. And to be totally honest, it scares me a little. Charles, I have too many things going on right now." Was she stupid? Was she actually trying to ward off any affection from Charles? Shelia couldn't believe she had said that. She finally looked up and saw her parents staring at them. "We're causing a scene."

Charles looked up, too, and saw his parents staring at them. Taking her arm, he led her to the VIP section on the third floor of the club. The winding staircase gave him time to formulate his next course of action.

"Shelia," he started to explain once they were seated in a corner booth, "I'm not trying to come between you and your plans or goals or dreams. I would like to be a part of them, if possible. All I want is to spend some time with you. Can't we get to know each other better? I'm not asking you to marry me tomorrow."

"Well, I know me, and I'm being honest with myself and you. I'm still in love with you, Charles." There it was. Shelia had let it out, all out. Now, he would have to deal with it one way or another. And so would she. "I have loved you for the last nine years behind the scenes. If we started to date or talk or whatever you call it, my feelings may be up here," she said, using her hands to demonstrate, "and yours may be down here. I know you're used to your little celebrity girlfriends. What could you possibly want with me?"

"You believe everything you see, huh?" His lips formed a cynical smile. "I don't have any celebrity girlfriends. I have friends who are celebrities. Some I have dated, but nothing serious ever came of it. Besides, if you've been in love with me for the past nine years, as you say you've been, and you've watched me, then you know that I could never care about any of those women."

"I just don't want to be hurt," she said again, stark fear glittering in her eyes.

"You keep saying that. Why don't you just enjoy the here and now? I'm not trying to pressure you into anything. I want us to enjoy each other's company and conversation, at your pace."

"Okay, but I'm still a little scared."

"Do I scare you?" he asked.

Giggling, she said, "Yes, you do. No matter how much you want to, you can never be just Charles Avery, neighborhood boy. You're a star."

"That's why I'm glad to be home for these two weeks. Being the recording star can get pretty tiring sometimes. Let's just be Charles and Shelia, okay?" he asked, running a finger down her nose.

"Okay," she reluctantly agreed.

"My car is in the parking lot. After the reception, can I give you a ride home?"

"I guess that's as good a start as any," she answered.

Hand in hand, they returned to the dance floor.

CHAPTER 2

Charles pulled in front of Shelia's house and put his rental car in park. He had a lot to say, but he didn't know where to start. Just looking at her made his heart beat faster. It had always been that way. He had yearned for this opportunity for the longest time, and now that it was here, he didn't want to move too fast and scare her away.

"So, where do we go from here?" She wanted to know what was on his mind; how he felt about things.

"Let's just sit here and talk for a minute, unless you're too tired. I'll understand. It's after eleven, and you've had a very busy day." Charles thought he was being considerate; Shelia thought otherwise.

"There you go treating me like a little kid again. I told you once, I'm twenty four now. I'm not Jeff's dependent little sister anymore. This year I will be in my last year of medical school. Funny thing is, your sister Devin and I are the same age, I graduated a year earlier because I skipped eighth grade, but she's treated like an adult. I guess it's because she has kids. That's not fair. Next year, I'll be a doctor, and my family will probably still be treating me like a teenager."

"Whoa, hold on a minute, girl. That sure was a lot to get off your chest. I'm sorry for the way you feel you're being treated. Maybe you just bring out a kind of protective instinct in people. You do in me."

"Well, I don't need to be protected, okay?" Shelia spat out.

"Okay."

They were silent for a minute, both feeling the need to reevaluate their thoughts. Shelia decided that another subject was in order.

"Charles, tell me about living in California."

"There's really nothing to tell."

"Yeah, right."

"No, really. I'm hardly ever there. With all the touring and promo- tions, I guess I could make a home practically anywhere and just travel when necessary. I was thinking about moving to New York. It's a little closer to home, and that's where I spend most of my time when I'm not touring."

"Well, tell me about some of the people you've met."

"Just usual folks. The stars that I have met I didn't get to know that well. I'm not into all the hoopla. I just want to make a career doing something that I love doing and am good at."

"Well, you're definitely a good singer. Your songs really touch people. You sing about things that people can relate to. You lift fallen spirits and mend broken hearts. People need that in their lives."

"Thanks, Shelia. Hearing you say that is more important to me than any of those awards I have in my den. Look, it's getting late. I don't want to keep you out too long."

Shelia looked at him. "What did I just tell you? I'll say when it's getting too late, Charles."

"Yes, ma'am," he laughed, yawning. "Would you like to go get something late night?"

"Sure, why not. I didn't eat much at the reception."

They pulled out and headed to the local diner. Twilight Haven was the only all-night diner in that part of town. On weekends, it was usually crowded with partygoers. The parking lot was always overrun with high-school kids. They used it as a meeting place and drove around the parking lot, wasting gas.

Shelia remembered the fun she and Liz used to have on Friday nights when they would beg Liz's older sister to give them a ride to the diner. They would sit inside at a booth near a window and watch the other kids huddle in their social cliques. She and Liz didn't have a clique; they had each other. Shelia had dreamed of the day that Charles would ask her out on a date and take her to the Haven for everyone to see. It never happened.

Instead, he paraded around with a string of cheerleaders, drama queens, and athletes before he settled on Caryn Thomas. That was her first real heartbreak. She went into a deep depression for weeks, and except for Liz, nobody ever knew it.

Then one day she overheard Jeff talking to Tia on the phone. Apparently, Tia had gotten into a fight that day at school with Caryn because she and Charles had broken up. Caryn had gone crazy. She had tried to fight Charles and kept calling the house at all hours of the night. That was the best day of her high-school experience.

Shelia brought herself back to the present day, having heard only part of the joke Charles had just finished telling. Shelia laughed anyway. This felt good to her; she was happy that he had finally brought her here. It had only taken nine years.

Inside, they sat in a booth near the back and looked at menus. They were enjoying each other's company, joking about things in the past, and about their families and friends. They were comfortable with each other. Probably because they were old friends.

"Can I take your order?" a waitress asked automatically as she walked to the table. She looked up from her order pad and realized who she was serving.

"Yes, I'd like…"

"Oh, my God…oh, my God," the waitress blurted out, dropping her pad on the floor and placing her hand over her mouth. "Do you know who you are?" she whispered, her hands shaking. She was drawing a lot of unwanted attention their way.

Charles smiled at her, saying, "Yes, I know who I am. I'm Charles, and this is Shelia."

"No, you're…you're Charles Avery. Oh, my God. Charles Avery, here in this diner."

"Yeah, um, I'd like to have the steak and eggs breakfast and a cup of black coffee," he said, wanting to save her, and them, from further embarrassment.

"Oh, I'm sorry. Of course you would," she said, retrieving her order pad.

"Make that two," Shelia said. "I'd like the same, please."

"Sure, right away. Oh, wait until I tell my mom," the waitress said, rushing off. But before handing in their orders, she stopped at two other booths. She also used the phone. By the time their food arrived, Charles had signed a handful of autographs, and the diner had mysteriously become crowded.

"Shelia, we can get our food to go if you want," he suggested, secretly hoping she would agree. This was one of those invasions of privacy that made him uncomfortable.

"No, I wouldn't dream of depriving these people of their chance to meet a hometown hero," she replied. She sympathized with his uneasiness, but didn't want to be seen as responsible for disappointing his fans.

He smiled at her and said, "I wouldn't quite put it like that, but thanks." Charles was ready to go, but he stayed, signing autographs and answering a stream of questions until he noticed it was after one in the morning. Shelia kept trying to stifle her yawns with her hand. "Okay, folks," he said to the crowd, "it's time for me to get going. Thanks for your support."

It took them another thirty minutes to make it to the car, because every few steps someone who had just pulled into the lot came running up to him.

"You sure did cause a ruckus," Shelia joked when they were finally back inside the car.

"I'm appreciative of my fans, but it gets harder and harder to find some alone time. I didn't come to Forest Park to stay locked up in the house. I want to visit the school and see Mrs. Jeffers, my old chorus teacher, without causing a scene. I want to visit friends and family without being disturbed. Most of all, I want to be able to be with you without people intruding on our time together. I can't even go to a restaurant without it becoming a mob scene."

"Well, that just shows you how much your fans love you. I think that you should go to the school and maybe give the kids a song or two, so they can see that someone from here can make it big if he tries hard enough."

"I know, but I can't give up every inch of myself. I have to keep something for me and the people that I care about, or I'll go crazy." Charles sighed, briefly looking out the driver-side window. He didn't want her to see how upsetting it was for him.

"That's true. I see your point. It must be hard. A lot of people just see the glamour of it." Shelia wished she could do more than feel sorry for him.

Back in front of the house, Charles said. "Your folks are home."

"Yeah, they had a great time tonight. They darn near did back flips when they learned Tia was pregnant—again."

"Is she?" he asked, surprised. "That makes number three. They sure don't waste any time, do they?"

"I guess they figure they've wasted enough time. I just hope she doesn't go through what she did the last time."

"Yeah, I heard she had a pretty rough pregnancy. I know it was hard on them both. Troy called me to tell me about it. It's times like those when I know I need to be here. Jeff and Tia are strong, though. That's why they made it."

"Charles, love makes you strong."

"Yeah, you have to definitely have love."

"Denise is pregnant, too."

"Really? Is that what Chauncey was running around hollering about?"

"Yeah, wasn't that cute? As big as he is, all muscles and stuff, running around crying like that. He was mush all day long." Shelia fell quiet for a minute. Opening up, she revealed a dearly held goal. "I can't wait 'til I can get started on a family. But my career is first."

"Shelia Daniels, I didn't know you wanted to have a family."

"Don't most women want families? Why would I be any different?" she added, offended. "Oh, let me guess, because I've been a bookworm all my life?"

"No, I just never thought about it," Charles apologized. "So tell me, how big a family do you think you would like?"

"A husband, of course, and maybe three or four kids. Two girls and two boys," Shelia firmly stated. "And I wouldn't mind a dog."

"Two girls and two boys?" Charles laughed. "And what if it doesn't work out that way? As a future doctor, I'm sure you know that you really don't have any control over that unless you plan to opt out of the usual route."

"Please. I am definitely going to go about it the normal way. That's half the fun, isn't it?" Shelia laughed.

"Okay, it's time for you to go," Charles said decisively. "You're starting to put thoughts in my head."

"Are you afraid of those thoughts?" she asked.

"Shelia, you're flirting with me, and that could be very dangerous for you." He got out of the car and went around to open her door. "It's better if you went in." She turned to face him as they walked to the front door.

"Charles, are you afraid of me?" She looked him directly in the eyes so that he couldn't evade the question.

"No, don't be ridiculous," Charles replied. "I'm just trying to get you safely in the house."

"I told you I was a big girl. Okay," she said, giving up, "I'll behave. When am I going to see you again? Next year at your family reunion maybe?"

"Don't be smart. What are you doing tomorrow?"

"I have to go to the hospital in the morning. I intern there during the summer. I don't get off duty until two in the afternoon."

"Well, I'll pick you up there at two o'clock, and we'll have a late lunch."

"Sounds good to me," Shelia readily agreed.

They stood at the front door of Shelia's house in silence. Charles didn't know how to go about saying good night. Should he kiss her or just walk off? If she were one of his regular dates, he would have her in his arms by now—or in his bed. But she wasn't just a nobody with a cute face and a nice body. This was Shelia Daniels, the woman he had been dreaming about for so many years. He just didn't want to make any mistakes. Plus, he felt himself getting excited by the simple promise of holding her. Not being able to control himself would be unbearably embarrassing.

Shelia was not going inside the house without a kiss; she had made up her mind about that. After waiting nine years, she was dying to find out how kissing him would feel.

"Well, are you going to kiss me or what?" she asked him impatiently.

"Shelia, could you let me do this?" Looking at her, he said, "It's not that easy, okay?"

In a challenging voice she said, "Okay, but what happened to just being Shelia and Charles and not the recording star and Jeff's little sister?" She stared him squarely in the face, waiting for a reply.

"You're right." Pulling her closer, but not so close that she could feel him growing harder, he looked into her eyes and slowly began to kiss the corners of her mouth. He was moving slowly and trying to keep control of himself. His hand tensed up on her arm. Taking his time, he covered her mouth with his own.

Shelia leaned into the kiss and put her hands around his neck. She could have sworn she felt an electric shock move down her back, reaching her toes. She moaned as his tongue slipped into her mouth, exploring. She impulsively moved closer to the warmth he was offering her. His manhood pressed against her stomach. She moved further into his embrace. Her arms pulled him closer.

With a groan, Charles began to run his hands up and down her back, coming to rest on her backside. He gave her a little squeeze.

Shelia's blood was boiling. She didn't want to stop because it felt so good. It was everything she had dreamed about for the last nine years.

"Um, Shelia, we had better stop this now," Charles urged. While he was trying to get his senses back on track, she was putting little kisses on his face and neck. His hands had moved to her hips, and she was grinding herself against him.

I'm only human, he thought. "Shelia," he whispered, taking a step back. Charles took both of her hands in his and held them together between them. They needed some space before the inevitable happened. "I'll see you tomorrow at two."

It took Shelia a minute to open her eyes and focus. "Oh, okay, I'll see you then."

He gave her another quick kiss and stepped back so she could open the door.

"Good night, Charles." She looked back, smiling at him as she closed the door.

"All right, good night, Shelia."

Closing the door behind her, Shelia leaned her head against the door with her hand still wrapped around the brass knob, trying to wipe the broad smile off her face. Her heartbeat began to slow down after she could no longer hear the sound of his car. She then moved to the staircase and went up to her room.

Taking the steps two at a time, she danced down the hall until she was in her room and reaching for the phone.

"Hey, girl," she chanted happily when Liz's phone was picked up.

"I ain't no damn girl, Shelia," a deep masculine voice answered.

"Sorry, Gregg. I didn't expect you to be answering," she said to Liz's live-in boyfriend, Chauncey's younger brother.

"Who did you expect?"

"My girl. It is her house too, ain't it? Gregg, I don't have time for you. Just put her on the phone." She and Gregg got along pretty well most of the time, but then there were those times when jealousy got the best of him. At those times, he didn't want Liz around anyone else, including Shelia.

"Shelia, it's after two in the morning. You woke my ass up."

"Then it must be important. Damn, Gregg, just put her on the phone."

"Hold on a minute, girl. Liz, your damn girl wants you."

Hearing the rustling and giggling in the background, she realized too late that she had interrupted something. She wished she had somebody to make her giggle like that.

"Hey girl, what's up?" Liz asked, dropping the phone and breaking into more giggles.

"You know what, girl. I'm going to call you tomorrow. You go ahead and handle your business."

Suddenly serious, Liz fell silent on the phone. "Are you sure, Shelia? If you have something to talk about, you know I'm here for you."

"No, it wasn't anything that can't wait until tomorrow."

"I saw you leave with Charles. Is everything all right?"

"Yeah. You go ahead. I'll call you tomorrow. Everything's all good. I'll call you."

"All right."

Shelia sat on the queen-size bed that was decorated with lavender and mint-green pillows, matching her comforter and curtains, and removed her shoes and clothes. Smartly, she had packed a bag so that she could change her clothes after the wedding rituals ended and the real party began. Grabbing her cleansing cream, she went to the white vanity table next to her white dresser and studied her chestnut-brown complexion, disgusted to see an outbreak of dark bumps on her cheekbones. Too much chocolate will do that to you, but the cleansing cream was her weapon in maintaining blemish-free skin.

She wasn't quite sure if this was the right time for them to act on their attraction for one another. He was in the middle of a recording career; she was away at college. True, she was in love with him, but was it still the same puppy love that it once was? But what if it wasn't? What if it was really love? It didn't feel the same as before. It was much stronger.

Smiling to herself in the mirror as she put on her silk shower cap, Charles' brilliant smile flashed before her. God, she loved his smile…and those soft lips. Stepping into the shower, she savored the memory of his smooth mouth caressing hers.

Sunday morning, still on cloud nine, Shelia found her parents in the kitchen eating a simple breakfast. About two years ago, her father Edward had been hospitalized for nearly a month due to a heart condition. He had a mild heart attack. After his recovery, her mother, Sylvia, had put the two of them on a strict dietary regimen. Shelia usually ate whatever they ate just to spare herself an argument. But today, a hard-boiled egg and rice cakes were not going to appease her stomach. As she took bacon, hash browns, and eggs from the refrigerator, her parents looked at each other, plainly curious.

"Shelia," her father started, "you sure did have a late night. I didn't think you would be going to the hospital this morning."

"Oh, no, Dad, you know that duty calls," she replied. "I can't afford to jeopardize my internship."

"Well, baby," her mother chimed in, "how was your evening? I noticed you and Charles left a little early."

"No, not really. It was nice." She smiled at her parents. Shelia knew they wanted to know what was going on between her and Charles. She decided she wasn't going to make it easy for them. She didn't know what was going on herself. Shelia started to whistle as she used the spatula to move her food around in the large frying pan. This really made them wonder.

"You sure are in a good mood this morning," her father ventured.

"Oh, yeah, just ready to start the day," she replied.

Her mother chuckled, knowing what Shelia was up to.

"Shelia, exactly what did you and Charles do last night that has you in such a mood?"

"Dad, you can't ask me that question anymore. I'm an adult now," she politely informed him.

"That might be so, young lady, but in this household—"

"Edward, let the girl be," her mother interrupted. "You forget that you were young once. What used to get you going?" she knowingly inquired.

Not answering, Edward looked at his wife and then returned to his newspaper.

"Thanks, Mom. I really have to hurry, or I'm going to be late." After stuffing herself, Shelia gathered her purse and keys along with a change of clothes and ran out to her car.

At the hospital, Shelia served as an intern and earned credits toward her medical degree. She had to obtain approval from the hospital's Board of Directors as well as Howard University College of Medicine Board of Trustees. She realized that Troy's letter of referral and recommendation helped sway the ultimate decision in her favor. Most of her time was spent at the various nurses' stations, but occasionally she did accompany doctors on their rounds where she was quizzed on diagnosis and procedures. Because she wasn't licensed, she was regulated to observing rather than touching any of the patients, but it would still benefit her in the end. She knew all of the medical terminology, and was also able to update patient charts.

Shelia had made a number of friends from volunteering at Oak Park Hospital over the years. She planned to do her residency there. The doctors, nursing and administrative staffs liked having her on the team, seeing her cheerful disposition, high-level efficiency, and solid work ethic as assets to the hospital.

Today, she was manning the third-floor station with a new nurse, Tabitha, fresh out of school. Tabitha was a really good worker, but she was a little on the ditzy side. She came on duty at eight, and already Shelia knew about most of her family and all of their problems.

By noon, Shelia had begun feeling a bit tired. Her best friend Liz, now a nurse at the hospital, was not scheduled to work, so her day went a little slower than usual. They always kept each other going with stories of the night before and general gossip.

With her long day drawing to an end, Shelia became increasingly eager to leave. Her stomach was starting to growl because she had skipped lunch, wanting to be hungry when Charles picked her up.

"Excuse me, is this nurses' station twelve?"

Tabitha smiled brightly at the handsome deliveryman and said, "Why yes, it is. What can I do for you?"

"I have a delivery for a Shelia Daniels? Is she around?" he asked, returning her smile.

"Shelia, dear, this delivery here is for you," Tabitha called.

A big smile on her face, Shelia signed for the flowers and carried them to the back of the station, Tabitha close on her heels. What a surprise! Two dozen red roses beautifully arranged in a glass vase tied with a red bow.

"Well, who are they from?" Tabitha asked.

"I don't know," she answered.

"What do you mean you don't know? Well, what does the card say?"

Shelia read the card aloud:

Thinking of you
Missing your smile
Holding my breath
See you in a while
Love, Charles

"Oh, my God!" Shelia shrieked. "They're from Charles Avery, a friend of mine." She instantly regretted blurting out his name. She wasn't thinking clearly, overwhelmed that Charles would do something this sweet and unexpected for her.

"Charles Avery…the singer, Charles Avery?" Tabitha asked. "I heard he was from here, but you're the first person I met who actually knows him."

Oh well, the cat was out of the bag. "Yeah, we're going to lunch today. He's an old family friend. A lot of people around here know him. He went to school with a lot of the people who work here." Thinking ahead, she pleaded with Tabitha to keep it quiet. "Please don't tell anybody about this, okay?"

But the new nurse was already itching to run to the first person she saw. "Okay, sure, our little secret," Tabitha reassured her.

At two o'clock Shelia headed for the exit. The stares and whispers directed at her the last two hours were a sure sign that Tabitha had not kept her word. Shelia had almost made her escape when she heard someone calling her name. Charles was walking towards her, his broad shoulders stretching the material of the silk T-shirt he wore, his straight-leg jeans hugging his taut thighs. He looked more like a base-ball player than a singer; more the athlete than artist.

The arrival of the roses had set off quite a buzz, thanks to Tabitha's loose lips. People who had been sneaking looks at her were now openly gawking at him. But Charles was oblivious to the whispers and stares, though he did hail a few people he knew from the neighborhood. When he reached her, he placed a hand on her back and led her to the car.

"Hi, stranger. Did you miss me?" he inquired.

"Not likely. Thank you for the flowers; they're beautiful."

"No, you're beautiful. The flowers, well, they're all right." She had occupied his mind constantly from the time he pulled away from her house the night before to right now. When he arrived home, his parents had already turned in for the night. Charles sat in the living room watching—but not really watching—a late-night movie. He was too antsy to sleep. Usually, at this time of night he was up recording or en route from one venue to another. But he wasn't thinking of music as he relived thoughts of the way she felt in his arms when he had held her.

Remembering the taste and feel of her lips when he had kissed her made his pulse rate jump.

He had sent the flowers on impulse when he had passed the florist shop on his way to meeting his father for breakfast. He was in a good mood and wanted to brighten her day as well.

More relaxed now that they were safely in the car, Shelia asked, "Okay, Mr. Charmer, where are we off to?"

"Someplace where we can be all alone. Someplace we can just relax and talk and get to know each other again."

Putting the car into gear, Charles turned into traffic and headed to the back roads leading out of Oak Park. They relaxed during on the ride listening to slow jazz on the radio. It was a breezy, sunny day—a perfect kind of day to just lie back and shut out the world. That was all Charles wanted to do. No pressures, no hassles, no tight schedule. He didn't want to think about the business. In fact, he didn't want to think about anything except enjoying Shelia's company.

"And by the way, Charles you didn't tell me last night that your car was a brand-new Mercedes. I don't feel comfortable. I'm afraid I might somehow damage these leather seats."

He laughed so hard his eyes watered. "Shelia, this isn't my car. I told you yesterday that my manager had rented it for me. I have a 2004 Land Cruiser. Cars are made to be enjoyed, not to be afraid of." He pulled over to the side of the road. "Here, you drive. I'll do the chillin'."

"Oh, no, I couldn't. I would be a nervous wreck."

"Well, at least take off your sneakers and put your feet up. Come on now, relax," he urged, returning to the road. Shelia played along, putting her feet up on the dashboard, and had to admit that it felt good to have the wind teasing her toes. She put them down after a second.

"You have very pretty feet. Anybody ever tell you that?"

"No, not lately."

Wondering if she could be baiting him, he felt a deep-down stirring of jealousy. Charles wanted to know if someone had actually told her that she had pretty feet, but he thought it was a question best left unasked. He drummed his fingers on the steering wheel, sorry he had ever bought up the subject of feet. Two minutes later, he was still thinking about her feet, and still drumming. It was getting on Shelia's nerves.

"Liz," she finally said, hoping to put an end to the racket. His finger drumming had always been a sign that he was either thinking extra hard or was frustrated. She had forgotten how often she had hear him drumming away while he and Jeff studied for exams. It would end only after Jeff had thrown something at him.

"Liz what?" he asked her, unaware she was answering his unasked question.

"That's who told me I had pretty feet. She told me last summer when we were getting pedicures at the salon. She said that I had pretty feet."

"Shelia, you didn't have to tell me that."

"Yes, I did."

"But I didn't ask."

"And you wouldn't have, but now you can stop beating your fingers against the wheel."

Charles was quiet for a moment before he saying, "Thank you."

"Here we are," he said, pulling onto an old road.

Charles drove slowly down a dusty, tree-lined, hole-filled dirt road. The road went down a small hill, then curved behind a big bush and ended at a wide field..

Shelia drank in the beauty of the hidden oasis unfolding before her. In the middle of the tall trees shielding this area from the highway was a small lake surrounded by a handful of smaller trees. The grass was adorned with an array of wildflowers. It reminded her of the open meadow that little Laura Ingalls ran through during the opening credits the television show "Little House on the Prairie." Birds flew overhead, and happy chirping was coming from the nearby trees.

"A long time ago," Charles began, "your brother and I found this little alcove back here. I don't think anybody in particular owns this land. It's probably still government land. I've been meaning to check into it. It would be a great place for me to build my dream house."

Not missing a beat, Shelia fired back, "A long time ago? I wonder how many girls you and Jeff have brought back here."

Laughing, he answered, "Who, me? Come on now, you know me better than that. I can't answer for Jeff, but I..." He could tell she wasn't buying it, so he changed the subject. "Let's get out and set up for our picnic; I heard your stomach a minute ago. Then we can take a walk."

"Who made all this food?" she asked, poking around in the basket.

"Oh, that's leftover stuff from the wedding. When I told Mom we were going on a picnic, she packed a basket and walked me to the door as if I was going to the first grade again with my lunch box in hand," he said, smiling.

"I know the feeling. Dad tried to give me the third degree this morning," she said, imitating her father's questioning tone. "Exactly what did you do last night, young lady?"

Charles laughed at her dead-on imitation, watching her all the while. The roots and ends of her shoulder-length hair were darker than the rest. With her thick eyebrows, it gave her an exotic look. He liked that, and he liked the way she tilted her head slightly to the left side when she laughed. He took in her smile and her jet-black eyes as they sparkled in the sunlight. His heart said to be careful he didn't lose it to her. But in that instant, he realized it was already too late.

They found a nice spot under a tree and spread the blankets out. It was beautiful. The grass wasn't overgrown; someone was obviously taking care of the grounds. Birds were singing their own songs of love up high in the trees. The sun was still visible, reflecting off the little lake in the middle of the field.

"Next time we come out here, you'll have to bring your bathing suit," Charles hinted, pointing at the welcoming water. "It's kinda cool, but once you get used to it, it's nice."

"Why next time? I have on a bra and panties. That's the same as a bathing suit, right?"

"Right." Charles said easily, unwilling to show his shock at her suggestion. "Well, let's eat first, walk it off, then go for a swim."

They ate cold fried chicken and potato salad. Mrs. Avery had also packed biscuits, ham, cheese and pickles. Charles opened a bottle of wine he had bought at a grocery store along the way and filled the two glasses his mother had stuck in the side of the basket.

Feeling stuffed, Shelia rested her hand on her stomach as she lay back on the blanket and looked up at the sky. What a wonderful day she was having with him. They were completely at ease with each other. They laughed about the past and talked about their future aspirations. Shelia started to drift off.

"Hey, sleepy head, want some of these?" Charles asked, drawing a strawberry dripping with whipped cream along her lips. She opened her mouth and took a bite. "Um…good. Give me another one."

"Okay, open up." He placed a strawberry against her lips, and when she opened her mouth, he leaned forward and bit into it. Juice from the strawberry ran down her cheek. Nibbling on her lips, Charles worked his way down her throat. Her eyes closed, Shelia arched her back and stretched her neck to give him a clear path. He returned to her mouth and covered it with his again. When he heard her moaning in pleasure, reality hit like a sudden dousing of cold water. He had to slow it down; he didn't want to make a mistake. He sat up abruptly, asking, "How about that walk now?"

His sudden withdrawal caught Shelia off guard, sending her emotions in a tailspin. First came confusion, then embarrassment, and finally rejection. What was going on? He was enjoying it just as much as she, wasn't he? Didn't he want to be with her? His intensity was palpable.

"Okay," she replied quietly, "but can I ask you a question?" Shelia continued without taking a breath. She wasn't one to hold back. "Why did you stop? Weren't you enjoying yourself?"

"Oh, of course, I was." Charles struggled to slow his breathing. The effect Shelia was having on him was dangerously close to spinning out of control. If he didn't get a grip, Charles knew that he could end up pushing Shelia into doing something that she might regret—they both might regret. He couldn't move too fast with her, although she seemed ready to go forward. "No, I just thought it would be best for us to keep it kind of simple today." Charles figured it would be best if he did the thinking for both of them for now. He stood, studiously brushing the pant legs of his blue and white track suit. He held out a hand to help her up.

"So in other words, you want more, but you're afraid to go after it?" she asked.

"I didn't say that. Stop putting words in my mouth."

"Well, why else would you keep stopping? This is the second time."

"Let's just walk," he said, drumming his fingers against his leg. Keeping her at bay was going to be harder than he thought. Charles couldn't believe he was actually thinking like that.

Charles began hastily putting things back into the basket. Shelia could make him burn with passion one minute and put him on the defensive the next. He hadn't wanted to stop, but he had to be careful not to frighten her away.

CHAPTER 3

Thirty minutes later, holding her hand, Charles lead the way through the maze of flowers, trees, and bushes. To put their earlier discussion behind them, he only talked about things they came across in the woods. He pointed out squirrels, a raccoon, a bird here and there as they walked along the nearly grass-covered path. Shelia held onto him tightly. Although he had said there wasn't anything dangerous around, she expected to see something come flying out of one of the bushes any minute. She didn't relax until they had reached the clearing and were near his car.

"I can see who wouldn't be any good to me if we were ever stranded on a deserted island," Charles joked.

"You got that right. I would stay right on the beach and pray for someone to come get me." Shelia wasn't lying. As brave and as strong as she appeared on the outside, wild animals, bugs, snakes, and strange foreign places were things to be avoided.

"Ready for that swim?" Charles asked, knowing deep down that it probably wasn't a good idea.

"Yep." She had already begun pulling up her shirt when he stopped her.

"Don't you want some privacy?" he asked.

"For what, Charles? The same shirt and shorts I take off here will be the same ones I take off from behind the car or that tree over there." Shelia wasn't trying to be immodest, but she did want him to be aware that she wanted him.

"All right, all right. Just don't do it so seductively. Have some mercy on me; I'm only human. I'll turn my back."

"You better not, and stop doing that. We aren't in high school. We are two consenting adults about to take a swim." *Maybe she was moving too fast for him. He either didn't get the hint, or was afraid to take it.*

"That's easy for you to say; you're not looking at you," he replied, not taking his eyes off her.

"Well, I'm going swimming." Looking him dead in the face, she pulled her shirt off.

He just stood there watching her, his hazel eyes twinkling in the five o'clock sunlight.

She was excited and her heart was beating fast, but she was determined to go through with this. Shelia had made up her mind years ago that if she had the chance to be with Charles she was going for it. They had been around each other all their lives, and she knew the kind of person he was. She might have to give him a little push if she wanted things to go her way. He wanted her, she was sure of it, but sometimes Charles was just too much of a gentleman.

Even though she, too, was unsure and was fighting to calm her own jumpy nerves, Shelia thought she was in control of the situation. She knew what she was going to do. She kicked off her sneakers, and with the sexiest smile she could muster, slowly pushed her uniform bottoms down and peeled it off.

Charles was still standing there, just watching her. He knew what she was up to, and it was working. She wore a pink silk and lace set under her uniform. It could have been a two-piece bathing suit, except it was sheer. No public beach in North America would let her walk around in that. He could tell that she was waiting for him to say something. But he couldn't; he didn't even want to move. Taking his time, he checked her out again from her face down. Meanwhile, his own shorts were becoming more and more uncomfortable.

"Well, are you coming or not?" she asked, further eroding his weakening determination. His looking at her filled her with heady excitement. It told her that he was at least interested, that he wanted her just as much as she wanted him. She felt his desire for her. Could see it too. He made her feel warm and secure. She felt comfortable with him, making her enjoy this experience even more.

Licking his lips, Charles tore his eyes away from her body. "Um…maybe I'd better wait a minute," Charles suggested, embarrassed. Using a towel, Charles tried to hide his excitement.

"Oh, please, I'm a medical student," Shelia said trying to appear mature and sophisticated. "I've seen an erection before. The water will cool you off. But you know what? Now that I think about it, skinnydipping would probably be an even better idea. That way our underclothes won't be wet when we get dressed."

"Oh, no. I don't think…" Before he could finish, she had unhooked the front of her bra and had thrown it to the ground. "Whoa, Shelia, I don't know if this is going in the right direction." A big knot was forming in his throat. Against his will, his eyes moved over her body, stopping at her perfect round brown buds.

"Do you need help, Charles?" she asked, walking towards him.

"Shelia, please, don't come over here." *How stupid did that sound?* Talk about something he thought would never come out of his mouth. "Look, Shelia…um…I can do it." Charles knew that she had no idea how much of a hard time he was having. If she came any closer, he wasn't sure he would be strong enough to stop the inevitable.

"Charles, I'm going to get you undressed so we can have a swim." Shelia was getting tired of his chivalry—if that's what it was. She pulled him close by his waistband, letting her breast rub against his shirt. She unzipped his pants and pulled his T-shirt over his head.

"Are you always so matter of fact? Don't you know that you're playing with fire, Shelia?" he asked, feeling his insides ignite.

"I've been waiting for this for a long time, Charles. I am not afraid of getting close to the fire. Besides, how am I going to get what I want if I don't go after it? You of all people should know about going after things. Isn't that what you did with your singing career?"

Her hands went back to his pants, pushing them down. Putting her arms around his neck and stepping closer to him, she felt Charles take a deep breath before bringing his head down and kissing her senseless. His hands moved to cover and squeeze her breast. She was in heaven. Charles was making her feel as if she was the only woman in the world for him.

Shelia let him guide her hand between them. She felt his slow intake of breath when she shyly wrapped her fingers around him.

"Shelia..."

Intriguingly, she massaged him. He groaned and began kissing her neck, his hands working their way down her back. When they reached her panties, he pushed them down her legs.

"Shelia, are you sure you want to do this? Maybe we should just get into the water." But he kept kissing her, and she was now pushing at his boxers.

Shelia couldn't tell who was breathing harder. She heard noises and at first thought they came from some unseen animal. Then she realized they were the noise makers. She wasn't seeing straight, and her thoughts were all asunder. She was losing herself in him when he spoke. Slowly, she reined herself in.

"Okay," she agreed breathlessly, "let's go into the water and cool off, but when we get out we are going to finish this, right?" She stepped back, keeping an eye on him as they headed for the cool water.

"It's getting late. We should probably head back."

Shelia stopped walking and turned to him. He was so sexy and masculine standing there in the nude. The sun was behind him silhouetting his chocolate-colored body. He was tall, lean, and muscular. She ran her hand over his chest hair, following the fine line past his navel to the forest that spread out around his maleness. Nervous as she might be, Charles was crazy if he thought she wouldn't try for more later.

The pond was refreshing and surprisingly warm. They swam, splashed, and played in the water like two little kids. They hugged and kissed and raced. Time slipped away as they enjoyed each other's playful side, a side that had never been explored. Occasionally, he and Jeff played pranks on her, but she knew he was only assisting in Jeff's revenge. That was before their time became hectic with the adventures of high school.

It was five-thirty when they finally came out of the water. It was still very warm outside. Shelia suggested they stretch out on the blankets and let the sun dry them off. Another bad idea, Charles thought, but he didn't argue.

Pulling her hair back into a ponytail, Shelia said, "I can't believe we did that, it was great. It was like being really free. Like being teenagers again, you know?"

"Yeah, it was fun. Those were the good old days." Looking pensive, he traced a droplet of water down the side of her face. He got blankets from the car truck and spread them on a patch of soft grass.

"Hey, do you think your mom will be mad if we miss Sunday dinner?" Shelia wasn't ready to return home. Anyway, they were already late.

"You and your folks still come over for Sunday dinner?" He stretched out next to her on the cushiony blanket, knowing a bad idea was getting worse.

"Are you kidding? They call it their excuse to visit old friends. You can hardly tear them away from each other. They'll have a lot to talk about today, what with the wedding just yesterday, Tia and Denise both pregnant. And don't think they won't be wondering where we are."

"Don't worry, we'll be back before it's too late," he assured her.

"I'm not worried, and we won't be back before dinner is over, either," she replied.

He looked at her. "Now, Shelia, I thought we settled this. Yesterday, you didn't want to be the one who gets hurt. What happened to all that?"

"Well, last night, I thought about it," she said thoughtfully. "You'll be leaving in two weeks, and I plan to get what I can out of our time together. And when you do go, you'll have some things to think about. If things don't go right, then I'll have to deal with the consequences." Shelia leaned over and kissed the corners of his mouth. As she stretched next to him, she felt his hand on her thigh.

"Shelia, you know I want to be with you more than anything, but I don't have any protection, and—"

"I have some," she proudly announced. From the inside pocket of the purse she had thrown to the ground earlier, Shelia pulled out a row of condoms and put them on the blanket.

Laughing, Charles said, "Girl, you're crazy. I hope you don't carry this many around with you all the time."

"No, I just knew that I would need them," she said smiling shyly.

"Shelia, we really do need to have a talk about some things, okay?"

"Okay, but that can wait until later, can't it?" She raised up on one arm and looked at him lying on his back. Shelia bent down and slowly brought her lips close to his, clumsily working her tongue around the corners of his mouth and causing him to expect more, want more of her.

Charles reached up and grabbed the back of her neck bringing her close to him. Putting an end to his torment, he pulled her into a crushing kiss before he rolled her over onto her back. His heart was beating so fast it scared him. All these years, he had wanted to be in this very position. And now he was afraid that if he messed things up, he would lose her; he didn't want to move this fast. But he was only human, and she was offering him heaven. Even though the sensible part of him wanted to take it slow, the more he touched her, the more he wanted to become a part of her.

Her breathing had becoming labored. His mouth controlled her neck, while his hands squeezed her breasts. Shelia closed her eyes, enjoying his unreserved attentions.

Her moans were like music to his ears. He wanted to please her. Placing his mouth over one nipple, he gently massaged the other. She arched her back and grabbed the back of his head.

"Oh, Charles, that feels so good," she blurted out.

He kept a hand on one nipple, while his other hand explored the sweet nest between her thighs. She gasped when he opened her with his fingers. She was so moist it made him groan, and he shook his head to keep the excitement that threatened to blur his vision at bay.

Shelia couldn't wait any longer; she wanted to be a part of him. She spread her legs wider, pleading, "Please, Charles, please…now," encircling his waist to draw him closer to her.

Charles fumbled for the condoms, eager to complete their union. Finding them, he tore one package open. But then he jumped up and covered himself with a towel. Shaking his head from side to side, he stumbled to his car. The sound of the condom wrapper is what stopped him cold. *What was he doing?* He didn't want to treat Shelia like this. She wasn't a cheap trick, a quick-fix freak, he could have picked up after a concert. He loved this girl, had always loved her. He had to treat her better than this; show her that she meant more to him than a quick lay on some back road.

He was bent over by the car struggling for air when she rushed up to him. "Charles, what happened? What's wrong?"

"Get dressed, Shelia," he responded harshly. "Please, just get dressed."

The ride home was quiet. Shelia sat in the passenger seat, angry and unsure of herself. No, not unsure. She was embarrassed. Hadn't she done everything she could to make him want her? Maybe he already has somebody. He had told her otherwise, but maybe he did. Had he lied when he said he didn't know about Miss April and Miss June? Perhaps there was already a "Miss" for this month. Why else wouldn't he want to be with her? *Another night of loneliness*, she thought to herself. But she couldn't make him want her any more than she could make the sun shine all night long.

Charles was also angry, but for very different reasons. He couldn't believe that he had almost lost control of himself—and so easily. But he wanted her so badly. How was he going to make it up to her? She sat wordless, quietly looking out the window and oozing sexiness. He still wanted her badly, but not just for sex. He wanted so much more from her.

"Shelia—"

"Save it, Charles," she snapped, looking at him briefly before turning back to the passing landscape.

"I think we need to talk about this."

"What is there to talk about? You didn't want to go there with me. I understand that."

"No, you don't understand. Shelia, please believe me when I say that I wanted to be with you today more than you could possibly know. But when we do go there, I don't want anything to be standing in our way." He knew he wasn't making sense.

"Listen, I don't know what you saw out there today, but Charles, we were all alone. The only person standing in our way was you."

"Shelia—"

"I don't want to talk about it. Just let it go for now, okay?"

Obliging, he fell silent. She was visibly deeply upset. He didn't want to cause her further pain by having their conversation turn into an argument.

Shelia was quiet for the duration of the long ride home. Caught up in her own thoughts, she really wasn't seeing the scenic route that Charles had taken. She didn't see the sun's decent into the horizon, made more beautiful by a surrounding purple and reddish haze. But despite the day's letdown, her mind and heart were surprisingly at peace. Her mind lingered on the past and on the long years of yearning to be held by this man. She daydreamed that one day Charles would be her man. In her mind, Charles Avery was already hers—only hers.

Minutes later, he woke her up, telling her that they were in front of his parents' house.

"As you can see, the house is still full of people," he said. "Would you rather go to the movies or something?" Charles asked, hoping he had been forgiven for their earlier disagreement.

"The movies do sound nice." Yawning, she sat up and began rubbing her neck. Their earlier mystifying conflict had been pushed aside, and Shelia was now ready to just enjoy the rest of her evening. "But we probably should put in an appearance first, especially since we didn't call. No point raising more questions than necessary; they already have enough. Let's just go in and answer their questions and get it over."

Shelia's neck must have been in an awkward position while she slept because it was very sore. She rubbed, rotated, and stretched it before getting out of the car and following him to the front door. Before opening the door, Charles bent down and gave her a quick peck.

"Are you ready for the inquisition?" he asked jokingly.

"I'm ready," she answered, squaring her shoulders. Their families were sometimes too close-knit, too crowded, too much in each other's business. By now you would think they would be tired of having their lives so intertwined. But they weren't.

"He what?" Brenda asked furiously, "Troy, what did it say, exactly?"

"Mom, calm down, this is nothing to get upset over. It's probably just a misunderstanding anyway," Troy said before calmly answering his mother's question. "It said that he was her latest beau and that the baby was born early this morning. It was a girl, six pounds, five ounces."

"That can't be true," Brenda said, refusing to accept this news about her son. She shifted her weight uncomfortably in her chair at the dining room table, ran her fat, wrinkled hand over her heavily graying hair and reached for another tissue, wiping the tears cascading down her face.

"He would have told us," Charles' sister Devin exclaimed, trying to think logically. They all knew their brother better than that.

"Now everybody just calm down," John Sr., the oldest sibling, said just as Shelia and Charles walked into the living room.

"Hey, everybody, what's up?" Charles asked cheerfully.

He and Shelia stopped dead in their tracks when all eyes turned on him. Each face showed either disappointment or disbelief. They were both confused by the reaction Charles' question prompted. Shelia tightened her hold on his hand.

"Whoa, who died?" he asked trying to lighten the somber mood of the room.

Moving to stand next to his daughter, Edward said, "This is no laughing matter, young man."

"Okay, would someone mind telling me what's going on?" Charles asked. He was completely confused, but from the way Shelia's dad was looking at him, he figured something very serious was afoot. But what?

Troy stepped forward to help his brother out. "Charles, have a seat. Everybody, please, have a seat and calm down."

Charles sat down on the love seat and pulled Shelia down beside him, holding her hand and feeling as if he were twelve again and about to be chastised for bothering one of his sisters. Everyone in the room seemed to be circling him. They all stood waiting for the answer to a question they hadn't yet asked.

"Your manager called earlier today," Troy explained. "He said for you to watch *Entertainment Television* tonight at seven. He said you wouldn't like what you saw and for us to have you call him as soon as you saw it."

"Well, it's almost fifteen after eight, so I missed the show," he said, looking down at his watch. Charles didn't really care. He had just had

the most incredible date of his life, not counting the little incident at
the end. Now wasn't the time for him to be dealing with work or
anything work-related. All he wanted to do was spend more time with
Shelia, but the way they were looking at him made him wish that he
had never come home.

"I recorded it for you when you didn't show up. Brother, I gotta tell
you, it's not good. Maybe you should watch it in private first," Troy
suggested.

"No," he said squeezing Shelia's hand. "We can all watch it
together."

"Man, listen to me," Troy tried to reason with his younger brother.
"You should look at it alone."

"Troy," Charles responded, standing to face his brother, "I know
what you're doing, but I'm telling you, it's all right. Besides, I don't have
anything to hide." He patted his brother's shoulder reassuringly, "It's all
right. We can all look at it together."

"Okay, if you say so," Troy said, giving up.

They all followed the new couple into the family room, taking
seats on the sofa, chairs, or floor. Earlier, all the kids had been ushered
into the back rooms to play. Troy started the tape.

One of the hosts of the TV show was ticking off the top-grossing
films of the week. Then a picture of his friend Kara came onto the
screen.

Kara was a supermodel turned actress, and one of the best as far as
he was concerned. She wasn't shallow or pretentious like many of the
other models he knew. And for a black woman in a business dominated
by whites, she was making a lot of waves. She was not only a runway
superstar, but also a star on television shows and in movies. And she
had multiple endorsement deals. She also had her own company, which
produced films, promoted new talent, and supported numerous chari-
table organizations. This opened the door for numerous minorities in
the entertainment and other fields.

They had been friends for a long time, ever since he had been just
a back-up singer struggling to be noticed. They had met at a big party

thrown by a record company to promote the new release of an artist for whom he was singing background on tour. She was struggling then, too. They had struck up a friendship and had even tried dating for a while, but he quickly realized that they weren't romantically compatible. Shelia was still heavily on his mind, and he couldn't commit to the kind of relationship Kara wanted.

Over the following year or so, he and Kara talked when they got a chance and lunched whenever they ended up in the same city. Charles tried to keep the friendship because it was important to have her in that corner of his life. Everett was his manager and agent, and even though they had forged a trusting friendship, Charles knew that the money he paid Everett was what kept him close. Kara had been there when he didn't have a pot to piss in. Loyalty was very hard to come by in his business.

"Congratulations to supermodel Kara Morning," the host gushed. "The model/actress delivered a healthy baby girl this morning in Beverly Hills. She's seen here with her latest beau, singer Charles Avery, at last year's Music Awards." A tape of her and Charles walking down a red carpet was showing in the background. They were both smiling and waving. "The six pound, five ounce baby girl was named Divine Noel. Both mother and baby are reportedly doing fine this evening. Again, congratulations to the family on behalf of this show."

Charles' mouth and eyes flew wide open. He sat back on the couch after bolting upright at the beginning of the tape. He couldn't believe what he had just heard. He just couldn't believe it. Troy reached over to turn off the tape. But he still saw the picture and still heard the words. Charles felt Shelia's hand slipping out of his. Turning towards her, he tightened his grip on her hand, shaking his head from side to side.

"It's not true," he whispered to her. Then he turned to everybody else in the room. "You got to believe me; it's not true." Turning back to Shelia, he pleaded, "Please, baby, don't cry. I swear, it's not true. I'll get to the bottom of this."

Tears ran down Shelia's face as she saw her dreams of a future with Charles quickly slipping away. She hadn't even realized she was crying.

ONE OF THESE DAYS

The tears started to fall as soon as she heard the news. In less than an hour, everything she had hoped for had crumpled. Charles had his hands on her face trying to talk to her, but she didn't hear a word he said. The voice of the TV host kept echoing in her head.

"Let's take Shelia to the bathroom, Devin," his sister Kristal said, moving closer to the pair. "She needs some air."

"Wait…" Charles protested. He was afraid to let her out of his sight.

"We'll be right back, brother," Kristal assured him.

Charles stood with her. He didn't want to let go of her hand. He felt that he had already lost her. Her eyes showed that she didn't believe him. She was so unsure, confused, and visibly afraid. And that made him mad as hell.

"I can't believe this shit," he hissed angrily. Charles spun around with both hands drawn in fists at his side and stomped a foot hard against the floor. After hearing his father clear his throat, he quickly apologized, "Excuse me, Mom, Mrs. Daniels. But this is crazy. I know what all of you are thinking, but that is not my kid."

Brenda went to her son and hugged him around the waist. "We believe you, dear. If you say it's not yours, then it's not yours."

"Mom, it's not that simple. Millions of people have seen this program. Everybody believes that I'm that kid's father. Why in the world would they do that to me? There is no way in the world I can be that kid's father."

"Well, you were dating her, weren't you, Son?" his father asked.

"Dad, we tried dating when I was first getting started. It didn't work out, so we decided to just be friends, and occasionally hook up." He felt uncomfortable talking about his sex life in front of his mother and Shelia's mother. "But that stopped two years ago. She was just doing me a favor by going to that awards show with me last year. We had a few drinks at the after party, but nothing happened. And when I won for new artist, it helped her career, too. That was it. We were not dating, seeing, or sleeping with each other nine months, a year ago."

"Sounds to me like you got a lawsuit going. That television program should never have aired that piece without more information, or at least some background investigation," Troy said, putting a hand on his brother's shoulder. "Good thing we got a lawyer in the family," he added, referring to their sister April.

"Exactly. But I don't think I need April yet. I've got some calls to make. But first, I have to check on Shelia. I don't think she believes me at all."

"Charles, I know my daughter," Edward offered from his bar stool. "She needs facts and proof. Until you can give her proof, she's going to believe what she saw and heard on that there tape." He didn't sound too sympathetic toward Charles, and he wasn't. Edward was privately hoping that the report would put his daughter's feelings in perspective. She was wearing her heart on her sleeve. He saw it as soon as she walked into the house. And he didn't like it at all. His daughter was going to be a doctor. School and studying needed to be her main focus, not Charles, if *they* were going to reach that goal.

"Edward, give your daughter some credit." Turning to Charles, Shelia's mom, Sylvia, said firmly, "I know my daughter, too, Charles. She really cares about you. She'll listen to what you have to say, dear. Now hurry up before she gets a chance to form too many ideas of her own." As Charles stood, Sylvia gave her husband a disapproving look. She knew what he was up to.

Devin and Kristal were trying to calm her down, but Shelia was becoming hysterical. She was crying so hard that twice she complained about not being able to breathe.

"If you don't stop, we're going to have to take you to the hospital. Now calm yourself down. Shelia, you know Charles. He cares for you, girl," Kristal said, wiping her face with a clean washcloth. "He's been caring about you for years. He tried not to let on, but I don't miss a thing. I used to see him looking at you when he thought nobody saw."

Devin added, "She's right, Shelia. Charles isn't the type of guy who would have a kid somewhere that nobody knew about. He would have come to us and said something. Besides, I don't think he would have gotten someone pregnant and risked messing up his chances with you. As Kristal said, he's been waiting a long time to be able to actually date you. You have to believe what he's saying to you. I don't believe it's his kid."

Blowing her nose, Shelia forced herself to be calm. She knew what they were saying was true, but why would the talk-show host lie? Charles was probably dating that woman around the time of conception. He had to have been dating someone. She was so confused. After she was willing to give herself to him, she didn't want to believe this.

Kristal lightly touched her neck.

"Ouch!" Shelia nearly jumped out of her skin.

"From the size of this passion mark on your neck, I'd say that my little brother knows exactly who he wants, and doesn't want anybody else to have her."

"A what?" Shelia screamed, looking in the mirror at the big black and purple patch of bruised skin on the left side of her neck. That's what had been hurting her earlier. She hadn't realized he had put it there, and was embarrassed by her naivety.

"Passion mark," Devin said, looking at Kristal curiously. "Haven't you ever had one? People put them on each other sort of to mark their territory. Now, if another guy sees you with that, more than likely, he's not going to want to talk to you."

"Yeah, right, marking territory. Seems like I should be the one marking mine," Shelia responded, crossing her arms and sitting back down on the closed toilet seat.

"That's the spirit, girl, now come out fighting," Devin laughed.

"Shelia, do you really care for him?"

Looking at her as if she was crazy, Shelia answered honestly, "Kristal, I love him. I've loved him damn near my whole life. And we almost..." Turning her head so they wouldn't see her blush, she stopped. "Never mind."

"We understand, but if you love him as you say you do, give him a chance to prove to you that this is all just a big mistake."

"I will. Let me get myself cleaned up here. I look horrible, and this mark's not going to make it any better. I'm going to catch hell when my dad sees it."

"Shelia, you're a grown woman. What can he really say?" Devin asked.

"Nothing, but I still have to hear whatever he does say. That's a pain in the butt." Hugging them both, she turned to fix her makeup and hair. Feeling better about her situation, Shelia decided that they were right. She knew Charles better than this. There was no way the man she knew would have a child out there without knowing about it. He was too responsible, too respectful. And if a kid of his was being born, Charles would be there.

CHAPTER 4

Charles passed his sisters in the hallway; each gave him a hug and kiss on the cheek.

"How is she?" he asked seriously.

"Really upset, which is understandable. She really loves you, Charles. The news was quite a shock to us. I can't even imagine what she's going through."

"Devin, you know that I would never do this to her." Charles said, defending himself.

"I know, I know. It's just the shock of it all," Devin replied with both hands held up.

"Do you love her, Charles?" Kristal asked.

"You know, I've been telling her that I wanted to take things slow." A mischievous grin came over his face as he thought of his day. "Yeah, I love her. I can't explain it, but I do. It's been there for so long."

"Well, then, get on in there and start fixing things." Kristal took a step and then turned back to him. "By the way, those mosquitoes are a bitch this time of year, aren't they?"

The women walked down the hall laughing, but the comment had gone right over his head. Charles just shook his head and watched them round the corner, then he went to the bathroom door. He stood next to it with his hand on the knob. "Shelia?"

"What, Charles?"

"Can I come in?"

"No, Charles, I'm a mess."

"Shelia, open the door," Charles said, his hand twisting the gold knob.

He waited until he heard the lock click, and then stepped into the large room. It had been newly remodeled after Devin had finally moved into her own house with her fiancé and twin daughters. The wall from the bedroom next door had been torn down. A new, much larger tub replaced the old, battered one, and the room was painted and the floor tiled over. His mom had placed candles and plants around the room. It was a place of tranquility, but today all of the good karma his mother often spoke of was missing.

She was sitting on the edge of the tub, wiping her face. His heart bled a little when she looked up at him. He could see the sadness in Shelia's swollen and reddened eyes. Charles walked over and knelt beside her.

"Baby, listen to me," rubbing her back, he soothed, "I am going to get all of this straightened out."

"How are you going to do that?" she asked.

"I'm going to call my agent first; hell, I'll call Kara herself at the hospital. The only thing that matters to me is that you believe that this is not my baby. I'm telling the truth."

"Charles, do you think that I want to believe you have a child by that woman? I don't want you to have children by anyone but me." Realizing what she said, Shelia quickly amended her last statement. "I mean, if we were to be together, later on, I would want to be the only woman to have your children. Look, I'm not thinking right. This thing that we have is new, and I know you've been with other women. I think that because of what happened today, my emotions are getting a little in the way. What happened today was pretty much my doing. You did want to wait, and I was determined not to, so I have to deal with the repercussions. Even though we didn't go through with it, I brought this all on myself."

"Wait a minute. Slow down. First of all, this thing between us is not new. It's been going on for a long time. We have just now decided to recognize it." He paused and took a deep breath. "Shelia, look at me. I've been with other women, sure, but I believe there was a reason I never found myself in any long-term relationship. I think that in the back of my mind, I've been just waiting for you to grow up. I don't want any other woman. I want you, baby, only you. What happened today…we did together, and there aren't any repercussions. I bared my heart and soul, my love, to you today. That's everything I have to give."

Tears were running down Shelia's freshly cleaned face. "Maybe I should go and give you time to straighten things out. Just give me a call tomorrow. It's getting pretty late, and I—"

"Oh, no, this has to do with both of us. I want you there with me when I make those phone calls. I'm sure my whole family will be staying late tonight." He stood and pulled her up with him, holding her close. When he felt the tension leaving her body, he began kissing her face. "Shelia, listen," he whispered, "I love you. I would never do anything to hurt you. Just give me a second to clear this mess up."

"Okay, but—"

"No buts," he said, taking hold of her mouth and caressing it with his tongue. Charles came up for air and kissed her forehead. He prayed that she truly believed him. After finally confessing their love, he couldn't let this lie separate them.

Edward was pacing the living room floor. He was very uncomfortable. Only the stern looks from his wife kept him at bay. They had been in that bathroom for a very long time. Any minute now he was going in there, even if he had to bust down the door himself. This was his baby girl, and she was a wreck. He didn't like it, not one bit.

"Edward, come over here and have a seat," John Sr. said, sitting at the bar with his two oldest sons, John Jr. and Troy. "Pacing back and forth like that will only get you more upset."

"How can you be so calm, John? They've been in that bathroom for a long time." Edward ran his left hand over his balding head, scratching himself just above his right temple. Walking to the bar stool, he folded his six-foot frame and sat down.

"I trust my sons," John Sr. answered, "plain and simple, especially Charles. He's not like his brothers. Now these two, I wouldn't have put anything past them when they were younger. Came home from church once and caught this one," pointing at Troy, "with that little Simmons girl from down the street. He was supposed to be sick. John, I caught him twice in the same month with two different girls. Just imagine the times I didn't catch them. But Charles, never had any trouble out of him. He has too much respect, and he's a very responsible man. That's why I don't believe a bit of this TV nonsense. Now don't get me wrong, he can be as mean as a pit bull when he has to be, but he really has a more gentle nature to him."

"Dad, please quiet down. We do have our wives and kids here, you know," John Jr. said.

Troy, shaking his head, agreed. "Yeah. The last thing I need to do is go home and hear about this until two in the morning."

"Well, it's different with girls. That's my baby locked in the bathroom with a man. Jesus, life used to be so much easier."

"With the girls I always just followed the missus' lead. She always knew what was going on in their lives, and from the smile on Brenda's face, I'd figure she knows what's going on in Shelia's. If she needs you, she'll let you know."

"Did that make it easier for you?" Edward asked.

"Hell, no." John Sr. turned his attention to the baseball game on the television.

Shelia found herself against the bathroom wall with her legs around Charles' waist. She was so wrapped up in Charles that she couldn't remember how she had gotten that way. He was holding her and kissing her. She couldn't think. All she knew was Charles. Every one of her senses was focused on him. She saw him, smelled him; was touching him and could taste him. And she heard him softly moaning her name.

"Oh, God, Charles, we can't do this. Our parents are right in the living room," she was finally able to gasp.

"I don't care." He placed more kisses on her face and neck. "Shelia, please, whatever you do, please don't ever think that I would mislead you. I would never jeopardize what we could have together. Shelia, I love you. You have to believe that. Please tell me that you believe that. I need for you to believe me when I say that I love you."

"I know you do, Charles. I love you, too." Shelia walked away from him, knowing in her heart she was telling the truth. She did love him, but his life was so different from hers. He knew the people she dreamed of knowing. He saw the places she dreamed of seeing. Even though she had told him she would except whatever it took to be with him, Shelia wasn't sure she was strong enough to deal with all the consequences of his celebrity.

"Shelia, sometimes my need to be with you is more powerful than it is rational. I know we have to get back out there, but I just wanted to hold you and make sure that everything's all right between us."

"Everything's all right." Shelia looked up at him and then down at the floor trying to hide her hesitation.

"Are you sure?" Charles asked, lifting her head. He waited for her nod. "Are you almost ready to go back out?"

"Yeah, I'm ready," she smiled.

They checked themselves and opened the door. Putting his arm around her, he led Shelia to the kitchen table and sat down to begin making his calls. One by one, family members began drifting into the kitchen.

Shelia didn't look at either of her parents. They would know that she was just in Charles' arms if she did. Her mother was especially good at knowing what was going on in her life. While she was away at college, Shelia couldn't count the times her mother had called to cheer her up on a bad day or check to see how she was dealing with her bad cramps. No, she would just sit back as relaxed as possible and watch Charles as everyone else was doing.

Charles picked up the phone and dialed the number to his manager's home office. His wife answered the phone. "Hello Marsha…yes…oh, better after I get a few things straightened out. Okay…hey, Everett, man, talk to me. How the hell," looking at his mother, he calmed down, "could something like this happen?…I know, but…please do and let me know right away what they say. Tell them that I'm already talking to my lawyer…no, I want a full retraction…so, what…I don't care about that. Look, my whole family is very upset about this. I won't have that. I'm calling Kara myself, right now…I don't know who the father is. I only know who it's not…all right. I'll talk to you later." Charles hung up the phone and looked around the table at his family members. He put his hand to his forehead, wondering why this was happening to him, right now, at this time in his life.

Turning his focus back to his family, Charles said, "Well, Everett is working on the show. He's already been in contact with them and is waiting for a return call. He admitted that they never looked into getting any background information before airing the piece. They said they would research it and make a retraction if their information is incorrect, which it is."

"Well, what are you going to do now?" Troy said, putting a hand on Charles' shoulder. Troy always had his little brother's back whether he was right or wrong. He spoiled Charles like crazy while they were growing up, often taking the blame—and punishment—for his mistakes. Charles put his hand over Troy's and squeezed.

"Don't worry, big brother. I've got to clean up this one myself. I'm calling Kara." Shelia didn't like that idea, and he knew it. He could tell by the change in her expression. Charles grabbed her hand and explained, "It's the only way to clear up this mess. I just want all of you to know the truth, tonight if possible. I don't like having this hanging over my head. I don't like the doubt I see in your eyes."

"Charles, we don't doubt you, baby," his mother replied, holding her husband's hand.

Picking up the phone, Charles called information to get the number to Cedar Seville Hospital, the hospital Everett told him where Kara Morning had her baby. Once he had it, he took a deep breath and dialed the number.

"Yes, may I have maternity, please?…Hello, I'm trying to get Ms. Morning's room. This is Charles Avery…um, thank you," he said hunching his shoulders because he saw Shelia's facial expression darken. "Yes, I'll hold. Hello, Kara. It's Charles. Listen, I'm putting you on the speaker phone. We need to straighten up some things for my family." He clicked the button on his parents' most recent prized possession and hung up the receiver.

"Well, Charles, how have you been? Can't say that I'm surprised to hear from you. Thought you would have called a lot sooner, though."

"I was busy. Listen, my whole family is here with me. I just saw a tape of that program *Entertainment Television.*"

"I'm sorry about that, Charles. I was just as shocked as you were when I saw it. I didn't think they would know so soon. I was hoping to let you know I was in labor."

Charles looked at the phone speaker. "Let me know you were in labor? I never knew you were pregnant."

"Well, my manager and I left the country as soon as I found out. We were trying to stay out of the public eye. I came back a week ago to have the baby here."

"I just called my manager, Everett. If the show doesn't retract the story, there will be a big lawsuit waiting for them on Tuesday morning. My, um, girlfriend," he said, nervously looking at Shelia and then their parents, "and both of our families were a little taken aback by the news that I was a father."

"Why would they do that?" Kara's voice was convincingly clear, but suddenly filled with attitude. Charles' confident facial expression changed to bewilderment.

"Kara, what do you mean? Who's the father?"

Her laugh filled the room as his family stared at him. "You are so silly. Are you mad because you weren't here to witness her birth? Please, everyone, accept my deepest apologizes." Kara cleared her throat. "Excuse me, Charles, but did you say *girlfriend?*"

There was a silence, and everyone all turned to Charles. He laughed a little and replied, "Yeah, that's what I said." He squeezed Shelia's stiff hand.

"Well, the baby's healthy, and Charles, she's so beautiful. I did a wonderful job. You'll be so proud when you see her. She's so very special." Kara spoke as if there was no one else around. She was in her glory.

"Kara?" Charles spoke. His patience was thinning. His anger growing. And he could feel his hold on Shelia slipping when the tears began to fall from her eyes again. "Kara," he repeated, "seriously, who is the baby's father?"

"You are, Charles."

"What?"

Shelia snatched her hand out of his grasp.

Charles was looking at her dumbfounded. This was not happening to him. He couldn't let it. He watched Edward put a possessive arm around his daughter's shoulder.

"Kara, this is not a joke." Charles' voice grew louder, deeper, more desperate. "I told you my family, my girlfriend are on the phone with me. Why are you lying?"

"Charles, are you denying your daughter?"

Without hesitation, he answered, "Hell, yeah." He looked around at his family. Their support showed in their eyes, but it was wavering. *This damn girl is crazy*, he thought. "It's not true," Charles stated, taking his mother's offered hand. "Kara, we both know that's not my baby. I haven't even seen you in a year. How can I be the father?" With his free hand, he began drumming on the kitchen table. *What could make a person turn on you like this? Why would she be lying to him when they both knew the truth? It was preposterous.*

"You still drumming your fingers, Charles? How many times have I told you to stop that?"

He stopped, slamming his fist down. "I want a DNA test. Your ass is crazy. How could you do this to me? I thought we were friends. You're lying, and now my family and Shelia are doubting my integrity. I can't have that."

"She's already been tested," Kara replied. "Against the hairbrush you left at the house."

"What hairbrush?" Charles yelled. He had never left anything at her house. He had only stayed there once or twice—two and a half years ago. Kara was lying, but the look on Shelia's face told him that she was starting to believe her. "I didn't leave anything at your house. I still want a test." Charles tried to figure out what kind of game she was playing.

"Charles, what did you say you're girlfriend's name is?"

"Shelia."

"Hi, Shelia," Kara greeted cheerfully.

Charles shook his head. The girl was nuts.

"Hi," Shelia mumbled reluctantly. She didn't like Kara Morning. And she didn't care if she was a big time fashion model. Kara wanted her man.

"Listen, Shelia, I really want to apologize for all the inconvenience. As soon as I get out of this godforsaken place, Charles and I can sit down and explain things to you."

"Explain what?" Charles questioned. "That you're a lying—." He stopped himself. Kara was obviously not the person he thought she was. He thought their friendship was genuine. The girl had issues. As his anger mounted, he became determined to get to the bottom of this.

"When are you coming back to California, Charles?" Kara ignored his statement and cleared her voice. "We need to discuss some things concerning the baby."

"What do I need to discuss about a baby that's not mine?" Charles asked, hunching his shoulders.

"If you keep denying the baby, I'm not going to let you see her."

"I think you're crazy," Charles shook his head. "Kara, you are lying to me and my family. My lawyer is also on the line. I don't know your reason behind this, but I'm going to get to the bottom—."

"Don't threaten me, Charles. I have lawyers, too."

"Why are you doing this?"

"Because you are my baby's father, and I love you, Charles." Kara's voice raised and became erratic.

"My lawyer will be in touch, Kara."

"Good night, Charles, to you and your family."

"She's a smart little snippett, isn't she?" Brenda asked, not waiting for the phone to disconnect.

"Shelia," Charles began as soon as he heard the phone disconnect. He reached for her arm, but she moved out of his reach.

"I think it best if we leave," Edward suggested, looking at his wife and tightening his hold on Shelia's arm. Inwardly, his joy mounted at the relief he felt. "Come on, baby."

Shelia let her father guide her toward the front of the house. Tears continued to fall down her face as she looked at Charles' hopeless expression. She didn't want to leave him, not like this, but her doubts crowded in on her.

After Shelia and her parents left, Troy was the first one to break the silence. "Man, I don't believe for a second—"

"Yeah, Troy. We know you don't." Kristal cut him off while moving over to the sink to get some water. "Any minute I expected you to jump up and say, 'It was me. I got Kara Morning pregnant.'" They all smiled, knowing how Troy felt about Charles. "Sorry, I was just trying to ease the tension. Charles, we know you're not that baby's father."

"Thank you. I know. I just wish Shelia did." Charles used his thumb and forefinger to pinch the bridge of his nose. "I just can't understand why Kara would lie like that about something so important."

"Well, we will worry about that later," April commented. "First things first. Tomorrow morning I'll call a friend of mine at Family Court and see about filing papers to petition paternity. We need to prove that's not your child before you go any further. I'll call you in the morning. Good night everyone, Mom, Dad." April kissed her parents, grabbed her brother's shoulder, then gathered her kids and husband and left.

Charles felt better knowing that soon he would be able to prove to Shelia that he was telling the truth. Her father said she dealt in facts. He was going to get all the facts she needed.

"You sure you're all right, Charles?" Kristal asked, also gathering her children to leave.

"Yeah, I know the truth. I'll wait for April to get the papers so I can get the blood test."

"Wow, just imagine, Kara Morning trying to blame my brother for her baby. Boy, I should have gone out west with you." A slap on the back of his head from his wife, Stephanie, had him hurrying to clean up his statement. "But I had already found the love of my life." He quickly grabbed her from behind. "Isn't that right, darling?"

"Save it, mister. You're already in the doghouse; none for you." She walked into the family room with an apologetic Troy close behind. His family was laughing and making jokes as they made their way into the other room to see the latest drama begin to unfold.

"This family is never short on action, I'll tell you that," John Sr. said, laughing and shaking his head.

"Devin, can you believe that woman? I wish she was here so I could—" Kristal was saying to her sister as they walked out of the kitchen and down the hallway.

"Girl, you're too old for all that violence. She'll get hers. Don't worry about that. Ain't it crazy that the people you envy are the ones with all the problems. Who wants to go to Hollywood? All the crazy people live there."

Kristal's husband, Richard, walked up behind them and patted Kristal on her plump backside, "Well, my baby doesn't need to go anywhere. Do you, love? She has all she needs in me. Right, hon."

"Of course," she answered, kissing his cheek. "My baby is definitely right." She gave Devin a side glance and a wink. "Matter fact, it's time for us to be heading out. School comes early and fast in the mornings. And I have to drive Kevin to school."

Charles heard the others getting their coats and heading for the front door. It was eleven o'clock. "Well, I had better head up to bed myself. I want to give Shelia a call," he said to his parents.

"Son, you know we believe you," John Sr. said. He turned Charles to face him and looked him in the eye. "You know that, right Son?"

"Thanks, Dad. I know you do. I appreciate it. Don't worry. I'm fine." He kissed each of their cheeks.

"Maybe," his mother added, "you should let Shelia stew for the night."

"I can't do that, Mom. I love her too much to let her think that this might be true. I have to call her." He watched his parents walk to their bedroom, then locked the front door once his siblings had finally left.

Shelia looked out the window because she could feel her father's eyes burning into her through the rearview mirror. Why try to hide her misery? She should be happy. She was in love, and Charles was in love with her. She believed that, and everything else he said in the bathroom, but in one swoop, their relationship had changed. She wouldn't start a relationship with Charles having a newborn by someone else. Why would she put herself in that kind of situation? She didn't want anyone to have Charles' babies, no one but her.

As more tears began to fall, Shelia waited to see how long it would take for her father to break his silence. All her life he had treated her like a baby, and it was nice when she was one. But now she was grown, and her life was her own. Jeff never had as hard a time leaving the nest as she had. When she had graduated high school, her father had fully expected her to go to the local college. He wanted her to stay under his wing.

Instead, she picked the best school she could that was far from her family. Shelia wanted to test her independence, and she found that she loved it. She was resourceful and intelligent. Her time away from home helped to build her confidence when she was faced with a challenge. And she had succeeded in overcoming her problems without the help of family or friends.

When she graduated from Howard University a semester ahead of schedule, they thought she would be content with something closer to home. She intended to transfer to John Hopkins' University, but she decided to stay at Howard University instead. Now she only had one year to go before starting her full internship, and he was still being the overprotective father. Shelia assumed that would never change.

"Well, I guess it's safe to say that you and Charles won't be seeing each other any longer." Edward Daniels looked into his rearview mirror in time to see his daughter's blank expression.

"And what would make you think that?" she asked, staring back into the mirror. "You can't honestly believe that." Shelia was struggling to hold onto the last strand of faith she had. Without being disrespectful, she wanted to let him know that not seeing Charles wasn't an option. The feelings in her heart, the love she had for him, were already too strong for that to happen. And if she loved him and knew the kind of man he was, she had to stand by him.

"I not only believe it, I expect it."

From the backseat, Shelia could see her mother's hand reach over to squeeze her father's.

"Just so that everybody knows and understands," Shelia said clearly. "I'm not going to stop seeing Charles. I have a private relationship with him, Daddy. I wish you would understand that." She didn't want to upset him, afraid that he might become stressed.

"Little lady…"

"Dad, you can't keep little-ladying me. I'm grown."

"Not as long as you're living under my roof."

"Look, you can't keep me under lock and key forever. Dad, I'm about to turn twenty-four years old. You still treat me as if I'm fourteen. And the worst part is that I fall right into the role. But not this time. I'm not your little girl. I'm sorry, but I can't be her any more."

"Shelia…" His voice boomed through the car. Her mother's hand stopped him.

"You're right, dear. Maybe we have been treating you like a little girl for far too long. Edward, dear, she does have a point. Baby, we'll try harder to treat you like an adult."

Her father didn't say anything, but Shelia saw the lines on his brow deepen, a sure indication that he was finding her declaration hard to swallow.

Charles was disappointed when Shelia's answering machine picked up his call on the fourth ring. "Shelia, this is Charles, baby. I wanted to talk to you before you laid down for the night. I wanted to tell you that for some reason Kara is lying. I can't tell you why because I'm not sure myself, but I will get to the bottom of it. I love you, Shelia. And, I need you to believe in me. I would never lie to you, baby. I'll give you a call tomorrow, baby. Have a good night."

CHAPTER 5

Despite the brief dispute with her father, Shelia had a very restful night's sleep, dreaming about Charles and their future together. After the message left on her phone the night before, she felt much better about their relationship, and she believed that he wasn't the baby's father. He couldn't give her a valid reason behind Kara's deceit; he didn't know himself. But she knew he would get to the bottom of it.

Now as she stretched in the tub and settled deeper into the scented water, Shelia tried to relax her sore muscles. She let the fragrance drift into her senses and take her to another place, a place where she could loosen the tension she felt in her shoulders and arms. Closing her eyes, she let the hot water work its magic on her body.

"You'll be late, Shelia." Her mother cracked the bathroom door. "You okay, honey?"

Shelia still couldn't look her mother in the face. This was the moment she dreaded. One on one, her mother could be merciless. She wasn't the sweet, salt-and-pepper haired woman everybody thought her to be. "Yeah, Mom. I'm fine."

"Can I talk to you for a minute, dear?"

Knowing she had no choice, Shelia answered, "Sure, Mom. Come on in."

Even though Shelia's bathroom was fairly large, with two chairs and a vanity table, Sylvia chose to sit on the commode. She wanted a clear, close-up view of her daughter. "Anything you want to talk to me about, baby?"

"Nah, I already called the hospital and told them I'd be late," she said, trying without success to change the subject.

Shelia took mostly after her mother, but she wasn't as direct or as impatient as her mother could be. "Well, since we don't have time for games, just tell me one thing." Her mother didn't even take a breath as she continued on. "You did use protection, didn't you?"

"Mom."

"Don't 'Mom' me. I'm not blind."

"I'm grown, Mom. I already heard enough from Dad last night."

"Last night your father was upset about that large mark on the side of your neck. Maybe he did overreact; you are an adult, but you have to remember that you are still his only daughter."

Sitting up, Shelia didn't even try to conceal her anger. "And that makes it all right for him to act like a Neanderthal? Mom, you of all people know that's not fair. All my life, I've been treated like this precious little baby girl. No wonder I had a hard time getting dates. Everybody was scared of Daddy and Jeff and his friends. Now I have a chance to be a little happy, find a little love, and have a little fun, and he still has a problem with that. I'm not going to stop seeing Charles, Mom. I've been in love with him for far too long and—"

"Oh, girl, calm down and shut up. You always were too hyper. Nobody is asking you to stop seeing Charles. You know we love that boy, and we know how you two feel about each other. Now listen to me. When I saw you walk into the Avery's house yesterday evening, I knew right off that something was different about you. I'm your mother, and I love you. Yesterday, either you made love with Charles or you almost did. I can just tell. I'm not even going to ask you which it was. It took everything I had not to pull you into my arms when you walked in, even with all that other mess going on. All I'm going to say is that when you're ready to talk, I'm here. I just want to know that you are all right."

With tears threatening to overflow, Shelia looked at her mother. "Mom, I am all right. I love Charles. All my hopes and dreams could never compare with the way he makes me feel."

"Well, that's all I need to know. If you really love him, then you do what's right for you. This baby mess will sort itself out easily enough. He'll have the test done, and we will know. I just want you to be careful, baby."

"Thanks, Mom. I do need to talk about it more than you know, but I'm just not ready to go into it right now. I guess I'm not as grown as I think I am."

"Honey, you will never be too old for a talk with your mother." Sylvia walked over to the tub and gave her daughter a kiss on the forehead. "Get to work."

As she dressed, Shelia wondered why she had been so reluctant to talk to her mother. All her life, even during arguments with her brother and father, her mother had been her constant ally. Feeling encouraged after Sylvia's pep talk, she left for work with thoughts of Charles and an positive outlook on her life.

"Hey, girl, everything all right?"

"Hi, Tabitha. Yeah, everything's fine. Why do you ask?"

Tabitha was standing at the nurses' station filing folders. "When Mrs. Kembla told me you were running late, I got a little worried."

"No, I'm fine. Just overslept."

"Must have been a late night."

"No, actually, I was home kind of early. Tabitha, did you tell anyone about Charles and me yesterday? I got a lot of stares as I was leaving."

"I'm not going to lie. I'm sorry, but I did tell my girlfriend. She promised she wouldn't say anything."

"Yeah, just as you did."

"I'm sorry, Shelia, but I've never known anyone who was dating a celebrity. Please don't be mad at me."

"I'm not mad, but I just wish you had kept it to yourself."

"I think that makes me feel worse."

The day was dragging by, and there wasn't much to do, so Shelia decided to spend the rest of the day visiting patients. She liked talking with older people and children the most. She would start in the geriatrics ward and end the day in pediatrics, where Liz worked. She needed to talk to her. On her way up to the fourth floor, she ran into Troy on the elevator. Reading a chart, he didn't notice her. "Good afternoon, Dr. Avery."

"Yes, good afternoon. Oh, Shelia, I'm sorry," he said, looking up, "I didn't realize it was you. What's up with this Dr. Avery stuff?"

"Well, we're at work, and I didn't want to be disrespectful."

"Are you kidding me? You're family, Shelia, even if you weren't seeing my brother."

"Thank you, Troy," she said smiling. Shelia saw him paying amused attention to her neck.

"I see that makeup still works for that sort of thing," Troy said, laughing. Seeing her blush, he quickly added, "I'm sorry. I shouldn't be teasing you like that. Charles certainly wouldn't appreciate it, and I can't blame him for making sure everyone knows how he feels about you." She kept blushing. The elevator arrived at his floor and he stepped out, "I'll see you around, Shelia."

"Good bye, Troy."

Shelia spent a half hour with the kids in the pediatric playroom, and then stopped by the nurses' station to see her friend, Liz. After filling Liz in on most of the events of the previous day, her friend hugged her.

"Girl, I knew it. Didn't I tell you that one of these days you two would be together? Wow."

"Liz, did you hear a word I said? Kara Morning is claiming that she just gave birth to Charles' baby. Can you believe it?"

"I heard you. He said it wasn't his. Don't you believe him?" Liz watched her friend closely. The response was slow to come. "Shelia?"

"I do, I do. It's scary, Liz. I mean, I want to believe it with all my heart. I do. But why is Kara Morning gonna lie about something like that?"

"Look, don't you let that woman do this to you, either of you. I don't care who Kara Morning is or what she does. Deep down, she's still a woman. And you know how sneaky and conniving they can be when they want to be."

"Calm down, Liz," Shelia said before Liz started one of her infamous tirades. Once Liz got started, sometimes it was hard to stop her.

"If that was my man, Kara Morning would have to give me proof—hard evidence. I damn sure wouldn't just give my man away."

"That's not what I'm doing, Liz."

"Make sure you don't. How long before you leave?"

"I have to be checked in by next Tuesday."

"Darn. That doesn't leave much time for you two to get reacquainted."

"I know, but tomorrow's my last day of work, so I plan to spend some quality time with him before I go. Look, I've got to get back to my floor. Tabitha's probably wondering where I am." She started down the hall then stopped and turned around. "Oh, before I forget. Tia and Jeff and Denise and Chauncey will be back in town Saturday, so they're having a little party at *Chauncey's* to welcome back the newlyweds. Can you make it?" Pausing, she continued, "Come on, Liz. You'll enjoy it."

"Count me in, and hey, call me later."

"Okay." Checking her watch, she saw that it would be another hour before her shift ended. This was the slowest day she had ever seen at the hospital. Usually, it was bustling with activity. Even the staff seemed thinned out.

Shelia walked off the elevator and saw immediately where everyone was—on her floor. Patients, doctors, nurses, and even housekeeping and cafeteria personnel were there. She pushed her way through the crowd to her station and asked Tabitha what was going on.

"One of the patients has a special visitor," she replied, smiling at Shelia. "Everyone is waiting for him to come out. We are lucky to be stationed right outside. Come over here and make yourself comfortable."

"Well, at least the hour will pass quickly with all this excitement going on. Does anyone know who the visitor is?"

"Sure, we all know who he is. That's why everybody is hanging around." Her smile grew wider.

"Well—" She stopped short as Charles, followed by Troy, stepped out of the patient's room. He smiled directly at her, making Shelia's heart leap into her throat.

Charles looked delicious in his tailor-made, mint-green linen suit. He wore a black silk T-shirt under it and had on black sandals.

Shelia couldn't stand to be this close to him and not be able to melt into his arms. She made herself stand still and watch the happenings with the rest of his fans. Tabitha stood next to her, close to bursting with excitement.

Charles saw only Shelia. The floor was packed with people waiting to see him, but he only wanted to pull her into his arms and kiss her. Distracted by his thoughts, he accidentally bumped into a candy striper who had come up behind him to ask for an autograph. He turned to excuse himself, but the girl fainted, collapsing at his feet. Troy and another doctor bent down to help her. Charles checked to make sure she was all right, but his eyes kept returning to a laughing Shelia.

After the commotion had died down, he signed some autographs and talked to a few people before getting to her desk.

Tabitha stood close by her, waiting. She wasn't a fool. He was going to make his way over to Shelia sooner or later. When she got home, she was going to call her whole family back in Warrington, North Carolina, and tell them she had met a real-life star. Maybe they won't believe her, but she had to share the news with someone.

"Hello, love," he said taking Shelia's hand. He wanted to touch her so badly it hurt. Bringing her hand to his lips, he slowly kissed each knuckle. She watched him intently.

"Hello, yourself," she managed to say, forgetting the staffers still standing around.

"Okay, guys, that's enough. Charles, behave; you're in a public place." Troy's warning snapped them back to reality. Even though the crowd had thinned out, there was still a small group of die-hard onlookers openly staring.

"Oh, sorry about that, man. Every time I get around my beautiful girlfriend, I seem to forget myself." Blushing, Shelia lowered her eyes. Trying to take the focus off her, she made introductions.

"Um...Tabitha, this is Dr. Troy Avery and his brother Charles Avery. Gentlemen, this is my friend Tabitha."

"Hi, I've seen you around, Dr. Avery. It's nice to meet you."

"Nice to meet you, too, Tabitha," Troy replied.

"Um...I know you're probably tired, but could I please have your autograph, Charles? I can't wait to tell everybody back home that I actually met you."

"Oh yeah? Where are you from?"

"Warrington, North Carolina. You've probably never heard of it."

"Sure I have. It's near Durham, right?" She nodded. "I know a fella from down there named James Alston. Know him?"

"No, but I know of the family."

"Well, it's nice to meet you, Tabitha," he said, turning to Shelia. "Now back to you. What are our plans for this evening?" Charles was reluctant to mention the previous night's drama. He was determined to make their time remaining enjoyable.

"I don't know. I have to stop by the house to make that phone call to the university, and then I guess I'm all yours."

Getting her meaning, his smile widened and his eyes twinkled. "Now I like the sound of that. How much longer do I have to wait?"

Checking her watch, Shelia saw that the time had flown by. "Well, it just so happens that you don't have to wait any longer. I'm off. Tabitha, I'll see you tomorrow."

"No, you won't. I'm off tomorrow."

Shelia was a little disappointed. "But it's my last day. I'm not going to see you."

"Well, even though it's against my personal policy, I'll come in for a minute at lunchtime to see you off."

"Great," Shelia said.

She got her purse and bag from the back room and caught up with Charles at the front desk talking to his brother. As she came up to them, he pulled her close, seemingly unconcerned that several people were taking it all in.

"All right, man, I'll see you later. You kids enjoy yourselves, now." Troy kissed Shelia on the cheek and gave his brother a quick hug before falling in with the slowly dispersing crowd.

"We're drawing unnecessary and unwanted attention to ourselves," Shelia whispered.

"Oh, nonsense. I don't see anybody around here but you." Charles turned so that they faced each other, looking into her eyes, he had to ask. "We are all right, aren't we?"

"Charles, I told you last night that we would get through this." She had her hands pressed against his chest, and his chest muscles were straining against her hands.

"We will?" He lowered his head and kissed her full on the lips.

She almost lost her equilibrium, as her legs were wobbling. He felt so good in her arms, and she could feel their hearts beating to the same accelerated rhythm. "We can't be kissing in public like this," she sighed. Opening her eyes, she looked at him, smiling, "I think we had better get out of here before we get arrested for indecent public display."

Laughing, Charles said, "Yeah, that thought occurred to me, too. Let's get you home so you can make that phone call. Then I'll take you out to eat."

"Okay, follow me. I drove today." She started down the hall, well aware that his eyes were stuck on her backside. "Can we go back to my favorite spot?"

He pulled her close and kissed her forehead, both oblivious to the stares directed at them.

ONE OF THESE DAYS

Charles and Shelia sat on wool blankets in the opening hidden from the road by a cluster of trees and bushes surrounding the meadow. It had become her favorite spot. Although somewhat apprehensive about the early-evening sounds coming from the dense woods, Shelia was quickly falling in love with the comforting atmosphere of this place. She relaxed against Charles as he sang softly into her ear.

Above them, an array of twinkling stars had a hypnotic effect on her. It was a clear summer night, and warm wind softly blew through the trees, creating a strange melody as it blended with the mating calls of four-legged inhabitants within the confines of the woods.

"Charles, I'm so glad you brought me back out here." Shelia sat between his legs as he rocked her slowly from side to side. The warmth of his arms encircling her was intoxicating.

"You said you wanted to come here, baby." He kissed the side of her face.

"I love it here." She closed her eyes and listened to their unseen companions. "You can hear the animals so clearly at night."

"They're all back on, settling in for the night. You're probably hearing their mating calls." He laughed and kissed her again.

"Is that what's going on?"

"Yeah, they're all trying to get some." They both laughed at his slightly bawdy comment.

"Charles, can I ask you something?" Shelia sat up and looked into his eyes, suddenly serious.

Charles leaned back from her, sensing what the question probably was. He had his reservations about bringing her back to this spot, especially in light of what had almost happened the day before. He thought he was in control of the situation. In the car, he was in control. In actuality, he felt himself losing control. Having her in his arms wasn't enough. It was a reality that he had been tussling with since they parked the car and decided to stretch out on the blanket.

"What's up, Shelia?"

"Do you want to be with me, Charles?"

"Now, what kind of question is that?"

"I think it's a fair question. Do you want to be with me?"

"Come on now, baby. You know I do. Haven't I spent time with you every day so far? Please don't be asking me this because of last night."

Shelia turned around and faced him. She was on her knees. "Okay, I'm going to make this as simple as possible. Are you not getting my meaning? Look, since we've been talking—what, a couple of days?— I've been practically throwing myself at you. And this has nothing to do with Kara or the baby. Why aren't you catching?"

Charles looked at her and realized she was dead serious. "Girl, how many times do I have to tell you to let me be in charge of some situations? Can I handle things, please?"

"I just wanted to make sure, you know."

"No, I don't know."

"Well, you know what they sometimes say about you entertainment types." Shelia smiled, clearly teasing.

"No, Shelia, what do they say about entertainment types?"

Charles knew she was joking, but he decided to take part in her game. When she flipped a limp wrist back and forth in front of his face, he grabbed her by the arm and pulled her on top of him. "Oh, is that what you think about me?"

Shelia hunched her shoulders and giggled.

"I guess I'm going to have to show you a thing or two."

"Charles, you don't have to defend yourself to me. You like what you like. I mean, to each his own, you know."

"Oh, really. No, Shelia. I'll show you what I like."

Charles kissed her on her nose and then rolled her over so that she was under him. He continued to kiss her until he heard her barely audible moan. As his lips blazed a hot trail of long kisses down her neck, he unbuttoned her shirt and pushed it off her shoulders. With his thumb and middle finger he unhooked the clasp in the front of her bra.

Shelia sighed as he squeezed her breast and then placed kisses on each inch of her skin, moving from one nipple to the other. She placed a hand on the back of his head as his hand splayed across her midsection until he felt the band of her jeans.

"Take these damn jeans off, Shelia," Charles demanded, urgently trying to unbutton them. She quickly obeyed. Charles' breath caught as she stood before him wearing only a pair of black lace panties. Her skin glowed in the moonlight. He held out his hand to her. "Come here, baby."

Shelia grabbed his hand and let him lower her onto the blanket. Goosebumps covered her body, and her pulse beat furiously. She wasn't just excited; she was past ready for this.

Charles shut out little voices in the back of his mind. He forced himself to forget about Jeff for the moment. As he watched her lying next to him, he decided to listen only to his heart.

His kisses slowly began to produce a longing for something more, something more intense. They hadn't quenched his thirst for Shelia. His hands had already felt her secret hiding spot. Charles couldn't take any more. He peeled his clothes off quickly and placed the condom over himself as her responses to his attentions increased his hunger for her. She was already on another level, floating between fantasy and ecstasy. He wanted to join her.

Charles spread her legs apart and knelt between them. Bending over to kiss her, he said, "Shelia, look at me." While he kissed her slowly on her face and neck, he whispered to her, "I've waited for you for so long, Shelia. I can't wait any longer."

"Hurry, Charles," she replied dizzily.

He pushed himself into her and froze. Shelia screamed out in pain, her body tensing. Charles felt the small barrier break.

"Oh, shit," he said, looking down at her. "Oh, shit, Shelia, why didn't you tell me?" He wiped at the tear that slowly slid from her eye and kissed her cheek. "Just relax, baby, and keep still. It will go away in a second. Relax." Trying to maintain control and soothe her at the same time was hard for Charles. "I'll stop, Shelia. I'm going to pull out."

"No." She grabbed him around his waist and stilled him.

"Well, you have to relax, baby, okay?" Kissing her temples, he continued, "I'm sorry, baby." Charles kissed her again, letting his tongue play along her lips, over her teeth, and into her mouth until he felt her muscles loosen. "You okay, baby?"

"Yes, please Charles, show me how to love you," Shelia pleaded.

He kissed her tears away and began to slowly move inside her.

Shelia was so caught up in the moment that she was unprepared for the wave of delight that started in the pit of her stomach. She began to move and match his thrust as if she was being beckoned by a divine light.

"Oh, Shelia, baby, you feel so good," he whispered.

Charles felt the rush of sensations starting to build inside him. Her moans and her thrashing told him that she was on the verge of her first strong orgasm. He wanted to be a part of it. Deepening his strokes and quickening his pace, Charles took her over the edge.

"Charles, oh, oh, God, Charles. I love you. I love you," Shelia screamed. Her orgasm sent Charles into a tailspin when he felt her muscles convulsing around him. With groans and pleas to her, he joined her in a realm of pure bliss. He bucked and ground through his release, collapsing on top of her.

When he could lift his head, he was still holding her tight, and she was caressing his back and hips. Kissing her slowly and passionately, he pulled her with him as he rolled onto his back. "Are you all right, Shelia? I didn't hurt you, did I?"

"No," she answered, tears falling. "It was beautiful. The pain caught me off guard, even though I was expecting it."

"Baby," he said, rubbing her leg, "if you had told me, it could have been better for you."

"Charles, it couldn't have been any better. I didn't tell you because I wanted it to be you, today, in this perfect spot. Oh, Charles, it was perfect. I loved having you inside me."

"You should have told me you were a virgin," he insisted.

"What would you have done if I had told you? You would have made up any excuse possible not to be the one to take my virginity. Or you would have tried to do the gentlemanly thing and talk to me about waiting for marriage. Well, you really should have known. I've been saving myself for you. I love you, Charles. I wasn't about to give my most precious gift to anyone else." She kissed his offering lips and looked into his eyes.

Looking at her, Charles knew she was speaking from the heart. "Thank you for this gift, Shelia. You humble me. I don't feel deserving of it." He kissed her face, cheek, and neck.

"Oh, Charles, you deserve this and more. I would have waited forever to be with you." She returned his kisses with all her love as he removed the first condom and replaced it with another.

"I'm glad I kept these in the car," he said, smiling.

Surprised, she said, "Again already, Charles? I'm really going to enjoy this relationship."

"Shelia, you haven't seen anything yet." Laughing, he made slow, lazy love to her the way he felt he should have the first time.

The moans and whispers of the two lovers mingled with the mating calls of the enchanted animals of the grove.

CHAPTER 6

The days leading up to Shelia's departure were some of the happiest of her life. Her stint at the hospital ended with a party given for her by the staff. It wasn't a surprise; they did it every year. But she liked knowing she was appreciated by the people who would be her colleagues.

She spent as much time with Charles as possible, having him over for dinner with her parents; cuddling in her parents' den, watching videos and eating popcorn. Because Charles drew too much attention when they ventured out, they mostly hung around their family homes.

A trip to the local mall for dinner and a movie was a total disaster once Charles had been recognized. They actually had to sprint through the mall and hide in the back of Macy's until security could rescue them.

Shelia was amazed at his fans' reaction to him. Teenagers, as well as grown women, were reduced to a state of near-hysteria around him. They screamed his name, blew him kisses, and tore at his clothes if they got close enough.

Friday, after making security arrangements with the local police department and the school administration, they visited their old high school, and Charles performed a mini-concert before an overflow crowd in the assembly hall. Shelia was so proud of him she could barely contain her excitement. Afterwards, a table was set up for him to sign autographs, and with Shelia and little Carlton—his oldest sister's son and a student at the school—helping, everyone received a signed picture.

It was two o'clock when they left the school. They were both famished, but stopping at a McDonald's was not a good plan. The last thing Charles wanted was to be bothered by people. They stopped at a small sub shop instead and had a quick snack. On the way to her house, Charles pulled over to the side of the road.

Shelia saw the look on his face. She knew exactly what was going on in his head because it was also going on in hers. Their love was so intense, the more time they spent together the greater their need to express that love. When they made love, it was uncontrollable, sometimes close to violent. Their climaxes were like an earthquake, shaking them to their very foundations. Afterwards, both she and Charles would feel numbed and stripped bare. It was as if they had been left wide open for all the world to look into their souls. Shelia reasoned that it was because soon they would be apart and were therefore trying to hold on to each other, trying to ensure that when they separated, a piece of the other would remain.

"Shelia, baby, why don't we go away this weekend? It's our last weekend together. You'll be gone on Tuesday," he suggested.

"Charles, you know we promised to be at the party tomorrow night."

"Damn, I forgot about that." He sat drumming his fingers on the steering wheel, deep in thought. Shelia turned and took his hand in hers.

"You know what we could do. Let's go stay in one of the hotels in town for the weekend. That way we can be together and still make the party."

"That sounds good to me. I just don't want to make love to you and get up and leave. I want to hold you in my arms all night." Making little circles on the back of her hand with his finger, he asked, "That sounds crazy, doesn't it?"

"Of course not. I want the same thing. I'm going to miss you so much. We'll be on different ends of the country."

"But I'm going to give you the number for the phone I carry at all times when I'm traveling. You'll be able to call me toll-free anytime."

"Okay. Well, let's go and get that suite and then get some clothes and dinner. We can pretend that we're married for the weekend." She smiled as she said it, but when she looked at Charles, she saw that he wasn't. "It was just a joke, Charles. For God's sake, lighten up." She mistook his serious look for one of fear.

Charles turned to her. "Would you marry me, Shelia?"

Now it was her turn to get serious, "Charles, why are you asking me something like that? Of course, I would marry you. What's wrong with you?" Shelia thought it was strange for him to ask a question that everybody already knew the answer to. Goodness, she had only been in love with him forever. Everybody knew that her whole life had revolved around that single-minded goal.

"Nothing's wrong with me. I was just wondering," he said, putting a smile on his face. "Okay, let's go."

Pulling back into traffic, Charles thought to himself that she must have thought he was speaking in the future tense. *Maybe it would be best if he let her think that*, he mused. But he had actually been proposing.

Charles had it bad, and he knew it. He was ready to do just about anything not to lose her. She still had another year of school to go, and it would be unfair of him to put that kind of additional pressure on her. So, he would bide his time; she was already his anyway. The year would go by pretty fast; he could deal with it. Or at least, he prayed that he could.

By eight Friday night, Charles and Shelia had settled into their suite at the Marriott. Lounging on the sofa, they watched an old movie on cable. Stopping at their houses for clothes and whatever else they needed for the weekend had taken longer than expected.

A terrible storm was underway when they finally arrived at the hotel. In the span of thirty seconds—the time it took to get out of the car and into the lobby—they had gotten drenched. As soon as they checked in, they got out of their wet clothes. Now in pajamas, they stretched out with a bottle of wine and a cheese and cracker platter that came from room service, compliments of the hotel.

The rain beat angrily against the double-glass doors leading to the balcony. The wind was blowing so hard against the furniture outside, Charles began to fear something would fly over the railing and land on the cars below.

He was tired, but too pumped up to sleep. Pulling Shelia close, Charles whispered in her ear, "I'm going to start a bath. You will join me, won't you?" Letting her go, he walked toward the bathroom.

"You must have been reading my mind. I'll be there in a minute. Do you want some more wine?"

Charles hollered yes over his shoulder. The bathroom was spacious and beautiful. A stand of twin sinks with a huge mirror above it was on one wall. A large beach-themed painting hung on the other wall. The stand under it was decorated with seashells, miniature lighthouses, and colored stones. Against the aqua blue walls near the tub sat an array of white candles. The commode was in the far corner, and next to it was a glass-enclosed shower with jet-spray fixtures. White floral designs ran along the base of the shower doors.

To the right of the shower was the sunken tub. It also had jet sprays. He turned on the water and the sprays, and poured in bath beads. He wanted the bathroom transformed into an enchanted setting, a place for love, before Shelia came in.

Moving quickly, Charles dropped rose petals from his mother's garden and set out red candles that he'd ordered from the hotel gift shop and had placed in the room before their arrival. He wanted the little time they had left to be special and unforgettable.

Shelia walked into the bathroom and clasped her hands to her chest in utter surprise. Charles stood in the middle of the room, totally nude, a bouquet of roses covering his private parts. Rose petals were laid over the sink counters and the floor. The sinks were filled with water with rose petals floating on top. Candles were strategically placed all around the room: on the sink counters, by the commode, on the floor, and around the edges of the tub. It was beautiful. She couldn't believe he had gone to this much trouble for her. He sidled up to her and pulled one rose from the bouquet. Putting it in her hair over her left ear, he bent down and kissed her softly on the cheek.

"I love you, Shelia."

"Oh, Charles, I love you, too. This is beautiful." Shelia was overwhelmed. No one had ever taken the time to make her feel so special.

He placed the remaining flowers on the floor near the tub. The flickering candles bounced over his lean, and powerful body. He's gorgeous. No doubt about it, she thought. His hands slowly unbuttoned her top and slid it from her shoulders. He lightly brushed her breasts and she felt herself shuddering.

Charles stepped closer and moved his hands to her waist. His lips were on her forehead as he pushed her pajama bottoms down. He began kissing his way down her body. He paused at her breast, biting and pulling on her nipples until they stood erect. Moving lower, he nipped at her stomach until he was on his knees in front of her and her hand was on the back of his head.

When she stepped out of the bottoms, he stood and pulled her into his strong arms. Running his hands up and down her back, he kissed every part of her body before returning to her mouth for a long passionate kiss that left her breathless.

Her arms encircled his neck, and she allowed herself to be engulfed by his passion. His erection was pressed against her belly; she wanted him inside her.

"Baby, join me," he said, leading her to the tub and helping her into the water. She settled next to him and let her body relax.

He wanted to savor the moment. If in all his dreams he could have believed that one day she would be his and accept the love that had burned for her all those years, he would have saved himself a lot of misery.

Shelia sat still as Charles began to sponge bath oil over her body, starting with her shoulders and neck and then moving to her back. He sponged down her arms and hands. Facing her and looking into her eyes, he dribbled water over her collarbone and breasts. Shelia couldn't hide the blush that crept up to her eyes. Not even in her wildest dreams had she thought a man would cherish her this much. Layer after layer of self-consciousness slowly fell away, and she allowed herself to enjoy this pampering.

"Stand, Shelia."

Doing as she was told, she let Charles wash her from the hips down. The attention overwhelmed her. Her body shook with excitement and anticipation of what was to come.

After she had sat back down, Charles poured them each a glass of wine. He turned the jet sprays back on, delighting Shelia and making them both laugh.

Charles poured wine onto her shoulders and began tasting. She gasped as his teeth bit into her neck, and she moved closer. She put her arms around his waist and held on. Charles moved to the corner and turned the radio to a slow-jam station.

On their knees, they slowly swayed to the music as he caressed her back. His lips moved down her body, stopping at her breasts. His hands massaged and squeezed them until she parted her lips, panting softly.

Capturing her mouth with his, he teased her with his tongue until she could stand it no longer and grabbed his head with her hands.

Charles rested against the back wall of the tub and situated Shelia so that she was straddling him. His mouth went to her breasts, and as she moaned and sighed, he covered each with tender kisses. Gripping her thighs with his hands, he leaned back to give her access to his face and lips.

Slowly, he stroked her inner thigh, moving closer to her center until he could feel the hair covering her.

She was trying to settle herself over him, but he wanted to play a little bit longer. Pushing aside her folds, Charles eased his fingers in to rub against her. Her eyes glazed over, making it hard for him to stay controlled.

Shelia didn't want to wait any longer. Pounding, the center of her womanhood throbbing, she wrapped her fingers around Charles, knowing he wouldn't be able to hold out for much longer.

"Oh, God, Shelia," Charles said. He shut his eyes and dropped his head, struggling for control. Pulling her closer, he bent his head into her neck and began to kiss her. Taking a couple of deep breaths, he pulled her down onto him. "Slow," he said through clenched teeth.

She could tell he was trying to keep control, so she leaned into him with her hands around his neck and let him set the pace. His hands were on her hips helping to guide her onto him. Their pace was so slow it seemed as if they were barely moving, but inside they were both struggling to keep control.

Charles was having a hard time. Even in all this water, the wetness she produced was all he could feel. The slower he moved the wetter she became, until it surrounded him. He held onto her and quickened his pace. His breathing became hoarse and heavy. She was calling out to him, but he didn't even understand what she was saying. All his attention was on the center of their universe. Then he felt her spasm and her muscles tightening. He opened his eyes and saw her bucking and grinding into him, reaching for her release. He was still holding onto a single thread of control when she exploded and her released wetness spilled over him. She held onto him, digging her nails deeply into his back; and he felt himself slipping into blackness. She felt so good.

With the last of his energy, Charles pulled her off him and held her close, kissing her face and eyes as he released himself into the water. It took him a second to get his bearings, but when he did, Charles thanked the Lord for little blessings. A mistake was something they didn't need.

Shelia was confused. She felt empty and alone. She melted into his arms, returning his kisses until they came down from the high they had achieved and landed back into the real world.

"Baby, are you all right?" Her answer was a kiss. "I had to pull out. We didn't have a condom, and—"

"That's all right. I understand. Let's get out of here and dry off. It was wonderful, but I don't want to be in the water again if you have to pull out. I felt so lonely afterwards."

Charles smiled at her as she walked out of the room. "That's my girl, direct and straight to the point."

"Hungry?"

"No, not really. Maybe some of that fruit would be nice. You'd be surprised what can be done with fruit, Shelia."

"I have a feeling I'm about to find out." Between drying off, kissing, and caressing each other, it took them twenty minutes to make it into the living room. Shelia was lying comfortably on the couch when Charles came into the room with a tray of grapes, strawberries, a banana, whipped cream, and a cup of ice.

"What's the ice for?" She looked at him questioningly. He answered with a sparkle in his eye and a wide grin on his face.

CHAPTER 7

Propping herself on one elbow, Shelia looked down at the only man she could ever love. He was her friend, her lover, her teacher, and her soul mate. How in the world was she going to survive away from him?

She was leaving Tuesday, and who knew when they would see each other again. Already a feeling of loneliness was working its way into her heart. She wanted to be optimistic, but her reality was a lonely existence without him.

Nothing would stop her from achieving her goals. Becoming a doctor was something that was going to happen, and she knew she was strong enough to succeed no matter the obstacles. But would she and Charles be able to rebuild the fire that was burning so brightly between them right now? Would this separation be permanent? When he returned to his celebrity friends and the supercharged environment they inhabit, maybe he would find someone else.

"Okay, okay, girl. Stop tripping. Just enjoy yourself."

Shelia looked down at him, not sure if he had heard her talking to herself. Easing closer, her thoughts drifted back to the night they had just shared, the things he had shown her and the way he had made her feel; and to the way he had held her through the night and how she felt waking next to him this morning. This was where she wanted to be, how she wanted to start every morning of her life. She felt safe and whole knowing he was there.

"All right, man. Thanks for letting me know." Charles was saying on the phone to his manager, Everett. He had called Charles' parent's house, then his cell phone when they informed him that Charles wasn't there.

In a good mood, he pulled Shelia onto his lap and hugged her. "He said a press release will be in all the major newspapers as of tomorrow stating it was mistakenly reported that I was the baby's father. *Entertainment Television* won't retract their story until the paternity test results come in."

"Maybe you should wait for the results before you put it in the papers, too."

"I don't need to wait. I already know I'm not the father. I already know what the results will say." He looked at her. "Shelia, I'm not the father."

"Charles, I know you're not," she said sincerely. "I believe you, baby."

He looked at her again. "Hey, let's get dressed and go do a little shopping. There's something I need to pick up downtown."

"I hope not at any of the malls. I don't want to have to share you with anyone during our last weekend together. Bad enough we have to attend that party tonight. We better get a move on. I want to be at your house when they come in. You know it'll be crowded. Everybody in the neighborhood will probably be there."

"It's not our last weekend together. We will just be separated for a little while. During the school year, we'll talk, and I'll visit you and you'll visit me."

She tried to put a smile on her face, but doubt weighed heavily on her mind.

The house was alive with activity; the resulting noise could be heard down the street. The front lawn was crowded with children and adults when Charles and Shelia pulled up. They had to park way down the street.

"Looks like we weren't the only ones trying to be here before the newlyweds." He smelled the burnt charcoal and saw the smoke rising up from behind the house. "Oh, looks like we're having one of the famous Avery barbecues. John and Dad must be back there *burnin'*."

"Well, I hope your mom made some of that potato salad with those real little bits of celery. I'm getting hungry just thinking about it." Holding hands, they made their way through the throng of people. Neighbors and business associates, old school buddies, and even some ex-boyfriends and ex-girlfriends were milling about. Charles didn't know what to think of the latter's presence.

Shelia was on cloud nine. Their little shopping trip was to an exclusive jewelry store in the shopping district. Standing at the front door of the store, Shelia considered reasons for the visit. Common sense told her that he was probably buying a gift for the newlyweds due back any minute. Or maybe it was something for his parents, since he hadn't been home in such a long time. But in her heart, she couldn't stop the little fourteen-year-old girl from coming forward with dreams of romance and marriage that had been stored away for so many years.

Charles waited patiently for the salesperson to buzz them in. He had taken off his sunglasses so he could be recognized by the store's salesperson; he knew when to use his celebrity status to his advantage.

"Ah, Mr. Avery, so good to have you back with us so soon," the lady said, smiling warmly as she opened the door wide. The petite redhead was sole owner of Steinberg Jewelers. "Oh, and I see you've brought a guest with you."

"Hello, Ms. Steinberg," Charles replied cordially, shaking her outstretched hand. "Let me introduce you to my girlfriend, Shelia Daniels."

"It's very nice to meet you," she said, shaking Shelia's hand as well. "I must say that is a lovely outfit you're wearing." She looked appreciatively at Shelia's pink and tan Capri set with a matching pink scarf doubling as a belt.

"Thank you." Shelia's smile faded as the lady pulled her into her arms. She looked at Charles, surprised by the gesture, but he only shrugged. He was used to seeing industry types hugging or kissing someone they barely knew.

"Mr. Avery, please come this way. I took the liberty of setting up a display table for your viewing. You and Ms. Daniels may take a seat right over there while I go to the back for your purchase." She pointed them toward a round table covered with a black velvet cloth.

"Thank you," Charles moved forward, his hand at the small of Shelia's back.

"So, what are you buying, Charles?" Instead of being coy, Shelia decided to have her curiosity satisfied.

He turned his hazel gaze on her as if weighing the question.

"Well?" Shelia asked again.

"I, um…"

"Here we are," Ms. Steinberg called out cheerfully as she rushed back into the room carrying a small black square case opened wide. "This is one of the most remarkable diamond engagement rings available in our store. Of course, if you don't find it appealing, I would be happy to help you find something else you might like."

"Thank you, Ms. Steinberg, but I made up my mind when I came in yesterday. This is the one I want."

"Very well." Turning on a small desk light, she set the ring against the black velvet. The stone sparkled brilliantly, reflecting a seductive array of colors when turned this or that way.

Shelia's heart started palpitating as she watched him pick up the ring and examine it closely. An engagement ring? What in the world…

He turned to her, smiling, his dimple seeming even deeper than usual, "Well, what do you think?" he asked, moving the ring in front of her for closer inspection.

"I'm not an expert on rings, Charles. It looks good to me." Could her dreams have become reality? She wasn't prepared to dare think that. Still, her eyes stayed on the huge rock sparkling enticingly in front of her.

"Do you like it?" he asked cautiously, not knowing how she would react when she found out that it was for her.

"Of course, it's a beautiful ring," she said. Ms. Steinberg stood nearby, smiling.

"I want you to have it." He waited for her to refuse his ring. He knew she would.

"Oh, no…I…No, Charles, I can't take this!" she exclaimed, trying to breathe evenly.

"Yes, you can. It's a gift from me to you. I want you to have it." His reassurances didn't do him much good; she continued protesting.

"But, Charles, it's an engagement ring. You can't buy me this. And it's way too expensive." But when Charles began to slipping the ring on her finger, she didn't move her hand away. She couldn't stop her dream from having a happy ending.

"Don't worry about how much it cost. If I couldn't afford it, I wouldn't have bought it." Watching her hold her hand up to examine the ring, Charles knew it had been the right choice.

Shelia froze, body and mind numbed by this symbol of his love. Trembling, struggling to steady her ring hand.

"But, Charles…" she sighed, leaving her thought unfinished as a sparkle from the diamond caught her eye.

"Shelia, please, just think of it as a friendship ring. I'm not asking you to marry me or anything. I just want you to know how much you mean to me. I want you to think of me when we're apart." After he had made his intentions and expectations clear, she eagerly accepted the gift.

It seemed as if everybody they ever knew had crammed into the house and yard awaiting the arrival of the newlyweds. The Avery family itself was large, but when extra people were added, any gathering became overcrowded. She recognized a lot of their former schoolmates, as well as a couple of Charles' old girlfriends. She would just keep an eye on them. There was no doubt in her mind as to why they were there. Word didn't take long to get around. Half of these people weren't even at the wedding, and probably didn't know the couples were due back today.

As soon as they stepped onto the front lawn, people began making their way toward them. Charles tightened his grip on her hand and led the way into the house, speaking to most and hugging others. He told them that he wasn't signing any autographs; he was just home to spend time with his family. A number of people left after taking pictures of him going into the house. Some of his old flames threw daggers at Shelia with their eyes, but she was too happy to notice. She was worried about only one girl, and she didn't see her around.

"Whoa, look at the size of that ring. Shelia, you been moonlighting or something?" Kristal hadn't given her a chance to get settled before jumping at her. "Oh, my God, that's got to be about five and a half carats." Shelia tried shrinking back, but Kristal was not having it. She pulled Shelia to the front of the living room, pushing her brother aside. "Devin, hurry and look at this. Charles, you really outdid yourself. My goodness, it's beautiful."

Only women were in the room, so Charles decided to go elsewhere. As he looked around he saw Caryn Wilson among the milling and chattering women. She was his high-school sweetheart, if you could call her that.

Since he couldn't be with the one he loved, as the old song went, he loved the one he was with. He hadn't given Caryn a thought since graduation day, but she had kept after him for some reason. Whenever he came home, she was there. He took her out a couple of times, but any feelings he might have had for her in high school had long faded. He leaned over Kristal and whispered, "Thanks, Sis," kissing her on the cheek. He then kissed Shelia full on the mouth and retreated to the back of the house.

Devin came up to Kristal and Shelia right on cue. "Damn, he must have broken the bank with that." She pulled April, one of their older sisters, into the group. Soon, other people made their way over to look at the ring.

Only one person in the room didn't move to gawk. Looking up, Shelia saw her. They hadn't associated with each other in school because of the age difference, but each knew who the other was. And they both knew that things could and would get pretty ugly if they let it. Right then, Shelia decided to let them think the ring meant more than she and Charles had decided on.

"Is my mother here yet, Devin?"

"Yeah, she was one of the first people to arrive. She and Mom are back there with Roberta and the rest preparing extra food. A lot more people came than were invited."

Devin had never cared for too many of their extended family members, and even less for Caryn Wilson. Age had never stopped her or Tia from voicing their opinions as far as that one was concerned. Tia had even fought her a couple of times for trying to make Charles look bad. She had come to the barbecue with one of their more rambunctious cousins, and their mother had made her promise to be nice. A smile on her face, Devin thought, *Tia hadn't been there to make that promise.*

In the kitchen, Sylvia and Brenda were boiling more meat and making more side dishes. Charles walked through and spoke to his sister Roberta and his sisters-in-law, Stephanie and Anna. He stopped at the counter to kiss both his mother and Mrs. Daniels on the cheek.

"Hi, Charles, is my daughter with you?" Mrs. Daniels asked.

"Uh…yes, as a matter of fact, she is." He didn't know what Shelia had told them about her arrangements for the weekend, and he wasn't going to volunteer any information. "She should be coming through here any minute. I'm going out back with the fellas." Stopping in his tracks, he turned to his mother and asked, "Um…Mom, what is Caryn doing here?"

If it had been one of his brothers, his mother thought, she would have been pulled to the side as if it was some big secret, but not her Charles. He didn't have a thing to hide, and she knew he wanted Sylvia to know that.

"I don't know. I think she came with your cousin Rema. I didn't want to be rude. She probably heard that you were home and wanted to see if she could catch your attention. Devin wanted to throw her out as soon as she said hi." She smiled at Sylvia, "Devin, Tia, and Kristal are all so easily set off. They don't take any mess, I'll tell you that. Just as bad as the boys were in school."

"Well, you should have let her," Charles said. "I don't need any headaches today. We only have two days before Shelia goes back to school, and I don't want to spend them arguing."

Sylvia laughed, "Charles, don't you go fretting about something so silly. Shelia knows how to handle things like this. You just sit back and enjoy your day. That girl of mine knows how to fend for what's hers." Looking back at the bowl of food, she added, "If it's hers?"

Charles knew it was a weak attempt at getting info. He started laughing and hugged both women from behind, "It's hers all right…it's definitely hers." Leaving them happy, he went out back to join his father and brothers.

"Man, where have you been? Your manager called here for you this morning. We've been here slaving since nine o'clock. Dad called me last night and told me to get over here first thing. He had the bright idea for this barbecue. You got off lucky this time."

"Troy, you didn't have to go to the hospital today?"

"Yeah. At six, I was waking patients up and checking stats." Lowering his voice, Troy continued, "So you stayed out last night, uh?"

"Yeah, something like that. I won't be in tonight, either."

"Well, good to hear it. You got yourself a good woman; smart, too."

"I know. Man, for the first time in my life I feel complete. It's like I've been waiting to feel this way forever. Even my music doesn't compare to her, and you know how bad I wanted this career."

"Charles, you've been waiting your whole life for her. Probably even longer than when you really started to take your singing seriously. Even when you were with other people, you were just passing time waiting for her. Everybody knows that."

They sat down at a table toward the back of the yard, "Troy, was it this way for you and Stephanie? Did you just know she was the one for you?"

"To be honest, I didn't even see it coming. But I was young and still in college. I got lucky when I met Stephanie because she kept me focused on my priorities. If it hadn't been for her, I probably wouldn't be a doctor today. We had two kids before I even started medical school. She's a very strong woman; that's what you have. Nowadays, a man needs a strong woman to make it. Shelia knows what she wants out of life, and even if a barrier arises, she's going to fight for it. Listen, you're a big-time celebrity. The last thing you need is some weak woman riding your coattails and who's going to complain every step of the way to boot."

Charles laughed, "You saw her, too, didn't you?"

"Yeah, I saw her walk in with Rema. Two peas in a pod." Laughing, they made their way back up the steps to the deck, where most of the men were standing around the grills drinking beer. Looking down, Charles saw people sitting at tables set up around the yard. Men were playing dominos or checkers, and a few of his younger cousins and nephews had a basketball game going. His nieces were jumping rope at the side of the house.

"I'm really going to miss you guys next week."

His father had moved over beside him. "Now, Charles, none of that sentimental stuff. You got a job to do. Your mother and me are so proud of you every time we hear one of your songs on the radio or see you perform on TV or get one of them awards. You just keep on making us proud, Son."

Charles accepted a beer from his brother and settled back to enjoy the day.

Shelia felt self-conscious after Kristal's overheated performance about her ring, but it was nothing compared with the show the mothers put on. She walked into the large kitchen ready to be put to work. She kissed her mother's cheek and spoke to Mrs. Avery.

"Afternoon, ladies, need any help in here?"

"No. We missed you last night, dear. Did you stay with one of your friends from work?"

Not missing a beat, Shelia replied honestly, "With a friend, but not one from work." She smiled to herself when she saw the mothers looking at each other. "Anyway, I'm here now and ready to help out anyway I can."

"Dear, if your neck is going to keep getting bruised like that, you should try to cover it with a turtleneck or something."

"Mom, it's about 80 degrees outside. And the bruises aren't my fault. Talk to her son about it." She smiled, putting her hand on Mrs. Avery's shoulder.

The scream was so loud people from the front of the house made their way to the kitchen.

"Oh, my God...Lord..." Sylvia was holding her chest. Brenda went to her and tried to get her to sit, but Sylvia was jumping around and crying.

"Sylvia, for God's sake, calm down. What is it?"

Her husband made his way through the crowd, "Sylvia, what is it?"

"Mom, what's wrong?" Shelia was beginning to get scared. Sylvia just pointed at her.

"Look, Brenda, look."

Brenda did look, and she started crying, too. Her hand flew to her mouth. The ladies hugged each other and started jumping together. "Oh, thank you, God."

Now, Shelia knew what was happening; once again she was the center of attention. Edward and John Sr. walked over to the women. "For God's sake, would you two get a hold of yourselves. You're causing a very big scene. Troy, you boys, clear some of these folks out of here so we can get to the heart of the matter. Nobody's hurt."

"All right, people. Let's make our way out the back door. There are plenty of seats outside. Dad, I'm going to put a sign on the front door telling people to come around through the gates. Too much traffic is coming through here."

"Sounds good. Now, everybody just calm down. Tell them kids to make their way to the back, too. More than enough yard out there for everyone. Don't want no accidents." Looking at his wife, John waited for her to settle down. "Are you all right now?"

"Lord, you kids have to stop surprising me this way. I'm getting too old for this." Sylvia stood up and walked over to Shelia. "Well, missy, you got something to say for yourself?" Just that fast, her mom was back to her normal self and moving straight in for the kill, Shelia thought. That's why she enjoyed it so much when her mother was caught off guard.

"No, I'm trying to figure out what's going on like everybody else," Shelia answered.

Charles walked over with a glass of water for each of the ladies. "Everything all right?"

"That's what we want to know, Charles," she said, turning her eyes on him. "Isn't there something you want to tell us?"

"Okay," Troy started to say, trying to take pressure off his brother.

"Troy Allen Avery Sr., you stay out of this one," Brenda interrupted.

Seeing that his mother was not to be played with, Troy backed off.

"Mom, what in the devil has gotten into you? I'm on the back porch with the rest of the guys when all of the sudden all hell breaks loose in here. And now it's my fault?" He stood next to Shelia, with both mothers advancing towards them. Sylvia grabbed Shelia's hand and held up the ring for everyone to see. After gasps from the women and admiring expletives from some of the men, realization finally dawned on Charles. Shelia just stood there, saying nothing. She pulled her hand from her mother's grasp.

"Oh, I see. All that noise was because I bought my girlfriend a going-away present." Charles scratched his head and received a smack from his mother.

"Explain. Now."

"Mom," he started cheerfully. "Mom, I just told you. I bought Shelia a going-away present."

Edward stepped forward. "Young man, we need to talk."

Charles immediately lost his smile. "But…"

"Dad, not now. This is just what Charles said it is—a going-away present."

"Shelia—," her dad started.

"Now, Edward, calm down," Sylvia interjected, placing her hand on her husband's arm.

"Calm down, calm down. My daughter has a $30,000 engagement ring on her hand, and I'm supposed to calm down. What in the world am I supposed to do, Sylvia?" He turned to his wife with both arms raised in exasperation. "You keep telling me to calm down. Why? Because she's an adult. To hell with that! This is my little girl we're talking about here. I didn't say anything last week when she didn't make it to dinner. I didn't say too much about Charles' new offspring. I didn't say anything when she came into the house with that big purple and black bruise on her neck, which by the way, is a lot bigger now."

"DAD!"

"EDWARD!"

Calming down was clearly out of the question. Edward was on a roll. "I didn't say anything when she didn't come home last night. But now I have to say something. She's a young lady and she's an adult, but she's also my daughter."

Turning to his old friend, Edward continued, "John, I know this is your son, and you are a very dear friend of mine. I value your friendship. But my daughter still has things to do before she's going to even think about settling down with anyone."

He turned his attention to the man who was trying to take his baby from him and finished his tirade. "Charles, I want you to know that I know you care about my daughter, and I know she cares about you. My wife and I also care about you. You're a fine young man; you always have been. And if I were to be honest with myself, I guess I always knew that you would be the one she'd end up with."

Sensing the seriousness of the situation, Charles decided that it was time for him to talk to this man. Mr. Daniels had every right to be upset. Charles probably should have talked to him first about buying the ring. It was an engagement ring, and it had been rather expensive, that was one of the reasons it took him so long convincing Shelia to accept it. So, he quickly interrupted Mr. Daniels.

"Mr. Daniels, if you don't mind, I would like to talk to you and my father in the den." He felt Shelia's hand tighten on his arm and bent to kiss her on the cheek. "It's all right, baby."

Watching the three men walk to the front of the house, Shelia was scared all of a sudden. She knew Charles wouldn't take the ring back, and she could bear that as long as he didn't come back to her saying he wanted to slow things down. Things would be slow enough in two days.

CHAPTER 8

While Charles talked to the fathers, the mothers were trying to calm Shelia down. Shelia was mad and felt that the whole thing was being blown way out of proportion. At first, she thought that the ring was a little extravagant; but after Charles explained to her that he meant for it to be a pre-engagement ring, she decided to accept it.

To Charles spending $30,000 on a ring wasn't a big deal because he had the money to spend. The price of the ring hadn't even crossed his mind. He saw it and wanted her to have it. He wanted to show her that he loved her and that he was very serious about their relationship. He intended to be with her in the future. And she loved him even more for it.

"Mr. Daniels, first of all, I want you to know that I love your daughter very much," Charles began.

The men were sitting at the bar in the den. John busied himself making them drinks.

"I probably should have spoken to you before I bought the ring, but it is just as I told you before. It is a going-away present. A friendship ring, if you will. I actually picked the ring out a couple of days ago. When we got to the store, it did take me a minute to convince her to accept it." Charles paused for a second, trying to figure out what would be the best way to handle the situation. "Listen, I know it's really an engagement ring, but when I saw it, that's what I wanted her to have. I didn't think that it would cause this big of a deal. And to be honest, I really didn't think of the price."

"Charles," Shelia's dad started, "this has to stop. It seems to me like you're moving kind of fast. It's only been a week since you two started seeing each other. Tuesday, she'll be leaving. Sounds to me like both of you are looking for heartache."

"He's right, Charles," John agreed. "You'll be on one end of the country, and she'll be on the other. Now how in the world is that supposed to work?"

"Dad, I love her. I've loved her for years. I can't just let her go like that." Charles was up for any obstacle these men threw his way. He wanted Shelia, and he would fight for her. He continued to plead his case honestly. "The last thing I would ever do is try to dissuade Shelia from completing her goals. Hell, I want to be a part of that, too. Just like I want her to be a part of mine. I'll give her all the support she needs."

"If you really feel that way," Edward countered, "you'll let my daughter be. This is her last year of school, and it's going to be her hardest. She doesn't need the added burden of missing you. It's just going to complicate things for her. Do you really want her to go through that? I'm sorry, Charles, but I have to forbid this. And, now, you have a daughter. She'll be a stepmother. This is too much. Way too much."

"I don't have a daughter. Why is it so hard for everyone to believe that?" Charles held his palms out in despair.

John put a hand on his son's shoulder, "Maybe it would be best if you gave her some space to finish what she has to do. It's only a year."

Charles looked at the two men as if they had spoken in some foreign language. He couldn't believe what they were asking him to do. He and Shelia would already be apart from each other for most of the year, but her father was asking him to just let her go completely. That was impossible. He couldn't do it. He stepped back from them and took a seat on the couch.

"Charles, I know that it's a lot to ask of you, but for my daughter's sake, I think it's for the best. Next year, she'll be back here doing her internship at the hospital."

"You say that like it would be the simplest thing in the world to do," Charles spat out. He ran a hand through his curly crop of jet black hair and let his head fall back on the sofa. "Damn it, that's not my baby. I'm tired of saying it over and over. Shelia believes me. She knows how much I love her."

"Well, if you love each other as much as you say, it's not going to go away in a year," Edward argued. "Then you two can pick up things where you left off."

Charles looked at his dad for support, but didn't detect any on his face. John handed his son a drink and said, "It's not like you were marrying her anytime soon. Just take a little step back. That's all he's asking of you. I have to say that if it were one of my daughters, I'd be asking the same thing."

"Exactly," Edward injected, glad to have someone on his side for once. "I just want her last year of school to be trouble-free."

Hearing a sudden commotion outside, they realized that the newlyweds had just arrived. The party was due to start, but for Charles, it was already over. Partying was the last thing on his mind at the moment.

"Well, come on, let's go and start this little celebration," John suggested, as if the conversation was over. "Charles, just think about what the man is saying." John gave his son a solid pat on his shoulder, knowing his decision was a difficult one.

The two older men rose to leave. Charles rose to shake Edward's hand when the man came toward him with his hand extended. "I'm sure you'll do the right thing, Charles."

I don't seem to have a choice. Charles sat down on the sofa, put his head back and looked up at the ceiling. He wasn't in the mood to celebrate. There were too many things going on in his head for him to be around other people.

Shelia had just come out of the bathroom when she heard everyone welcoming the newlyweds home. Thinking that the men were still in the front room, she went out to the porch with everyone else instead of sneaking into the front hallway and ease-dropping on their conversation, which had been her plan. Standing at the back of the crowd, Shelia waited until people started leaving the deck area before greeting her brother and new sister-in-law with a kiss.

"Hey, squirt. Wow! Look at you. You look so different." Jeff was pulling her into a brotherly hug and noticing that his sister seemed to have a glow about her. This was something new, something he wasn't used to. Jeff sensed that his sister had been changed forever.

She hugged him back and held onto him a little longer than she intended. When she stepped back, his eyebrows had a question mark, and he looked deeper into her eyes. "What's wrong, squirt?"

"Nothing," she lied. "I'm just happy to have you guys home. How was your trip?" She asked trying to change the subject.

Not fooled for a minute, Jeff replied, "It was nice. Later, okay?" He squeezed her hand to give her some much-needed reassurance.

"Yeah, later." The last thing she wanted to do was unburden herself on him so soon after his return home. She smiled up at him, loving the idea that he was still there for her when she needed him and knowing it would always be that way.

"Where's Charles? Looks like somebody got a little too hungry while I was away." He smiled, drawing his wife's attention to the mark holding its prominent position on Shelia's neck. "Tia, we've only been back five minutes, and I already have to go after one of your family members. Just look at this girl's neck."

Tia put her arms around Shelia, "Jeff Daniels, if you so much as touch a hair on my brother's head, you'll be sleeping alone for a very long time." She pulled Shelia close to her and jokingly finished, "So, what's it going to be? Mind your business or sleep with your son. It's up to you."

"Thanks, Tia," Shelia laughed.

"Well, I didn't think the situation was that drastic, Tia. Maybe he just made a mistake, right?" Jeff replied, prompting the three to have in a group hug. "Anyway, look at that ring she has on her finger. Be careful you don't get a hernia, girl." Jeff lifted her hand to watch the magnificent diamond sparkle in the sunlight.

Tia took hold of the hand in question. "Does this mean what I think it does?" She glanced at Shelia, hope in her eyes.

"No, it doesn't. It's just a going-away present. I'm leaving Tuesday morning to go back to school. I'm finally in my last year."

"Jeff, maybe I need to go away for a while," Tia suggested.

"If you're waiting to get one of those, you'd better not leave until I get about sixty-five," Jeff replied.

"Cheapskate. Where is my big brother, anyway?"

"He must still be inside. Dad and Mr. Avery pulled him into the family room for a serious talk about this ring about a half hour ago. They should be just about done; at least, I hope they are."

"Uh-oh," Jeff said, looking and pointing at his dad standing by the grill. "That means he didn't like what was happening with his *baby girl.*"

"Exactly. He was so embarrassing, Jeff. I wanted to crawl under the kitchen table and pull all the chairs in." She reined in her frustration when she realized her father was outside. "They're already done. Good. Let me find Charles and make sure everything is all right." Shelia turned to go inside the house and look for her beloved.

Charles had fixed himself another drink, still upset because he didn't know how to go about explaining to Shelia that they should remain casual friends until she finished school. Mad at himself because he was a grown man letting other men make decisions about his life with Shelia. Fathers or not, they didn't know everything. He really didn't see what difference it made. They wouldn't be together either way. He just wanted them to have an exclusive relationship while they were apart. The last thing he needed was to be on the other side of the country thinking about some college punk trying to get his hands on her. He wouldn't be able to get any work done.

He certainly wasn't interested in being with anyone else. Sex wasn't his main purpose in life anymore. Those teenage urges were long behind him. All he wanted was a mature relationship with a mature woman. Shelia. And they were trying to stop him from doing just that. *What am I going to do?*

He didn't hear her walk up behind him. His head was down when her arms circled his waist, but Charles knew right away that something wasn't right. She didn't feel right to him. He turned around and knew why.

"What are you doing, Caryn?" The frown on his face should have been a clear indication of his displeasure. She chose to ignore it.

"I just came in to speak to you. You sure are touchy these days. What's going on?"

"Nothing's going on. What do you want?" A look of mistrust crossed his face. She chose to ignore it.

"That's a silly question. What do I always want when you come home? Why didn't you call me so we could spend time together while you were here?"

"Because I'm with someone now."

"Charles, you know I don't care about that." She put a hand on his chest, causing him to take a step back closer to the bar. Caryn stepped forward.

"Well, Caryn, I do care. I have a girlfriend. So, could you step back, please?"

"Now, Charles, you are beginning to be downright rude. I've never seen you like this before." Smiling lazily, her plush velvet lips and sparkling teeth, which were usually a turn-on, beckoned him closer. But instead of feeling a tingle of excitement in the pit of his stomach, Charles felt the rise of bile in his throat. He was repulsed by her triflin' behind.

"I'm serious, Caryn. I don't have time for your games." He lightly pushed her to the side and tried to move past her. Not one to be dismissed, Caryn stumbled, tripped over a stool leg, and fell onto the love seat. He leaned over her to see if she was all right. Charles didn't think he had pushed her that hard, but in his state of mind, anything was possible.

"Are you all right? Caryn, are you all right?" He spoke as his voice became slightly filled with nervousness. *Damn, did I hurt the girl? Now, I'll never get rid of her.*

Quickly, her arms went around his neck, and she opened her eyes smiling. "I am now."

"Oh, you..." He should have realized it was a trick. Charles was trying to straighten up when he saw a movement in the doorway.

Shelia stopped, her feet suddenly feeling like cement blocks. She couldn't believe her eyes. Charles was lowering himself onto the love seat next to Caryn. The surprised look on his face only made her madder. Her hands balled into fists clutched at her side, Shelia stepped into the room ready to do battle. She was not going to go out like this. After all the promises he had made to her, all the dreams and plans they had talked about, how could he do something like this to her? She was not leaving without an explanation—a helluva good explanation.

Charles damn near jumped out of his skin trying to get away from Caryn, who had a slick smile on her face. She continued lounging on the couch. He moved away from her.

"Baby, it's not what you think," he said, pleading eyes looked nervously from Caryn to Shelia. A deer caught in the headlights couldn't have looked more like the end was near.

"Oh, and what do I think?" Shelia stepped past Caryn, who really didn't matter to her one way or another right now. Caryn didn't owe her anything. Charles seemed to have lost his tongue. "Well, Charles, what do I think?"

"You think that I was fooling around with Caryn, and it wasn't like that. Why in the world would I do something like that? Caryn, tell her."

When they looked at Caryn, she just sat there smiling at them. "Charles, Shelia knows about our past. It's perfectly—"

"Just shut up," he yelled, dismissing her with a wave of his hand.

"No, let your little ho talk," Shelia turned to her, daring her to say something else.

"Shelia," Charles grabbed her arm, "look at me. Do you think I would mess up what we have for her? She's nothing but a chick trying to get my money. You think I don't know that?"

Caryn stood up and looked at them. "Look, it seems to me that you two have some issues to iron out in your little, um, relationship." She stepped back when Shelia started towards her. "I'll just be leaving now. Charles, call me when you get your problems straightened out." She smiled because she saw that Charles was still holding Shelia back. She was not afraid or anything, but fighting wasn't something she had ever been particularly good at. She was much better at just creating drama and then getting far away before any violence could befall her.

Because she didn't have anyone else to vent her anger on, Shelia jumped on Charles.

He thought the matter was over once he had explained himself. He was wrong. Pouring himself another drink, Charles tried to figure out what had just happened.

After Caryn left, Shelia had turned into a pit bull. She cussed him up and down, broke up with him, and even tried to give him back his ring. Tears were streaming down her cheeks, and he felt bad even though he hadn't done anything wrong. He wanted to console her and make her believe him, but then he got pissed off because she didn't believe him. By the time it was all over and done, they both had been screaming at the top of their lungs, and once again, their parents were eyewitnesses to the crisis.

"Maybe it would be best if we took you home, dear. You both need to calm down," Mrs. Daniels said to Shelia.

"I do want to go home. I need to be alone." She looked at Charles with hurt in her eyes.

Charles was looking right back at her, "Shelia, this is ridiculous."

"Oh, now I'm *ridiculous*." Again, her temper seemed to take over her mind, and again she was on a rampage. "You know what? Forget it. I'm out of here." She stood up and looked at him one last time. "I'm ready. Good-bye, Charles."

He didn't want her to leave like that. She was clearly upset. Now, he had really done it; he had lost her. Charles was about to stop her from leaving, but his father put a hand on his shoulder to stop him. Mr. Daniels looked relieved, and as he walked out, Charles couldn't help feeling resentment towards the man.

CHAPTER 9

Troy whispered sweet nothings into his wife's ear as they danced at the welcome home party thrown after the barbeque at *Chauncey's*. As infatuated as he was with his wife and the prospects of the splendid night ahead lavishing her body and mind with love, his brother's situation wouldn't stay dormant in his own mind. Occasionally, he would glance toward the bar, where his younger brother sat drowning his misery in alcohol.

After things died down at the barbecue, he had tried to talk Charles into staying home, but Charles insisted on going out with the rest of the family. They all knew he was already well on his way to being intoxicated, so an agreement was made to keep a close eye on him. But they all also knew that it would be Troy who would watch his brother like a vulture. Because whatever Charles went through, Troy went through.

He was hurting, and nobody wanted Charles to cause a scene or any embarrassment to himself. Even if he wasn't thinking about it at the moment, his career and reputation still had to be protected.

Charles sat down at the bar as soon as he walked into the club and stayed there. The other patrons and his many fans must have sensed his dark mood because, for once, they stayed clear of him. He had plenty of time to think about his life and the way things had turned out with Shelia. And it seemed to him that he had been the one who ended up getting hurt.

Suddenly, he didn't want to be at *Chauncey's* anymore. *What am I going to do to get this girl back? I can't let her leave thinking the worst of me.* He was extremely drunk and already had the beginnings of a major headache. Shelia's face kept popping up in front of him, the look of surprise when he gave her the ring, a look of pleasure from a long, hard lovemaking session, and the look of disappointment at seeing him in the arms of another woman. Charles had to get to her. An overwhelming urge to be near her filled his being.

Charles started to stand and wobbled a little. Accidentally, he bumped into a petite woman who was standing next to his seat, causing her to spill her drink. He immediately apologized and offered to buy her another. The woman graciously accepted his apology and the drink with a smile. Then, she realized who he was and tried to get a little friendlier. Charles talked to her for a second, trying to be polite, but kept to general conversation.

"Yo, man, that's my wife you're trying to get next to."

Looking up from the woman, Charles searched for the face that matched the voice. A tall, dark, burly man with broad-shoulders was rushing toward him. Because he wasn't even the tiniest bit interested in the woman and was only being nice, Charles didn't feel it was that big of a deal. To keep things calm, he picked up his drink and lifted it up in acknowledgment.

"I'm sorry, brother. We were just talking. No need to get upset." Turning to her, he said, "It was nice meeting you, Miss." Charles tried to walk by, but Hercules stepped in his way with both hands on his hips.

Stephanie, Troy's wife, felt her husband's arm tense up around her waist and, leaning back, saw worry in his eyes. She followed the direction of his gaze.

"Get the guys, Stephanie," Troy said simply, leaving her on the dance floor to go to the bar. She quickly went to find Jeff, Chauncey, and her brothers-in-law.

Troy moved as fast as he could without bringing attention to himself. Most people thought he was always trying to take up for Charles, sort of like babying him. Only immediate family knew the real reason he watched after Charles as he did. Once, he had seen what could happen when Charles' control was pushed to the limits.

Though he was the youngest boy and had a sincerely sensitive nature, when provoked, Charles could lose himself in his anger and become impossibly and aggressively hostile. In his younger days, he had easily beaten up guys both younger and older than him, leaving some with short-term hospital stays. It was always in self-defense, but Troy also saw it as something that caused his brother a great deal of pain. Charles didn't like confrontation, and he hated hurting people, even when they deserved it. Unfortunately, there were a lot of people who had faced his wrath.

Troy often thought that it was probably what drove him into the medical field. He probably wanted to shoulder some of his brother's pain or at least ease it.

This fool will not move out of my way. Charles wasn't in the right frame of mind to be dealing with a knucklehead. When a finger kept digging into his chest, he felt his temper start to rise. He saw Troy out of the corner of his eye, but the man kept taunting him, and his patience was rapidly wearing thin.

"Yeah, I know who you are. You're that punk who sings all those love songs. Right?"

Charles just looked at him. *Easy man, keep it together. Don't do anything. Just wait. One, two, three....*

"You don't look like much to me. Trying to talk to my girl. Where's your girl? Can't get one?"

Let it go. Just let it go. Four, five, six...

The man's wife tried to step between them, but there wasn't any room. Instead, she placed a hand on her husband's bulky shoulder, trying to tell him to stop. He gave her a hard shove that caused her to bump into the wall near them with a nasty thud.

In one instant, he was in Charles' face; in the next, he was down on his knees, trying to pry his finger out of Charles grip. He screamed out when he heard the snap of his finger breaking, but it was drowned out by the classic hip-hop music the DJ was playing.

"Charles, let up, man," Troy stepped over to him, speaking directly into his ear. Jeff and Chauncey soon followed him. Charles did as his brother said, not wanting to hurt the guy any more than he had to.

"What the hell is goin' on?" Chauncey asked, not wanting any altercations in his club.

"He broke my finger. This son of a..."

Stepping forward, his wife spoke apologetically, "I'm so sorry, Charles." She explained to Chauncey, "It was self-defense. I tried to stop him."

"Let me take a look at it. I'm a doctor." Troy led the man to the VIP section. He stopped briefly and told Charles to have a seat and wait for him.

"Man, are you all right?" Jeff stepped in front of Charles and put a hand on his shoulder.

"I was trying to leave. Chauncey, I'm sorry about that."

"Hey, no problem. The girl said it was self-defense," Chauncey replied.

"Yeah, but I shouldn't have done that."

They laughed at him. "Hell, it's a lot better than sending him to the hospital with broken ribs or a caved-in chest like you did the Stewart boys that time. But, I do think you've had more than your share of my alcohol tonight."

Charles smiled, feeling a little better. "Well, I started taking some anger-management classes out in California. Not to stop my anger, because that wasn't my problem. I just had to learn to think of other ways to handle some situations. Now, instead of going in for the kill, I think of less harmful solutions."

"I bet half this town wishes they had that class for you while you were in school." Chauncey laughed, patting him on his leg.

"Right now, I'm so drunk I probably couldn't defend myself if I tried."

"Yeah, well, tell it to that dude." Jeff looked at him. "Getting drunk because of today, huh? Listen, don't let my father get to you, man. And Shelia, she'll come around. She loves you. Right now, she just thinks she's been betrayed. Trust me, I know those kinds of women."

"Yeah, I guess you would, with that sister of mine," Charles laughed.

He convinced Troy to take him to the hotel instead of his parents' house. He wanted to be alone. In the morning, he knew he would have a terrible hangover, and he wasn't quite up to playing twenty questions with his mother.

The ride over was quiet. Charles was half asleep when Troy finally broke the silence, unable to hold his feeling in any longer.

"Charles."

"Uh…" Charles moved his head closer into the headrest of Troy's Lincoln Navigator.

"Charles, wake up. I want to talk to you." Troy nudged his leg hard enough to make it move sideways.

"Wha—what, man?" He moved his head from side to side, opening and then closing his eyes.

"Are you awake?"

"Yeah, man, damn, what?" Opening his eyes fully, he turned his head toward his brother.

"I just wanted to tell you that I'm proud of you." This statement had Charles sitting up and looking at his brother. "I mean at the way you handled things back there. Those classes we talked about must have really helped."

"Yeah, I guess they did. I tried to hold out as long as I could, Troy. I tried not to hurt him, especially because I knew you were there. I talked to myself, hell, I even tried to count to ten. Being a doctor and all, I must have put you in an awkward position."

"Well, it wasn't that bad. His finger was just slightly dislocated. The splint I made will help until he gets to his doctor. And listen, make no mistake about this; if ever you're in any kind of danger, my doctor status goes right out the window. Defending yourself is different from hurting people for fun. Family comes before all else."

"Thanks, man." Charles held out his hand for a pound.

"No doubt. Now get some sleep."

Charles sat back and realized what he missed most when he was on the road. His sense of family. Many times he had thought about moving back to Chicago. He could sing and record from anywhere in the world. He already traveled a lot, and most of the time he was on the East Coast, anyway. He needed his home base to be where his heart was, and that was in Chicago. No matter how big a celebrity he became, he knew his family would keep him grounded. That was what he needed. No, that was what he wanted.

Sunday morning, Shelia climbed out of bed and wearily made her way to the kitchen. Jeff was sitting at the table waiting for her. But she was intent on one thing—making herself a hearty breakfast.

"Good morning, squirt." He sounded too happy to her. She didn't like it.

"Morning," Shelia mumbled, making quite a racket tossing things about.

Jeff was amused and decided to help put an end to her misery— but not the easy way.

"So you decided to stay in last night, huh?"

"Wasn't in the partying mood," she replied, grabbing a bowl from the cabinet, and slamming the door shut.

"Well, you missed a nice one." Jeff smiled at her.

"Oh, yeah?" Shelia said, bending to clean up the two eggs that had fallen out of the carton when she had thrown it onto the counter.

"Yeah, it was bumpin'. Even when Charles got into that fight, people just kept right on partying." He had to wait only about half a second for her response.

"Fight? What fight? Charles was in a fight? Is he okay? Was he hurt?" She leaned over him the way a detective would on his favorite show, "Law and Order". It was mildly intimidating.

"Yeah, I mean, I guess he's okay." Hunching his shoulders, he decided to let her think whatever she wanted. "Troy got him out of there before I really had a chance to see him."

"You didn't check to see if he was all right? Damn, Jeff, he could have really been hurt. What if something's wrong with him?"

"Well, Troy is the doctor. Besides, he was so drunk he probably didn't feel any pain last night. But this morning he's going to be hurting."

"Is he at the hospital or at his parents?" she asked frantically, trying to remember where she had thrown her purse when she stalked through the door the night before.

"Neither. I heard him tell Troy to take him to some hotel or another." He put down his head and smiled into his coffee as he heard his sister race up the stairs to her room.

Ten minutes later, Shelia rushed out of the house, leaving her brother to clean up the kitchen.

With heavy metal music beating behind his eyes and a jackhammer boring its way into his skull, Charles struggled to rouse himself and focus on the sounds he heard in his room. The glare of the sun made his eyelids hurt. He awkwardly turned on his side and mumbled, "God, have mercy on me. Please turn off the sun." He put his hands over his eyes and slowly realized that his prayer was being answered. The curtains to his room were being drawn. He gratefully rolled to his side.

"Thank you," he said aloud.

"You're welcome."

Charles lay absolutely still. Now, unless he was going crazy or had died in his sleep, somebody was in his room. He tried once again to open his eyes, but they were heavy, feeling as if crazy glue had been dropped into them.

"Who are you?" he questioned.

"Surely, you're not that drunk. Open your eyes, sleepy head."

He willed his eyes open and beheld the beauty standing over him. "Shelia?"

"Yes," she answered.

"Shelia," Charles whispered, grabbing her hand and closing his eyes. "Thank God."

"Charles…Charles." She looked him over, making sure that he hadn't keeled over from alcohol poisoning or something. The heavy rise and fall of his chest, not to mention the shrill whistle coming from his nostrils, confirmed that he was alive and well.

He was fast asleep, and he had a vise-like grip on her hand. Unable to escape, Shelia quietly lay next to him until she finally drifted off, too.

When Charles woke up in the darkened room, his senses told him he wasn't alone. Well, that and the warm, curvaceous body nestled half under him. *Lord, what in the world have I done?* Jumping out of bed, he saw that the sun was already starting to disappear beyond the horizon. He had slept the whole day away.

Charles went around the room turning lights on. Then he tip-toed to the side of the bed. *Well, the young lady would just have to call a cab if she didn't have a car, but she absolutely had to get out of his room.* He prayed that if they had done anything, he had used protection.

Charles reached across the bed and shook her leg. She buried her face deeper into the pillow. Light-brown hair spread over the pillow covered her face, and the sheet covered her body.

"Hello…excuse me." *Oh, shit…what am I going to do?*

She stirred a little.

"Hey, wake up." *Why me? Why me? Why me?*

Turning over, she looked up at him.

"Shelia? Oh, shit," he said, caught completely off guard; he had forgotten that she was there earlier. "Shelia, what are you doing here?"

She smiled, asking, "Did you expect someone else?"

"Uh…" Relief spread across his face. "Of course not. I just didn't expect to wake up next to you, either."

"Well, I was told that you had been in a fight last night, and you may have been hurt." Taking in his puzzled expression, she continued, "Obviously, my brother still has a little trouble determining the difference between a lie and the truth."

"He told you I was hurt?" Charles asked, taking a seat next to her on the bed.

"No, actually he just let me believe that you were."

"So, I owe him one, right?"

"I guess you do. Earlier I stopped by the front desk and added another day to your stay. I didn't think you were going to make check-out time."

"Thank you. Shelia, how long have you been here?"

"Since this morning or early afternoon. You grabbed hold of me, and I couldn't get up so I fell asleep. I didn't get much sleep last night, anyway."

"That's right. I grabbed a hold of you, and I don't ever want to let you go."

She was not sure how to reply. "Charles—"

"No, don't say anything, Shelia. You grabbed a hold of me, too." Suddenly uncomfortable, Charles changed the subject. "Well, are you hungry? We could order something from room service."

"Okay. You know we've missed dinner again, don't you? We should go over there."

"No, I don't feel like being around anyone right now. I'll call Mom and let her know I'm all right. What's your father going to say when he finds out you're here with me?"

"I don't see that it's any of his business," Shelia answered, still angered by her father's interference in her relationship.

Charles reached for her hands. "Shelia, last night your father asked me to stop seeing you until after you finished school."

"But—"

"Wait, let me finish. He and my father both thought it would be best so that you could finish this last year without any of the additional pressures that our relationship might cause. And I agreed with them because I didn't want you to be stressed out about where I am, what I'm doing, who I'm with, or when we might see each other again."

"Charles—"

"Hold on. After you left last night, I realized that I am miserable without you. I need to have you in my life. Last night, I thought you hated me, and I couldn't handle it. So, I got drunk."

"Charles, I could never hate you. What nobody seems to realize, including you, is that I'm going to worry about all of those things whether we're going together or not. Even if we break up today, I'm still going to love you tomorrow. That's not going to change. This is going to be a hard year for me; but if I don't have you in my life, it will be a helluva lot harder."

Pulling her close, Charles kissed her face, cheeks, and neck. He whispered softly, "Shelia, marry me."

Shelia held onto him. In this man was everything she needed to complete her. Tears ran down her face. "Oh, Charles—"

"Please, Shelia," he leaned back and looked into her eyes. "For both our sakes. I can't let you go back to school without having something to take with me. I know I'm being a selfish bastard, but I need you."

"Charles, I need you, too. But—"

"No, buts. This way we'll have a part of each other. We'll be connected. And when you finish school, I'll move back here or wherever you want to do your internship. I can make music anywhere. The house in California will be ours to use when I, or we, have to go out there. I'll have a house built for us here. All I need to do is put a studio inside. Please, Shelia," Charles finished in desperation. He sensed she wasn't as convinced of the practicality of his proposed engagement as he was, but he had to convince her to be his.

"It's not that I won't marry you, but how and when? And what about our parents? Dad isn't going to go for it."

"That's true," Charles sighed, sounding defeated. They both seemed to lose the wind they had been riding on.

"Unless," Shelia said, "we don't tell anybody."

"Shelia, I can't ask you to do that."

"Charles, I'm asking you to. It's the only way. If we go to the justice of the peace—"

"Are you kidding? Do you know how fast news will travel? Plus, there is a three-day waiting period. You leave Tuesday morning."

"Well, could you visit me in Washington? Maybe then we—"

"No, I have a couple of meetings here on Wednesday morning, then I leave Saturday for the West Coast. Wait. What if I come to Washington Wednesday afternoon, and we drive to Elkton. There's no waiting period down there. We would just have to get a license and see a preacher or justice of the peace. People do it all the time, and it would be even more private."

Charles tried to think more clearly, "On the other hand, I'm not sure if I like sneaking around. And to be honest, I don't know how long we would be able to keep it a secret even in Maryland. All hell will break loose if our relatives hear about it over the news."

"Charles, it's only for a year. And the sneaking around is really for my benefit, not yours. I heard enough of that last night. He forbade me from seeing you. This will save me from hearing my dad's mouth. If it comes across the news, we won't deny it. Besides, it'll be too late for anybody to do anything about it."

"Okay, but only if you're sure," he agreed, happier than he had been in a long time. *Keeping a secret wasn't a problem for him; he had his share. But Shelia would be missing out on all of the things that brides do on their wedding day.*

"I'm sure, but school starts Thursday. I'd have to be right back. We won't have time."

"I could stay in Maryland until Saturday morning then leave for the coast from there. We could stay at a hotel there, and you would just have to leave your husband every morning and go to school." Smiling down at her, he went to the phone to order room service. They talked the whole plan through once more before calling their mothers.

As she answered her phone Sunday evening, Brenda checked the caller ID feature she had recently installed. Hushing the kids, she put the phone to her ear.

"Avery residence."

"Hey, Mom."

"Charles?"

"Yes, Mom. Listen, I'm sorry for not making it to dinner. I had a really bad night."

"So I've heard. Is everything all right, dear?"

"Perfect, Mom. I just wanted to call and let you know that I was okay."

"Well, all right. It's still not too late. I could have a plate waiting for you."

"No, I'm just going to order some room service and rest a bit."

"Okay, dear. Will you be home tomorrow?"

"Yes, definitely. I love you, Mom."

"I love you, too, baby."

Charles replaced the phone and started for the bathroom. Shelia had agreed to wait twenty minutes before she called her mother, who was also at his parents' house.

"Avery residence."

"Hello, Mrs. Avery. This is Shelia."

"Oh. Hi, dear." Brenda checked the caller ID and did a delayed double take.

"Is my mother around?"

"Of course. Hold on one minute," Brenda said, motioning for Sylvia to come to the phone.

"Hello."

"Mom."

"Shelia, are you okay?"

"Yes, Mom, perfect. Listen, I'm not going to make it there tonight for dinner. I just didn't want you to be worrying about me."

"Well, all right, dear. I'll see you at home."

"Mom, I'll be there in the morning, okay?"

"Okay." Sylvia paused for a moment, trying to put some things together in her head. "I love you, and be careful."

"I love you, too, Mom."

Sylvia was still a little confused when she hung up the phone. Brenda was standing beside her, smiling.

"They're together," Brenda whispered to her friend.

"What are you talking about?"

"My son and your daughter are together."

"How can you be sure?"

"Look," she said, pointing at the caller ID. "Charles called me twenty minutes ago from this number saying that he wouldn't make it tonight." Pressing the display button, she added, "Shelia just called from this number. Same number, Marriott Suites."

They hugged each other, laughing.

"Good for them," Sylvia said, as they sat back at the kitchen table.

"Hey, what are you two so giddy about?" Edward asked as he and John came in.

Sylvia answered, "Oh, nothing. Just talking about being grand-mothers again."

"Yeah, well, don't encourage them. Jeff and Tia had better slow down and pace themselves. John, have a talk with that daughter of yours," Edward joked, putting a hand on his friend's shoulder.

"My daughter? Tell your son to keep his hands off her," John responded.

"Can't. Too much like his old man. Look at 'em. They're perfect together." They all peered down the hall at Jeff and Tia standing in the hallway hugging and whispering whatnots to each other.

Brenda and Sylvia shared a secret smile as they called the families in for dessert.

CHAPTER 10

Things had gone exactly as planned. Tuesday morning, Shelia's family took her to the airport to see her off. She was starting her last year of school and, in one more day, beginning a whole new life by secretly becoming the wife of Charles Avery. Her emotions were mixed—happy and excited but also worried and sad. She was leaving her family, and in one more day, betraying their trust by secretly marrying Charles.

Once on the Howard University campus, she checked into Mays Hall, her home away from home for the next year. After unpacking, she immediately began taking care of routine new school year rituals. Catching the shuttle, she crossed the large campus and went to the bookstore. She purchased her books and supplies she would need using the list sent with her class schedule. She also ordered two white uniforms and five name badges, a requirement for fourth-year medical students.

Wednesday morning, she received a large bouquet of flowers and a message with Charles' arrival time. Unfortunately, two of her friends were visiting and went into a tizzy wondering who could have sent her such an elaborate arrangement. Although Shelia was beautiful, she was known to be a bookworm and had never dated much. Her new flipped hairstyle and the glow of her skin set them buzzing the minute they stumbled into her at the Blackburn Student Center. Now, she was getting flowers. They knew something was definitely going on.

Charles came to pick her up Wednesday at one the following day. The Mays' Hall student lounge turned into a mini-autograph session/photo shoot. One girl, a biochemistry graduate student from New York, answered the door and couldn't control herself. She cried the whole time he was there. The normally extremely serious students vied frantically for attention—except for Shelia, who took her time getting ready so they could enjoy themselves. No one bothered to ask him why he was there. They just gathered around him trying to get his autograph.

He watched her cross the upstairs balcony and come down the stairs. Not taking his eyes off her, he thought what a fool he would have been if he had not come today. Talking her into waiting had been going through his head. When she smiled at him, he knew he made the right decision. *God, she's beautiful.* This was the woman that he was meant to share his life with.

To everybody's astonishment, he walked past them and took Shelia into his arms, kissing her breathless. He held her to him as if he hadn't seen her in years, all but deaf to the chants and cheers coming from behind her.

Whispering into her ear, he asked, "Are you ready, love?"

"Yes, Charles. Did you meet everyone?"

"Yes, I think I did," he replied, giving them one of his heart-stopping smiles, both dimples showing.

The luxury limousine waiting at the curb was filled with roses. About a half-dozen boxes filled the back of the limo. She was speechless. Each box or vase had a little note from Charles expressing his love for her. He knew exactly how to make her feel loved. And she loved him so much for trying to make her day special. An attentive, romantic, and good man was hard to find. At least that was the mantra many single women chanted. Maybe they were looking in the wrong places. Every man she knew was a good man. She had been brought up and raised around good men. Shelia was so thankful, so happy.

She sat back, enjoying being treated like a princess. They drank champagne and snacked on crackers and cheese as the car rode through town and made its way onto Interstate 95 North.

They arrived in Elkton at three-thirty and went straight to the county office building, where Everett was waiting, to get their license.

Shelia was surprised to find the paperwork already filled out. All she had to do was show identification and sign. Then they went to the chapel, where a justice of the peace awaited them. Shelia was so completely caught up in the moment, she didn't even think about how all the arrangements had been made.

Although the ceremony was fast and simple, Shelia couldn't contain the emotional roller-coaster that it produced in her. Tears streamed down her cheeks, leaving black streaks on her cream-colored pantsuit.

It wasn't what she had dreamed of for herself. She had always assumed that she would have a traditional wedding—like Jeff and Tia. She used to make lists of the names of her bridesmaids and guests. Shelia had even started drawing pictures of her wedding gown when she turned fifteen.

If she were to be honest with herself, she would have had to admit that she regretted not walking down the aisle in a flowing white gown instead of standing in front of this small town justice in a pantsuit. She wished her mother had been able to give her the unnecessary advice most mothers try to pass on to their departing daughters. And she did want her father to be eagerly waiting in the wings to walk her down the aisle, but she understood that this was the best way to handle her present situation. Her father would never have walked her anywhere to get married to Charles, or anyone else, at this point.

No, her wedding wasn't the perfect fairy-tale that she had read about in a wedding planning book, now resting at the bottom of the hope chest she had started the year she turned seventeen.

Charles and Jeff had been home from college at the same time that year. She remembered how they had unexpectedly shown up at the school's homecoming dance. Charles had danced with her that night for the first time. He hadn't been the only one she had danced with that night; her dance card had been pretty full. But that dance with him changed everything for her, making her focus on her future.

That night Shelia had prayed that she would end up in this exact position one day—married to Charles. And it was exactly how she wanted it. Exactly how it should have been. And it was right because Charles made it right.

Looking into his eyes, she could see how much he loved her. When the justice of the peace told him he could kiss his bride, and she felt his lips meeting hers, she got a glimpse of heaven that was all the reassurance she needed.

He presented her with a wedding band that looked as expensive as her engagement ring, if not more so. It seemed to be of the same carat size. It was a cluster of small diamonds in the shape of a half-moon to surround the engagement ring. It made her wonder just how much money Charles had made over the years to afford such expensive gifts. But she let it go.

When they left the chapel, the limousine was waiting to pick them up. On the way back to Washington D.C., they stopped at a small but impressive restaurant in Havre de Grace. They had the salmon with steamed vegetables and broiled potatoes. There was also champagne and a small wedding cake.

Charles had put a lot more thought into her wedding day than she had, Shelia thought, feeling more appreciative by the second.

As they were leaving the restaurant and heading back south on Rt. 40, Charles told her to look up at the sky. She burst into tears when she saw a small private plane, displaying a banner reading, US. TODAY, TOMORROW, FOREVER.

He had told her that he had made reservations for them at the Hilton Hotel. Shelia didn't expect the large suite, but with all his other surprises, she should have.

The suite was breathtaking. The sunken living room area was wide and spacious and had a high ceiling. A bedroom was on the second-level loft. It had a king-size oval-shaped bed. Down the hall from the living room was the bathroom, and next to it was a kitchenette. Shelia loved the suite.

A bottle of champagne and a fruit basket, compliments of the hotel, were on the living room table. She stepped down into the room and spun around like a little kid. Charles came up behind her and pulled her to him.

"Are you happy?" he asked in her ear softly.

Turning in his arms, Shelia replied, "Oh, Charles, I love you."

"I love you, too," he said, pulling her with him onto the couch. He undid his shirt buttons and stretched out on the sofa, hoping to loosen some of the tension gripping his weary body, "It's been a busy few hours, huh?"

"Charles, I can't believe that we are actually married. I'm about to bust with happiness." She stretched out her ring hand. "Mrs. Charles Michael Avery. Oh, God, I can't believe it."

"Well, soon it will be Dr. Avery," Charles said, basking in her glow.

"There's already one of those."

"That's Dr. Troy Avery. I'll be glad to call you Dr. Shelia Avery anytime."

"Charles, I was just thinking. I'm not going to be able to change my name."

"Why not?" he quickly asked, disappointed.

"Well, if I do, Mom and Dad will know."

"Shelia, you're hundreds of miles from home. How are they going to know? Your school mail goes to the dormitory, doesn't it? All you have to do is use your maiden name whenever you write to anyone at home."

"Yeah, I guess you're right. I don't even know why we should hide it now. There's nothing they can do."

"True, but just as we're making it easier on ourselves, we need to make it as easy as possible on them, too. And them not knowing is the only easy way for now. I mean, now that it's done, I feel a lot more guilty than I thought I would, even though I realize that we did what we wanted to do, what was best for us. But at the same time, we were being just as selfish as your dad trying to keep us apart."

"I know what you mean. I was thinking the same thing. He was being selfish trying to keep me to himself, trying to keep me from becoming a fully independent woman. And we were being selfish by sneaking off to get married, keeping them from enjoying our wedding."

"Well, it'll get better. As you said, we'll just keep to the plan, and after you graduate, they'll see that I'm not an obstacle in your career path in any way."

"I don't think they really meant that, Charles. They know you're a good person. And I'm sure they know you love me."

"Shelia, that night at the house, your dad made it very clear that he didn't want me bringing you down. With the money I make, you would think he would know that you would be very well taken care of. But all the money in the world wasn't going to make him change his mind. He forbade me to keep seeing you."

"He has a lot of pride. I think the whole baby thing made matters worse. Don't worry about it. My dad does like you, deep down inside."

"Yeah, way down inside. The baby has nothing to do with it. Shelia, he doesn't see me as Jeff's best friend anymore. I'm just another man after his baby girl. He sees me in a totally different light."

"Don't worry about it, baby," she repeated, running her hand down his arm and linking her fingers with his. "I feel bad that I didn't buy you a ring," she said, changing the subject. She refused to let the bad vibes she was starting to feel worm their way into her happiness.

"We have plenty of time for that. Besides, I wouldn't be able to wear it. Too many people would notice, believe me. Too many questions. The only person who knows about this wedding besides the justice of the peace and the woman at the license office is Everett, my agent. And he wants to keep it a deep, dark secret because he thinks that once it leaks out, especially after the baby story, my record sales will drop. At least you'll be able to wear your rings while you're here. Please don't forget to take them off when you go home for your breaks." They laughed, but they both knew that their deception was no laughing matter.

"I won't. Lord, can you imagine what would happen if I did that?"

"Listen, after May we can forget all this sneaking around mess and have a real wedding if you want. I suppose our mothers will feel cheated."

"Well, that's too bad. I had always dreamed of having a big fancy wedding with a dozen bridesmaids and flowers everywhere, but I don't want another one. This was the best day of my life."

"What about the wedding night?"

His smile was bright, his dimples deep. She loved him. "We'll have to see."

"Come here, wife. Let me show you something." Charles pulled her alongside him on the couch cushions. "Shelia, I want you to know that I love you more than anything in this world." He kissed her hands and face. "I plan to do anything and everything I have to do to make you happy."

"Charles, I love you. You know, all my hopes, dreams, and wishes came true today. I've known you're the one for me since I was a teenager. I love you."

Kissing her as he picked her up, Charles carried Shelia to the bed and lay her down. Unfastening the button on her blouse, he kissed her shoulders as he slowly spread the blouse open. When her bra was unfastened and removed, he stood and removed his own clothes.

"Shelia, I love having you in my arms." Kissing her neck and shoulder, he slowly bite her lips, burning a path to her breast. Charles felt himself drowning in her essence. She felt so good, and she was his. This woman that he had secretly loved for almost half his life was finally his.

"Charles…mm, Charles." Shelia couldn't make her mind work beyond murmuring his name. He was showing her so much pleasure. She could scarcely control herself.

Charles worked his way down her body, lavishing attention on every inch as if he was trying to memorize the contours of her body. He bit at her hips and licked her inner thighs. He kissed her feet and sucked her toes. He was adding a new and exciting dimension to their lovemaking.

Reversing his direction, he worked his way up her body. She was already overcome with desire and wanted him to take her to the next level. As his lips leisurely kissed her inner thighs, he used his fingers to open her paradise of pleasure and gently massaged her.

All Charles could think of was pleasing Shelia, claiming her heart and her soul as well as her mind and spirit. When they parted, he wanted to make sure that she thought of him often. He wanted her to miss him as he was surely going to miss her and to count the days until they would be together again. This was his woman, and he wanted it to stay that way forever. He decided to brand himself into her.

"Charles."

Shelia was out of it. Her legs were shaking, her eyes were glazed over. But she could see her husband, and she could feel what he was doing to her. Her hands were on his shoulders, trying to pull him up her, but he took her hands and placed them over her head. And he held them there. Spreading her legs wider, she opened herself to receive him. But that wasn't what he had in mind. Instead, as he lowered his head to her boiling point and took her into his mouth.

"CHARLES!!"

She jerked forward, but he held her in position and made slow love to her with his tongue. Shelia was transported into a world of hazy colors swirling before her eyes. One of her hands escaped his hold and came to rest on the back of his head. The pleasure building inside her was so strong it bordered on pain. Finally, she was ready to cross the threshold of ultimate release.

Her whirlpool became a tornado as she held onto him, screamed his name, and rode through the storm.

Charles kissed her and pulled her close, finding comfort and pleasure in the sexual release he was able to give her. He was content to just lie beside her and hold her for the rest of the night, but Shelia had other plans.

She wanted to please him back. Her inexperience made her a little timid, but she was willing to learn, and she learned fast. She began to rub his chest and kiss his neck. Then she made small lines across his chest with her tongue moving from nipple to nipple. Charles let out a little moan, and that was her incentive to press on. Shelia placed her hand around him and began massaging him gently. She felt him jerk. His hand played in her hair as his head eased back into the pillows. His face told her she must be doing something right. Working her way down, she licked his navel. But then faltered, not knowing what to do next.

Sensing her hesitation, Charles pulled her up to him. He kissed her cheeks and tasted her tears.

"Shelia, baby, what's wrong?"

"I just wanted to please you." She was embarrassed because she didn't know how. *How was she going to keep him if she couldn't please him? If she didn't know how?*

"Baby, you don't have to do that to please me. *You* please me." He nestled his face between her neck and shoulder, kissing her.

"I'm afraid I might hurt you," she said, looking up at him innocently.

"Oh, baby, you wouldn't hurt me." He brought her lips down to his and kissed her with all the passion he possessed. Shelia still had her hand around him, gently massaged him as he filled her mouth with his tongue. Sighing, he struggled to stay focus.

When the kiss ended, she whispered, "Charles, show me what to do."

"Um…Shelia, that's not something a husband should instruct his wife to do. I guess some do, but not me. When you feel more comfortable, it will happen. I don't need you to do it. Let's just enjoy each other, have fun, and become more comfortable with ourselves. It takes time, you know."

But Shelia's determination was strong. She had seen movies. *How hard could it be?*

Forcing Charles to lie on his back, she made her way down to his groin. She massaged him and kissed him. She licked him and blew over him. Using her secondhand knowledge, she slowly took him in. It was some time before she felt at ease. She heard his moans and groans, and her confidence grew. She felt him shaking.

"Shelia…oh, Shelia," Charles moaned.

ONE OF THESE DAYS

Shelia realized that she got pleasure out of giving him so much pleasure. She loved the way he called out to her. But she was so caught up in pleasing him that she didn't realize how close he was to an orgasm. Charles quickly pulled her off him. His breathing was heavy, and he had a savaged look on his face as he hurried to place the condom over his erection. As soon as he was covered, Charles pulled Shelia closer, helping her to straddle him and lower herself over him smoothly.

Both of them were chasing a phantom of desire. They pulled, pushed, clawed, and bit until, finally, they tumbled together over the horizon.

Snuggling close to her husband, Shelia thought of all the girlish dreams she had kept tucked away deep within her heart. How close to reality had her dreams been? She had never really thought much about loving a man so much. All she had wanted back then was to be around him. Now she loved him as a man should be loved. She loved him with her body and soul, her heart and mind.

Thursday morning, Shelia was on her way to her first class as Mrs. Charles Michael Avery. She had spent a wonderful night with her husband and was riding high. Getting off the shuttle in front of the College of Medicine, Shelia peeked repeatedly at her wedding band. Charles must have visited the same jeweler as he did before because it fit perfectly. She smiled to herself as she relived the most important day of her life.

She only hoped that their families would understand their decision to marry and be able to forgive them for having followed their own path. The love and support of her family were very important to her. She wouldn't have made it this far without them. Now that they were married, Shelia didn't think that she could bear hurting her parents by telling them the truth right now. Charles was right; it would be best to continue keeping their marriage a secret until she graduated.

CHAPTER 11

The first month of school had been hard for Shelia, but she had managed. She missed Charles so much. They talked everyday, but that only made her miss him more. She had become very popular on campus once everyone found out who her boyfriend was. She was constantly invited to join different academic groups. But she declined all offers because of her hectic course load. She had just began the first of her intramural electives, General Surgery, which required her to make daily rounds with surgical teams. There were conferences and clinics she needed to participate in, and the possibility of research projects. She seemed to live between the College of Medicine and the Louis Stokes Health Sciences Library.

Shelia didn't know how to handle her new-found friends, either. She realized most only wanted to talk to her to fish for information about Charles. She didn't like being used.

Instead of dwelling on how miserable she was, Shelia focused all her energies on her studies, which kept her too busy for social activities or to think nonstop about Charles.

Only a few of her friends knew that she was married. They found out accidentally when a dozen roses arrived at the house. The card was not in an envelope, and it was signed, "All my love, your husband, Charles." She swore them to secrecy, but didn't expect them to keep their word. When she talked to him that night, she told Charles about it, and he told her not to worry. If anything came of it, he said they would handle it together.

"We were finally able to get the paternity test done," Charles wanted to cheer her up, relieve some of her tension.

"That's good. I know Kara was putting up a fight."

"You can only do that for so long. But when she went for sole custody, April told her that before I gave up custody of my daughter, I wanted the blood test. If she was my daughter, then I would want partial custody. Kara's lawyer couldn't argue that in front of the judge. So, the test had to be done, and of course, it came back negative."

"Well, we knew that much."

"Yes, we did. Anyway, Kara called me earlier today to apologize. She said that she thought we could be together. I really think the girl is crazy. There's no way I would have believed that was my child. I never thought her feelings for me were that strong."

"Maybe they were. You never know. Or maybe she was just used to having things her way, getting what she wanted. And she wanted you. If you broke off things with her, she probably didn't like that too much."

"I honestly thought the breakup was a mutual decision. Either way, it's over with now. I told her about our marriage. She didn't seem to happy about that, even though she did offer her best wishes."

"Do you think she was sincere?"

He laughed, "Probably not, but that doesn't matter. We're together. That's the important thing. Everything will work itself out as long as we stay strong. I love you."

But it wasn't that easy for her. Shelia realized that their secret wasn't much of a secret. People knew. Trying not to think too much about the accidental outing, Shelia decided to believe that everything was going well. Instead of letting her guilt and fears get the best of her, she put even more effort into her studies. She didn't want to think that they were betraying her families.

Shelia had been calling her parents weekly. But gradually she stopped calling home even that much, unable to deal with the guilt talking to them caused. If she didn't talk to her parents, then she wouldn't have to think about her lies.

Her emotions were becoming topsy-turvy. One minute she felt happy and carefree, and the next, she felt blue and heavy-hearted. Seeing pictures of Charles in magazines or on TV made her a hopeless wreck.

Charles was on a tour to promote his latest CD. He was making a lot of stops on the talk-show circuit. Every day, she saw one of his videos on MTV. By the time November came, she was ready to sprout wings and fly to California. But, she didn't have to do that.

In November, she was on a commercial flight to California to attend an award show with Charles. She was very excited at the prospect of meeting stars she had watched on television and in the movies and musicians she listened to regularly. Even though she was in the same age group as some of these people, their lives were far removed from her own reality. There was almost an unreal quality about them.

Charles had told her that she would have to get used to having a lot of money. Not that it had to change them, but some of the people they would have to associate with wouldn't understand everything about them, and vice versa. It was a totally different way of life. He explained that some of the people she would meet wouldn't seem to be on her level, financially or intellectually. It wasn't their fault, but in Hollywood, people thought differently, especially those born and raised in the lifestyle of the rich and famous. Where she would think twice about spending large amounts on something frivolous, they wouldn't hesitate. And their priorities were a lot different. But Shelia found that most of his friends were not stereotypical show-business types because he had surrounded himself with like-minded people.

He was at the airport to pick her up. Standing by the luggage area for arriving flights, Charles attracted only an occasional flash of a camera.

Shelia's flight had already appeared on the incoming-flight board, and he stood near the conveyer belt looking around for her. It had been a couple of months since he had seen her, months that seemed like years.

He felt his hands begin to sweat as his anticipation grew. Then he looked up and saw her walking towards him. His heart skipped a beat; her beauty still stunned him.

She swayed down the terminal simply dressed in a floral print blouse and black dress pants. He could tell she hadn't seen him yet, because she looked a bit uneasy.

Shelia had stepped off the plane, excited and doubly anxious to see Charles again. At the end of each phone call she told him that she was doing fine, but that was not entirely true. Time was her enemy. And time seemed to be winning the battle. Her medical training, her marriage, her life were all waiting for time to pass so that things could become as she wanted them.

As she walked further into the terminal, Shelia began nervously looking for him. She couldn't wait to hold him in her arms again and look into those magnificent light-brown eyes.

Then there he was in front of her, causing her heartbeat to quicken. Overjoyed, she ran into his waiting arms.

As Charles held her in his arms, the loneliness of the past three months seemed far away. She was again complete. But she knew it would be harder to leave him this time.

"Baby, I'm so happy you're here," he exclaimed, holding her tight.

"Oh, Charles, I've missed you so much," she whispered, tears of pleasure and relief in her eyes.

After fighting the airport traffic, Charles' driver took them straight to Rodeo Drive to select a dress to wear to the award show. At first, Shelia felt self-conscious shopping alongside celebrities and Hollywood types. But her confidence rose as she paraded the latest fashions on the mini-runway for her husband. She tried on a number of designer dresses before they decided on a cucumber-green, long, straight dress with spaghetti straps that crossed in the back. The body of the low-cut number had rhinestone designs across the center of the bodice, accentuating her slim waist.

As she headed to the register with the dress and accessories, Charles handed her a credit card. She was going to refuse it and use her own card even though the total would be quite high. She knew because she had already calculated the total cost of her purchases. But then she looked more closely at the card. It was a platinum Visa card with her name at the bottom.

Shelia hesitated, but accepted the card. Her card, actually a bank card for a joint account her parents had opened when she started school, had been her bread and butter for the past seven years. Trusting her judgment, her parents made sure that there was always funds available for her use, knowing she would have expenses during her college years. They didn't want her to have to work when her main focus should be her studies. And Shelia made an effort to keep her expenditures to a minimum.

Charles saw her hesitating. They were going to have to talk again about their financial situation, he thought. He wanted to share his wealth with her, not make her feel as if she would owe him later. She was his wife, not his mistress.

Shelia realized she would have to get used to a lot of things. Unlike people back home, nobody really bothered Charles here. They looked, and a few stared and pointed, but none of them went into hysterics. Most of the people who noticed him were tourists happy to see a celebrity—any celebrity.

They decided to spend her first night in California by themselves at home enjoying each other. After seeing what was now *their* house, Shelia was nearly speechless.

"Charles, this is beautiful," Shelia enthused. She kept looking as they drove up the long driveway. The house was built on a hill and could be seen clearly between the palm trees lining either side of the driveway.

"I'm glad you like it, baby," he said, both pride and pleasure in his voice.

"Like it? No, hon, I love it," she corrected, tugging on his arm every time she saw a different aspect of the landscape.

Charles just smiled as she excitedly bounced in the passenger seat.

Seeing the house from the driveway was nothing compared with the effect of seeing it up close. It was a beautiful, large two-story house with a three-car garage on about four acres of land. The immaculately land-scaped grounds included a perfectly manicured lawn, a variety of trees, rose bushes, and a flower garden.

The driver let them out at the front of the house with her luggage and shopping bags, then pulled the car toward the garage. Charles led her through a side gate to the backyard portion of the property, which had a swimming pool, a cabana, changing rooms, and a full-length basketball court. A wide deck had an awning covering half of the area.

The back sliding-glass doors opened to a large lounge area. A fully-stocked bar took up one wall. The game room had a pool table, game table, and a large-screen TV loaded with the latest video games. A state-of-the-art stereo system occupied one corner of the room.

She followed Charles from the lounge to the library, then to an office, and finally, to a gourmet kitchen. When she came to the living room, Shelia stopped dead in her tracks and looked around her.

Painted in soft mauve and cream colors, the living room was filled with paintings and sculptures by African-American artists. She knew he was a collector of arts, but had no idea he had so much. Large ceiling-to-floor windows made up one wall, allowing the sunlight to enter into the room in even streams. In the foyer, a crystal chandelier hung from a high ceiling. A wide staircase ran along the left wall of the room. Plush white carpeting covered the entire area.

Upstairs, the first three doors Shelia opened were fully furnished guestrooms. The fourth opened to a bathroom; the fifth was an exercise room, and the sixth was a nursery. The last room was the master bedroom, which had a connecting door to the nursery. Charles carried her suitcase into this room and put it inside an empty walk-in closet. She opened the connecting door and stood in the nursery.

"That was here when I bought the place. I figured I might need it one day, so I left it."

She smiled at him as he walked in the room. "Well, I guess one day we will. I told you I wanted four kids," she replied, putting her arms around his neck and kissing him. "Charles, I missed you. It's going to be even harder to leave you this time."

"Shelia, we only have six months to go. Then we will be together always." He held her hand and led her back into the bedroom. "I want to talk to you for a minute."

"What's wrong, Charles?" she asked, seeing the suddenly serious expression on his face.

"Nothing. I just want you to know some things, that's all. First, I want you to know how much I love you. Since you've become a part of my life, only sunshine has fallen on me. I want you to know that what I have is what you have. This is a 'we' thing. This is not my house; it's our house. I'm not a millionaire; we are millionaires. That card I gave you earlier is a joint account. I know that you have your own, and it's okay if you want to keep it. I understand that you have a strong independent nature. You have your own checking account, and so do I, but I plan to open a joint one. We can change our own accounts to savings. Well, we don't have to go too deep into it. I wanted us to go by my accountant's office before you leave so he could explain things to you. Because of the money we make, it might be easier to have a joint account that we can withdraw money from or make purchases with using a checking card."

"Gosh, Charles, I'm used to just balancing my own account. You don't even get to see your checks?"

"No. I really don't have time for it."

"Well, that's going to change. From now on, I will be handling our money. The only thing we need an accountant for is taxes—until I learn how to do them, too."

"But you don't understand the kinds of checks that have to be made out, or the number of people who have to be paid."

"I'm just going to have to learn. These people could be robbing you blind. Exactly how much money do *we* have?"

"Actually, I couldn't give you an exact figure." He knew she had made her point. "Don't look at me like that. It's close to $125 million.

Probably more, because I started to produce my own records on this CD, and I also did some producing for another artist on my label."

"Did you say $125 million?"

"Yeah, maybe more. I'll call later to get an accurate balance."

"Charles, you don't see that something is wrong with that? You have to actually call someone to find out how much money you have. See, I'm going to have to find time to read up on financial management."

"Shelia, you can do that anywhere and anytime. I thought we were going to meet at home during your winter hiatus."

"Yeah, we are, but when I go back to school, I'm going to read up on it."

"You're too much." He stood and kissed her on her forehead.

"What do you expect? You just dropped a bombshell right into my lap."

Charles ran a finger through her hair and played with an end strand. "I wouldn't expect anything less from you. I love you, Shelia."

"I love you."

"Do you want to do more shopping or maybe go sightseeing?" It was close to six p.m., and she was beat.

"No, I just want to have a light dinner, a nice hot bath, and a little bit of loving from my husband."

"You got it," he said, pulling her out of the room. "Oh, by the way, tomorrow morning, Everett and a couple other people will be here to get us together for the award show."

They were making their way to the kitchen when Shelia stopped on the step. "I don't need anyone to come help me get ready. I can dress myself."

"Shelia, this is different. It's just my assistant, my stylist and barber. They make sure I'm where I'm supposed to be and looking my best. Remember, to everyone but Everett, you're my girlfriend. Why do you find it so strange that they would help you?"

"Because I'm just Shelia Daniels. Nobody knows me."

"Baby, you're Shelia Avery. And tomorrow we're not going to the movies. We'll be at one of the biggest award shows of the year. Stop putting everybody but yourself on a pedestal. Truth be told, some of them need to be in ditches. A lot of the stars people idealize are the worst human beings. They are cruel and inconsiderate, crawling all over each other to get to the top. And they make mistakes just like everybody else. Besides, you don't get that excited when I come around," he finished, jokingly.

Shelia looked at him, took one of his hands and placed it over her left breast. He could feel her heartbeat increasing. She licked her lips and whispered, "No, I get very excited when you are around."

It took him a minute to tear his eyes away from her lips. He smiled at her. "You're getting good," he said, laughing as he continued down the stairs.

"I've been practicing," Shelia stated.

"Oh? Who with?"

"Don't be jealous. I've been practicing alone in the mirror, and I've been thinking of new ways to please you."

Charles missed the bottom step and stumbled. They laughed when she caught him.

"Girl, stop teasing me. You know it's been a long time."

"Who's teasing?" A solid pat on his behind produced a sound that echoed through the lower level of the house.

With a sneaky look on his face, Charles came towards her. He lifted her over his shoulder and ran back up the stairs to the bedroom. "We'll eat later."

Shelia woke up the next morning sore and very hungry. But she was the happiest she had been in months. It was only six-thirty, but she was wide-awake and ready to start her day. Charles pulled her closer to him when she tried to get out of bed. She slowly moved out from under his arm and went to the weight room. She did her morning stretches, jogged on the treadmill, and lifted some free weights.

Checking the bedroom, she saw that Charles was still resting. She took a shower then ran out to the swimming pool for a few laps. When she stepped out of the pool, Charles was sitting in one of the lounge chairs watching her.

"I was wondering what you were swimming in."

"Well, I was going to keep my underclothes on, but when I saw how secluded it is around here I decided to be free."

"Very nice."

"Thank you," she replied coyly as she sashayed up the steps.

Shelia tried to walk past him, but he grabbed the middle of her leg. He pulled her down on the lounge chair and kissed her neck and shoulder. His hands were spread across her breast and stomach.

"Charles, we don't have time for this."

"Yes, we do. We always have time for this." He pulled on one of her nipples and tweaked it with his fingers.

"Um…you have to get ready for the awards show."

"I have plenty of time." He moved his hand to rest between her legs. "So beautiful, Shelia."

She relaxed against him, awaiting an onrush of pleasure that always resulted from his attentions. They heard a door sliding open and the smell of food from the kitchen.

"Damn, Ms. Holden, the housekeeper, is here." She couldn't see them because the cabana blocked her view. "Come on, let's go inside the changing house."

"No, Charles, that was a sign for us to get up from here. You're so horny," she laughed.

"I have to get it while I can. I won't see you for another month and a half after this."

"Poor baby," she said, leaving him to tame his erection.

The award show was held at the Shrine Auditorium in Los Angeles. From the moment she stepped out of the black limousine, Shelia felt like she was the star, not Charles. Although she knew the screaming fans were there to see the stars, she was glad she had allowed his stylist to help her dress and accessorize and have someone come to the house to give her a facial and apply her makeup.

Charles stood next to her dressed in an ivory tuxedo; a cucumber-green, ivory and black striped tie and matching handkerchief were his only accessories.

The walk down the red carpet was slow as Charles was stopped for a number of interviews. He was questioned more than once about Kara Morning's baby and the baby's paternity. Each time he answered the same way: he was not the baby's father, which was public knowledge, and he wished Kara the best. Only two interviewers bothered to ask who he was escorting. Charles pulled her to his side each time and introduced her as Shelia and joked that he had begged her to accompany him. He never said girlfriend or wife, as they had agreed. Charles didn't want to call her girlfriend, and they knew they couldn't use the term wife.

Once they were settled inside waiting for the show to begin, Shelia watched as other celebrities filed into the auditorium. Eric Benet, Toni Braxton, Usher, she named them all in her head, occasionally tapping Charles' shoulder when she couldn't contain herself. She tried not to embarrass her husband by acting like a stereotypical fan. She was doing quite well until he introduced her to Will Smith and Jada Pinkett-Smith. She had to ruefully admit that she may have acted a bit of the fool when the couple spoke to her as if she was an old friend. When LL Cool J walked in and sat in the row ahead of theirs—well, her earlier resolve all but disappeared.

Suddenly she saw Kara Morning walking down the aisle. She was beautiful in a soft yellow ballerina gown fully beaded across the bodice. Next to her was an actor named Dontane Blue. Shelia had seen him in dozens of movies. Shelia sat still, her nervousness replaced by quick stabs of jealousy and apprehension. She was jealous of Kara and her supermodel star status, the sparkling lights, and the lavish award show, and apprehensive about her future with Charles. Could she ever live up to this glamorous part of Charles life?

Those thoughts left her mind when she saw that Kara had seen Charles and instead of taking her seat, walked further down the aisle toward them. Charles was looking in another direction and didn't see her coming. Shelia squeezed his hand tightly, making him look her way. With her eyes, she tried to warn him.

"Well, well. What do we have here?" Kara came to a stop right next to Charles' seat.

"Hello, Kara," he spoke to her cordially.

"Charles," she replied, drawing unnecessary attention their way just by talking to him. A few celebrities and attendees turned toward them. They had no doubt been following the story. "And who do we have here?" She glanced in Shelia's direction.

Shelia smiled at her, determined to let this woman know that she didn't intimidate her.

"This is Shelia," Charles replied, squeezing Shelia's hand.

"Is this her?" Kara stood back on her hips just as an usher came to stand next to her.

"Ms. Morning, can I help you find your seat?"

"No, I know where my seat is. I'm just talking with a friend."

"We're done, Kara. Don't make a scene," Charles said. He nodded to Dontane as he approached. "Dontane."

"Charles. Come on, Kara," Dontane urged. "It's time to take our seats." He guided her toward their seats, glad she followed willingly.

"It's all right, baby," Charles said, reassuringly. "Don't worry about it."

It was hard for Charles to remember to treat her like a girlfriend. He was so glad to have her with him. Throughout the evening he could feel Kara's eyes on him, but he didn't let that spoil his time with Shelia. Kara had issues that she had to deal with on her own. He had no idea why he was the object of her affection, attention, or crazy obsession. Charles was determined to show Shelia the time of her life while she was with him. He looked at her enjoying the show, clapping at his nomination for favorite songwriter. Charles lifted her hand and kissed it, bringing her attention to him. He loved her.

The after-party lasted longer than they had expected. He had wanted to take Shelia on a quick tour of the city before her flight home the next day, but there would be no time for that in the morning.

Their last few hours together were spent making love in the cabana under the stars. He held her close and talked about how much he loved her, how he had first started loving her, and how he would love her forever.

Charles and Shelia stood in one of the airport lobbies, wrapped in each other's arms. She still had fifteen minutes before heading to the security checkpoint and her terminal. It was as if they were the only two people there. As her time neared, she turned in his arms and held him tight. She put her hand on the back of his neck and pulled him down for one last passionate kiss.

They focused on each other and on that moment. Neither saw the man who came up behind Charles and took the picture that would almost turn their well-thought-out plan inside out.

CHAPTER 12

It was the third week in December, and Shelia was excited to be going home. Walking across campus, she saw that signs of winter had slowly worked their way into the landscape. Trees were desperately hanging onto their last few leaves. The wind was sharp and crisp, and by five-thirty, it was dark outside. Rushing students carrying last minute Christmas gifts and suitcases were clearing out the dorms for the holidays. As she walked, she made a list of last-minute chores.

In the last month, she had adjusted well to being Charles' wife. Actually, her life hadn't changed that much. The loneliness was still there, but she had learned to work around it. The guilt of keeping secrets from her family was still there, but she had learned to live with it, too. Holding fast to the dream of their life together, she regularly counted the days until they could be open about their relationship.

Her grades had suffered slightly during the beginning of the school year. After her first examination period, she saw them drop from honors status to satisfactory, but now at the end of the term, they had returned to their usual levels. And she was once again on the right track. All in all, everything was going just as planned.

Shelia still talked to her husband daily. Although she could detect loneliness in his voice, he, too, was dealing with their separation. That was all they could do, anyway—deal with it.

On Wednesday of the last week of school, all hell broke loose. Shelia was in her room packing when she received a phone call from Charles. She thought nothing of it, even though she had already talked to him once that day.

"Hey, you. What's up?" she asked cheerfully.

"Shelia, you're not going to believe this. Are you sitting?"

She became alarmed. "Charles, what's wrong?"

"Baby, remember when we were at the airport the night you left here?"

"Of course, I remember." Especially that kiss, she said to herself.

"Somebody took a picture of us kissing and sold it to the National News, that rag magazine." His voice was thick with disbelief and disgust.

"Well, that's no big deal. Everybody knows that we go together." Shelia shrugged and kept folding her clothes.

"No, baby, you don't understand. The picture shows your arms around my neck; your wedding rings can be seen. They even had the nerve to show your ring finger in an inset."

Shelia sat down, her legs suddenly weak. "Are you sure?"

"Baby, I'm sitting here looking at it. Everett got me an advance copy when the magazine called the agency for information. They wanted to know whether I was married or if I was involved with a married woman. And they wanted to know her name. Listen, this issue goes to the stands first thing in the morning. I don't know if our parents will see it or not, and I don't know if one of the entertainment shows has gotten wind of it. But I'm sure they will."

"Oh, my God, Charles," she said, putting her hand over her mouth. Shelia had often told herself that she didn't care if her parents found out, but now was not a good time. She wasn't ready to have another argument with her father or answer his questions. She couldn't even confess to her mother as she wanted to. Whenever her mother called, she would cut their conversations short because she didn't trust herself. But now that the possibility of her finding out was real, she realized that she didn't want them to know yet.

Unfortunately, Shelia's father had always been a bit possessive with all his kids, but especially with her. It got worse after Brian died. When Jeff refused to marry Tanya, a girl who claimed to be carrying his baby, he and Edward had stopped speaking for almost a year. It got much worse during that time. When the baby was found not to be Jeff's and they reconciled their differences, he promised to stay out of Jeff's business. But he never made that promise to Shelia.

"We'll get through this, but I need you to be strong. Now, if nobody calls you tomorrow asking questions when you get home Friday, just don't bring it up. I'll be there early Saturday morning. And make sure you take off your wedding band."

"Charles, if our parents do see it, what are we going to say?" Shelia began to panic. Her voice was tight with worry. Charles tried to reassure her that all would be well.

"I'll leave that up to you. I understand that you don't want to be at the receiving end of your father's wrath, and we don't want him getting too upset because of his heart condition. But maybe we need to tell them. Both of our families will be upset, but we'll get through it. Once we explain everything to them, they'll understand, support us, and continue to love us as they always have. Everett is having a fit. He 's thinking that it's bad publicity. And I guess it is if people assume I'm messing with a married woman. But I think, if anything, it will bring me a whole new audience if they think I'm married—a more mature group. Anyway. That's not even important to me right now."

"I don't think the publicity will hurt your record sales at all. Mature people already buy your CDs." Shelia paused. "Look, I don't want to ruin our holidays over this. My father will absolutely hate me."

"Shelia, I don't think you give your father enough credit. He just wants what's best for you. Granted, he is a little too possessive of you. Maybe this is your chance to be that independent woman you were telling me about. I mean after you graduate, you still have to take your exams, do your internship and your residency. He won't want you dating then, either. He'll say you need to start your practice first. When will be the right time to tell him? When we have daughters, I hope I'm not that way."

"Okay. I'll just take the wedding band off and pray that the subject doesn't come up. If it does, can we say they must have painted the other ring on or something to get a story."

"Okay, if that's what you want to do, but I warn you. This magazine is not going to stop at a little story. They are going to try to find out, first, who you are. And then second; they'll start looking for a marriage license."

"Do you really think it will go that far?"

"Baby, I know it will. All I'm saying is that the lies are going to start building up. It's one thing to keep a secret, but one lie will end up being two, then three, just to cover up the first two."

"I walked into this with my eyes open. And I don't want to lie, but…damn. To be honest, the only reason I'm afraid for our families to find out is my father. He'll be upset, lecturing me, and we'll start arguing. I know I'm wrong for this. How can I argue with him about being a mature woman and keep this secret? That's crazy. I wish there was some way to tell them without him getting overly upset. He just wants me graduated and my career started before I get married."

"I know."

"But I don't regret anything. I had to do what was right for me. And you are so right for me, Charles."

"Baby, everything is going to be all right. I'm going to get some sleep. I have to get up early tomorrow. I'm scheduled to appear on a morning show. Let's just hope they haven't gotten wind of this thing. If they have, I'll tell them that you are my girlfriend, and I don't know where the picture came from."

"Okay, yeah, yeah. Charles, I'm so sorry that I'm asking you to lie."

"I love you, Shelia. Keep your chin up."

"I love you, too."

Lord, Shelia thought to herself after she hung up, now I'll be nervous all day tomorrow. Too scared to even answer the phone. To her a little lie would be worth it to keep her father's peace of mind. Or maybe, it was her own peace she was trying to keep. After she graduated in May, she would confess everything to their families; hopefully, her father would be able to deal with it because school would be behind her.

Shelia made herself believe that they were doing the right thing, praying that these two weeks would go fast.

Jeff tried to call his sister Friday morning after going to the supermarket for the one breakfast cereal his kids absolutely had to have. He had picked up a copy of the National News and was leafing through it while in line at the checkout counter. What he saw caused him to drop the half-gallon carton of milk he was carrying. As he came through the front door of his home, he called to his wife, Tia. For once, she was stunned into silence after she read the article. It didn't name the woman in the picture, but Jeff could tell it was Shelia. He knew she had gone to California to see Charles. There was no doubt that it was Charles in the picture. The ring, enlarged for the public's viewing pleasure, confirmed his suspicions. The wedding band was new, but it matched the engagement ring perfectly.

"Tia, how can you be so sure that it's not true?" he asked his usually reasonable wife.

"Because I know Charles…and Shelia. They wouldn't have gone and gotten married without letting someone know. Besides, they know how your father would blow his stack."

"Maybe that's why they didn't say anything. But I have to believe that they would have at least told Troy. You know how close he and Charles are." He picked up the telephone and dialed Shelia's number.

"Now you're using your head. You know those magazines get stories wrong all the time, always trying to make a quick buck off someone. I bet they probably didn't even investigate the picture. They just print that kind of stuff to sell magazines. Charles should sue their pants off. Remember how they messed that story up a few months ago about him and Kara's baby? I would have sued them for that."

Jeff redialed and got a busy signal again. Relaxing, he decided to wait 'til she got home.

Shelia took the phone off the hook around seven Thursday night because it seemed everybody they knew wanted to ask questions. The few people who were left on campus—most of whom she didn't even really know—made pest of themselves by coming by and staying way too long. Everyone at the dorm still had last-minute packing to do and wanted to do it as quickly as possible. A couple of people had attended late classes and were tired, so they closed the dorm down to outsiders. Shelia was able to have a quiet night before she left for home the next day.

Shelia arrived at her parents' house early the next morning, nervous and anxious. After unpacking her suitcases, she lowered herself into a hot bath and took a long, relaxing soak. She expected her mother to burst into the room any minute with a billion and one questions. But the feared interrogation never came.

As the week wore on, things seemed to be moving normally. Charles came home Saturday morning as he promised, and they resumed the boyfriend/girlfriend roles that both families had believed before school started.

Her father wasn't too happy about it and made no effort to hide his displeasure. He even pulled Charles aside. "Charles, I thought that we had an agreement." Edward Daniels looked stern sitting on the sofa in his family room. He took another sip of the juice in his hand.

"Mr. Daniels, I know what you asked me to do, forbade me to do, but I never agreed to stop seeing Shelia. I said that I would think about it, and I can't do it. I can't let her go. I love her too much. But she's still doing well at school. I told you that I don't want to hinder Shelia's education or her career, and I won't." As he looked Edward in the eye, Charles hoped for a smidgen of understanding from this proud man.

Edward stood, one hand in his pocket, the other around his glass of juice, and looked at Charles. He liked the young man a lot. He even hoped that one day Charles and Shelia would marry. Right now just wasn't the time. Shelia had things to do.

He had lost his son Brian at an early age. Jeff was practically lost to him over a misunderstanding. Some fast girl, Tanya, had said she was pregnant by

Jeff, and he and his wife had tried to force Jeff to marry her. When Jeff told his father that he couldn't go through with the wedding, Edward's pride and stubbornness caused him to stop talking to his son for a long time. He had lost his friendship with John Avery behind that incident, too, again due to his pride. But as glad as he was that the situation had been resolved and Jeff was now happily married, he couldn't keep quiet about this. Things just had to be done the right way.

A long time ago, he and his wife had agreed to stay out of their children's business, and he had tried, but Shelia was his daughter. His wife kept telling him that it was the 21st century, and he knew Shelia was a grown woman, but surely, the rules were different where a daughter was concerned. Maybe it was foolish, but try as he might, he couldn't wholeheartedly give his seal of approval to this relationship between Charles and Shelia, even though she had only six months to graduation. But he obviously couldn't stop it, either.

"Okay," Edward said.

"Sir?" Charles questioned, unsure of how to take the response.

"I said okay. I realize that you and Shelia love each other. I also realize that there's nothing I can do to stop it. I never really wanted you two to completely stop seeing each other. I just wanted Shelia to accomplish her goals. Charles, I admit that I'm a little stuck in the past, but I know that it is hard for a woman out there. Then and now. Every since Shelia was younger, I've known the girl was special. She's smart, Charles. And I knew she could be something, someone. I wanted her to be independent. In my line of work, I've seen so many single-mothers, hard-working women struggling to take care of their kids. And they do a good job, but it's a struggle that I never wanted Shelia to have."

"I understand."

"I'm not sure you do. Not until you have your own children. Boys are special, but girls, girls melt your heart, Charles. I know everybody thinks I'm too possessive of Shelia. I agree. I love my baby girl. I'm glad she has you, Charles. But having you doesn't stop her from having to complete herself."

"Yes, sir," Charles agreed, seeing Edward in a totally new light. He admired the man and his convictions, and he hoped when he had a daughter, he was the same.

"Mom, I don't understand why Dad is making such a big to-do about me dating Charles? I'm still doing everything that I'm supposed to do. I'm finishing my studies."

"Do you think that's all it's about, Shelia? Your grades? You graduating?" Her mother put down the paring knife she had been using to cut the rolled-out dough into square shapes for a chicken and dumplings dish, a favorite of Shelia's.

"What do you mean?"

"Shelia, you're his baby girl. He doesn't just call you that for the fun of it. He means it. You are his *baby girl.* He's so proud of you. I think he wants your career more than you do."

"But, Mom, I'm a grown woman now. Sooner or later, the baby girl grows up."

"That's easy for you to say. Wait until you and Charles have your own kids, then maybe you'll understand what he's going through. Now that Charles has straightened out all that paternity business, I'm sure your father will come around easily. He truly likes Charles." There had been many a time when she had to remind her husband that Shelia was grown. He would sometimes become testy if he didn't know her whereabouts, but Sylvia had always managed to keep the wolf at bay. She had her own agenda for her daughter's future, and becoming a doctor wasn't necessarily at the top of that list. Happiness came first, and she saw a lot of happiness and love between her daughter and Charles.

Shelia and Charles both needed to do last-minute Christmas shopping so they went to downtown Chicago and bought a lot of stuff. All their Christmas gifts had both their names on them. They figured that they could get away with that much.

ONE OF THESE DAYS

On Christmas Eve, Shelia was sitting in the family room of her parent's home wrapping the last of their gifts. She was bone-weary. She made herself a cup of coffee and then settled on the family-room couch to watch television. As she flipped through the channels, barely paying attention, she caught a glimpse of Charles. Quickly, she switched back to the channel.

"National recording artist Charles Avery seems to be rapidly making a name for himself in the music business, as well as in the rumor mills and romance departments. Recently the singer, who earlier this year was erroneously reported as being the father of supermodel Kara Morning's daughter, was caught on film in a sensual embrace with this unidentified woman in a California airport. In the photo provided to this station, the woman is wearing an exquisite and very expensive wedding band and engagement ring set."

The picture showing Shelia's hands draped around Charles' neck flashed onto the screen. "And these photos, taken just a few days ago, show him Christmas shopping with a woman identified as longtime friend and new girlfriend Shelia Daniels of Chicago, Avery's hometown. Is R & B's newest heartbreaker beginning to be just that?"

She picked up the phone to call Charles, but he was out with his brothers. So she sat back and willed herself into relaxing. But she kept returning to the magazine photo and the TV images. What kind of reporters were these? If they were so smart, why couldn't they figure out that same woman was in the magazine and on TV? Maybe it was more profitable to keep the public guessing. Probably more money in having people believe Charles was a two-timing dog.

Suddenly more angry than rational, Shelia called information to get the station's number and dialed it.

"WXTZ-TV, how may I help you?" the operator asked. "Hello, WXTZ-TV?" she repeated, now sounding irritated.

Shelia hung up the phone, realizing she had just stopped short of making a huge mistake. *Besides, wasn't she asking her family to do the same thing—believe the lies?*

Anger had almost become her undoing. She vowed to not let them get to her—to not play into their hands. As mad as she was, had she stayed on the phone, anything could have come out of her mouth. She had to learn to ignore them.

"Hey, baby." It was 1:30 in the morning, and Charles sounded tipsy, having just returned from club-hopping with his brothers and friends.

"Hey," she replied, pressing both hands to her weary eyes.

Hearing fatigue in her voice, Charles asked, "What's wrong? You sound miserable," concern instantly overriding the numbing effects of the alcohol. "Talk to me, Shelia."

"Did you watch the report tonight on WXTZ?"

"Shelia, don't let that worry you. My mother told me about it already. She stayed up until I got in. I'm going to tell you the same thing that I told her. Don't worry about it. We already talked about this. Baby, don't let them get to you. I'm not sure if this will be the end of it, but as long as we know the truth, we don't have to worry about anybody else."

"It's easier said than done, Charles. I don't like to hear them talking about you or me."

"I know this is all new to you. And, baby, if I could, I would stop it, but I can't."

"I know…"

"Shelia, please believe—"

"I know it's not your fault, Charles. But it's still a hard pill to swallow. I don't blame you; I was just pissed off."

"Don't let it get to you like that. Are you all right now?"

"Yeah, I'm over it. I'll see you tomorrow morning."

"Okay, baby. I love you."

"I love you, too. Good night."

"Good night, love."

By the time Shelia got up the next morning, Christmas day was in full swing. A light snow was falling. Beautiful, white Christmas, she thought, anxious to start her day. She realized how late it was when she heard her brother and his family at the front door. She must have overslept. Moving quickly, Shelia showered and dressed, and then went downstairs to join her family.

Every Christmas her small family ate breakfast together, afterwards going to the cemetery to place a holiday wreath on the grave of her older brother, Brian. He had died nearly ten years earlier in a drunk-driving accident. It had been so long ago. Even so, the pain of the loss renewed itself as soon as the car crossed under the wrought-iron arch at the cemetery entrance.

At first, she hadn't wanted to go because it hurt too much. Brian was like her guardian angel. He had protected her, disciplined her, and spoiled her rotten. They were all close, but Brian was the one who watched over them all. And when he died, Shelia was mad at him for a long time for leaving her. As she got older, she understood that the family needed that time at the cemetery to make peace with Brian and with themselves. Jeff used the time to tell his kids about the uncle they never knew.

Her father always stayed after everyone else went to the cars. As kids, they used to watch him talking to Brian, and would wonder what was being said. Their mother would wait patiently in the car, wiping at tears, and watching her husband just as she was doing today, but she never told them what he said to his son.

As the day wore on, Shelia became aware that her brother was watching her intensely. She found it vaguely disturbing, wondering if he knew anything. She decided to take the easy way out and pretend she hadn't noticed his staring. It was one thing for them to be unsuspecting, but quite another if they started asking questions. She had no doubt she would crack, especially under pressure from Jeff.

Jeff knew his sister almost as well as he knew himself. Something was going on. He couldn't put his finger on it, but he knew it had something to do with Charles and the rumors he had been hearing.

Last night, when they were out with the guys, someone had mentioned the articles to Charles. Charles had swallowed hard and had tried to come up with a reasonable explanation. In the end, he told them that they were not to worry and that in his line of business, gossip was big money.

This was true, but now Shelia was acting weird. Jeff didn't believe the stuff about another woman or the baby because he knew that Charles loved his sister and that she loved him.

Jeff and their mother had talked about it before Shelia arrived home and had decided not to mention any of it to Edward. Ten chances to one, he would never hear about it unless someone brought it to his attention, anyway. He didn't watch anything on television except sports, and he rarely read the papers. They didn't feel there was any need for Edward to get upset over something so silly, possibly causing him and Shelia to get into a pointless argument.

CHAPTER 13

The Daniels and the Averys usually ate together on holidays, as well as on Sundays. The tradition had started when Tia and Jeff first started seeing each other again. They had been high school sweethearts, but had broken up shortly after Jeff went off to college. Now it seemed all the more appropriate since one of the Daniels' children had already married into the large Avery family, and everyone expected Shelia to follow suit.

On this Christmas Day, the crowded Avery house had a joyous aura, the aromas of turkey, ham, and other holiday dishes wafting through each room. Besides the Averys and their eight children and their spouses and children, there were aunts, uncles, and cousins who frequently dropped in for dinner. Sometimes even friends of the family were invited, fitting comfortably into the welcoming atmosphere.

Today, the men were sitting in the large but congested den watching whatever football or basketball game they could get on the tube. This was John Jr.'s idea, following a losing snowball fight with the grandkids. He had been the first to admit that he was old and tired. Soon, his brothers, brothers-in-law, and most of the other men joined him. It was cold outside, and there wasn't any point in risking catching a cold. Excuses for ending the game varied. The kids had teased and mocked them, but when the first blast of warm air hit their faces as they walked into the small foyer, all the teasing was instantly forgotten.

Most of the Christmas gifts had been exchanged and put away. The laughter and excitement of the kids could be heard coming from the basement as the boys played their new hand-held video games and the girls took turns singing with the help of a karaoke machine.

The house was beautifully decorated with garlands of green leaves and red holiday flowers. Miniature white lights were strung around doors and windows throughout the house, and mistletoe hung invitingly over every door. A small tree stood in the living room. A much larger tree, gloriously decorated, was in front of the bay windows in the den.

Brenda Avery still had all the ornaments made by all of her children over the years. They were her most treasured gifts, and each Christmas she decorated the main tree with them. Thanks to the ever-expanding Avery brood, new ornaments were added to the tree every year. And mistletoe hung over every doorway.

Tia stood at the sink rinsing a bunch of grapes to snack on. "So, Shelia, what did my brother get you for Christmas?"

Shelia looked up at her sister-in-law. "I don't know yet. We are going to exchange our gifts later tonight. He was so excited buying everything he could for the kids. And I was excited, too, so, I didn't give it much thought."

"Christmas is really all about the kids, isn't it? Well, what did you ask for?"

"I didn't, because if I started asking for things, he would have been keeping a list. It doesn't really matter. I know whatever it is, I'll love it."

Tia nodded approvingly. "So, how are things going at school? I wanted to ask you this morning, but the kids kept me kind of busy."

Tia and Jeff had two kids, seven-year-old Kevin and two-year-old Kayla. Kevin was born while Jeff was away at college. When she and Jeff parted ways, Tia failed to tell him that she was pregnant. He didn't find out about his son until four years later, when he came back into town. Shelia was glad that Jeff and Tia were able to overcome their past mistakes and rekindle their love.

"Oh, fine. I've finished two of my elective courses, General Surgery and Surgical Intensive Care Unit. I love doing daily rounds with the surgical teams and participating in the conferences. And I learned a lot about operative techniques and fundamental diseases." She sat at the table, concentrating on the eggs she was preparing for her mother to devil.

Kristal and Devin, who were making potato and pasta salads, joined in the conversation.

"So on top of the hectic schedule at the medical college, you have to make rounds with the doctors?" Kristal asked with bewilderment. "That's impossible."

"Not for Shelia," Devin said. "It's a wonder she doesn't have three or four degrees by now. She was always a whiz in school."

They all laughed. "Well, to be honest, they keep you pretty busy. But to me it's a thrill. Every morning I wake up excited to see another patient, do another case study, attend another lecture, because there is so much to learn. Procedures and techniques are changing every day."

"You sure do make it sound exciting," Tia replied.

"It's as though medicine is what I was meant to do, but it's too serious an occupation for me to take lightly. So I deal with it and learn as much as I can."

Devin said, "Well, that's no surprise."

Charles breezed into the kitchen just then and pulled Shelia into his arms, kissing her chin and neck.

"Charles, she's not under the mistletoe," Devin scolded with her hands on her hips.

"Sh, nobody has to know," he said, grinning.

Kristal stepped forward. "Well, we know. The rule is only kiss under the mistletoe. That's cheating, and I'm telling."

"Tattletale. Tia, Devin, y'all wouldn't tell on me, would you?" he asked the two sisters most likely to take his side.

"Do I look like Troy?" Tia shot back, ignoring his hurt expression. "If I can't kiss, you can't kiss."

Pretending to be mad, Charles left the room. "Oh, and Tia, yes, you do look like Troy," he said once he was safely down the hall.

"He's too sneaky," Kristal chimed, pointing at her departing brother.

"Kristal, leave him alone," Devin said, defending him. She had idolized Charles since she was a baby. He was her handsome older brother, her hero and protector. "You were the same way when you and Richard first started out."

"I know. I just like messing with him. I'm really happy that he's found someone special to love."

"Me, too," said Tia, moving to the table to help Shelia finish. "As soon as Shelia finishes school, they can get married and start making some babies."

"Whoa," Shelia said, "getting married is one thing. Having babies is something else entirely." She looked back unblinkingly when they turned surprised stares on her.

"Don't you want kids, Shelia?" Tia asked worriedly. She knew her brother wanted children; he had made no secret of that. Charles was the only one of the siblings without children.

"Of course, but not right away. You all make it seem like it's the easiest thing in the world to do."

"Well, it's not the easiest thing in the world to do," Anna corrected and Stephanie and April joined in. "It's painful and tiring and shocking, and oh, did I mention painful? Your hormones are jumping all around inside, and you don't know whether to be happy, sad, or just miserable. But it is the most natural thing in the world. And it's so rewarding—after all the pain has gone away."

"Shelia, as a soon-to-be doctor, you know how the female body works and what it's for," added April.

"And surely money will not be an issue for you," Devin added. "Besides, you have all the experience you need right in this room. We have almost twenty kids among us. And between our parents and yours, you'll never see your kids, anyway."

"Yeah, but who's going to have my kids for me? I'm scared to death. I could have thirty doctorates, and I would still be scared," Shelia laughed, trying to lighten the moment.

"Well, that's natural, too." Tia understood completely and put a hand on her sister-in-law's shoulder. "Tell you what. Both Denise and I are due in April. I'll talk to her. Whoever delivers while you're home on spring break will let you into the delivery room so you can see first-hand what it's like."

"I don't know," Shelia replied, excited about the offer but still apprehensive. "Especially with Denise. This is her first baby. I wouldn't want to intrude on her and Chauncey's moment."

"That's true," Tia agreed. "Well, you'll just have to make sure you're home when your niece or nephew is born and come in with Jeff and me."

"Okay," Shelia said, "but I'm still in no hurry to have kids of my own."

Later that night Charles talked Shelia into going for a relaxing ride. He knew this would be the only way to get her alone and away from the endless stream of extended family members who were making their holiday rounds and ending up at the Avery house. Practically no one had left the house, as they were all enjoying each other's company. It was Tuesday and work was on the horizon for almost everyone, but nobody seemed to care.

Shelia settled back in the passenger seat of the rented Cadillac Escalade. She loved this truck. It was roomy and comfortable and had all sorts of extras included. With the touch of a button, she could watch a movie, play a CD, or map the easiest route to another city. The seats were heated and sent out soft vibrations at her request.

She leaned back, feeling the warmth of the heated seat rising up and enveloping her. After a minute of enjoying the car's little luxuries, she looked over at the blessing God had bestowed upon her. No material luxury could possibly compare. How lucky she was to be sitting next to this man she loved so much. Although her marriage was a secret, she felt luckier than a lot of women. They hadn't spent a lot of time alone this trip, what with last-minute shopping and visiting friends and family.

"Shelia, we need to talk." He drummed his fingers on the steering wheel.

"What's wrong?" Shelia looked at him closely; something was wrong.

"Your dad talked to me the other day. He said he was glad we were together. Now, I understand why he was giving us such a hard time. He loves you."

"I know that."

"I, um, think we should tell them the truth. He only wanted to make sure I wasn't a hindrance to your plans."

"And you're not. I've been telling him that from the start. It's hard for him to give up control."

"Well, now, he has given it up, and he's trusting you to make the right decision."

"I'm not telling him yet, Charles. He'll be more upset than before, especially after he thinks he's giving us permission to date."

Charles saw her point. "Okay, but I just thought now would be a good time to put it all on the table. I didn't mean to make you mad."

"I'm not mad." Shelia sat back deeper in the seat. "I'm just disappointed."

"In my suggestion?"

"No, in myself." Leaning into her seat, she shut her eyes and ended the conversation.

"Hey," Charles began two minutes later, breaking into her solace. "What do you want to do this weekend?"

"I don't know," Shelia said, abstractedly.

"Do you want to go on a little trip?"

"Sure, where to?" She liked the idea. "It would be nice to spend a little time with you alone."

"How about we go to the Bahamas for the weekend, a brief getaway?"

Sitting up straight, she asked, "Are you serious?"

"Of course, I am."

"I always wanted to go there."

"Good. Call and make the reservations. We can leave first thing Friday morning."

"Really? Oh, Charles, that would be perfect. Make the reservations? How am I supposed to do that?"

"What do you mean?"

"I can't make the reservations. I don't have that much credit on my card."

"Sure you do. Remember, Shelia, you have two cards now."

"Oh, right." Shelia hadn't used the card he had given her, although she knew its credit line was unlimited. She still thought of it as his.

"Besides, Shelia, I want you to start getting used to handling the money. I know you haven't used the card since leaving California. You can't be scared to spend your own money."

"Charles, you just have to understand that—?"

"I know it's hard for you to let go of your independence, and I understand that it's going to take some time. But I just want you to know that this is our money, not mine. I'm here to support you."

"I know, baby, and I do appreciate everything you're saying. I'll make the arrangements first thing in the morning, and I'll work on letting go of some of the independence." In fact, there had been times she needed to use the credit card, but she had always resisted, always finding a way to make her money stretch. She kept forgetting that her husband was a millionaire, and she was now one, too. Once he had reminded her of the reality, her eagerness overrode her other emotions.

This would be her first trip to the islands. As an undergrad, she had been unable to join her friends on trips during spring break to Miami. She wasn't as financially stable as most of them were; the majority had well-to-do parents who had also attended Howard University. But now her time had come, and she was going to enjoy it.

Shelia knew where they were headed. It had been a long time since they had been there, but the memories of the grove were still fresh in her mind. She had given him her virginity there, made him her best friend there, loved and laughed with him there, shared her hopes and dreams with him there, and thanked the Lord for him there.

As he pulled onto a blacktopped road lined with light-posts on either side and drove up the wide lane, a spacious two-story, three-car-garage house came into view.

Her eyes were like saucers as she took in the massive landscaping that had converted her peaceful cove into a modern Garden of Eden.

The mansion was complete with a front porch holding Roman columns and a swing. The driveway widened as it neared the garage. There was a walkway leading to the porch. Rose bushes littered the landscape, and flower gardens lined each side of the walkway. It was breathtaking.

After he stopped the car, he sat quietly waiting for her reaction.

A sad look came over Shelia's face as indelible memories of their time there crowded her mind. They won't be able to come there anymore. People didn't take too kindly to trespassers.

"I'm sorry, Charles," she said, laughing lightly to cover her sad regret. "I thought we were coming here to exchange our Christmas gifts. I didn't know that someone had bought the property."

"Do you like it? The house, I mean," Charles asked mysteriously.

"Yes, I do. It's going to be something else when it's finished. Guess we're going to have to find another special place that's ours and ours alone."

He tucked a strand of hair behind her ear. "Baby, what's wrong? Why are you so sad all of a sudden?"

"Here," she said tensely, looking at him with eyes full of love. Her hand held a small jewelry box. "Merry Christmas."

Charles took the box, smiling his thanks at her. Untying the ribbon and opening the box, his smile widened when he saw the thin rope chain with a gold wedding band encrusted with diamonds at the end.

"Thanks, baby," he grinned, kissing her on the cheek and lips. "I love it."

"I'm glad. I figured that if you can't wear it on your finger, at least you can wear it around your neck, under your shirt or something," she said wistfully.

"You're right, baby," he smiled, raising his arms and fastening the chain around his neck.

"Now let's hurry up before we get into trouble for being out here."

"Why would we get into trouble? We can be out here."

"Come on, Charles. Do you know the owners or something?"

"Of course, I do. So do you." A wink of his eye finally elicited the reaction he had been waiting for: She jumped into his arms.

Her questions came faster than he could answer. "You bought it? This is our house? You had all of this done?" Questions came out of her mouth so fast, he was unable to answer.

"Merry Christmas, baby. This is our house."

Almost choking with tears of happiness, she wrapped her arms around him. "I can't believe it. Charles, it's beautiful. Thank you, baby."

"I knew you would like it." He returned her hug then they they admired their new home. "I worked with a contractor in California. He sent a crew here with specific designs that we had decided on."

"Oh, I love it already. I can't wait for it to be finished. And you've been keeping it a secret from me all this time? That was pretty sneaky of you."

"Well, it wasn't hard with neither of us being in town. Troy helped me with the real estate company. He's the only one I told about it."

"Why am I not surprised?"

Feigning innocence, Charles flashed those dimples that made her melt every time. Then he got out of the car and walked around to help her out.

They walked around the front of the house, with Charles pointing out many decorative changes he had made. He couldn't take her inside because last-minute work was still being done. It didn't matter; she was already in love with it.

After they looked around, Charles took blankets from the trunk of the car, and leaning against the hood, they talked about decorating, moving in, and eventually raising a family there. Snuggled together and warmed by their love, they took little notice of the night's coldness as new snow began to fall, covering the landscape with a thin coat of pure whiteness.

CHAPTER 14

Stretched out in one of the reclining chairs on the luxury private jetliner, Charles snored, the soothing sound of Kenny G's saxophone in the background.

The aircraft's interior had carpeting wall-to-wall, extending from the front of the plane to its rear. Wood paneling covered all the walls except for the state-of-the-art entertainment center, which occupied nearly one entire side of the plane. A thirty-two-inch flat television dominated the area, which included a DVD player, VCR, video-game systems, and a surround-sound stereo system. A wet bar was next to the doorway leading to the kitchen in the back, which was equipped with a microwave, refrigerator, toaster oven, and sink. The kitchen also had cabinets fully stocked with food.

The bedroom was to the back of the plane, tastefully decorated in sage and cream with cream-colored paneled walls. It was beautifully accented with vases of greenery and decorative candles. They had been offered use of the room, but had declined because their flight would not take more than five hours. A small bathroom, complete with a shower, was in the back next to the bedroom.

Shelia's eyes burned due to broken sleep the night before, but her excitement made it difficult for her to give in to her weariness. She suppressed a giggle as she thought of her earlier conversation with her husband.

"Shelia, baby, are you sure you don't want to use the bedroom?" he had asked, a devilish grin on his face.

"No, Charles. We're not joining the mile-high club this trip."

"Baby, it's only me and you and the wide—"

"It's me and you, a pilot, and a flight attendant."

"They're not paying us any attention."

She had walked toward the front of the plane, Charles hot on her heels. "Are you kidding? They'll be all in our business. They probably have cameras hidden in that room."

"Shelia, they transport celebrities all the time. These people are professionals. They're used to being inconspicuous." Coming up behind her, he had placed an his open palm on each of her hips. "Don't you want to be with me?"

"Don't try to make me feel guilty. That's not going to work. When we get there, we'll have plenty of time to be together. Now, sit down there and enjoy the flight."

Charles had done as told, keeping a seductive eye on her until he drifted off to sleep.

She occupied herself with magazines and crossword puzzles that did not hold her interest for long.

"Ma'am, would you like a drink?"

Shelia jumped at the sound of his voice and nodded, then clearing her throat and weakly answering, "Yes, I would. Thank you." Her face flushed a soft red when she realized that the flight attendant had to repeat his question. "I'm sorry. I'm just so excited," she offered in the way of an excuse.

"I understand. Are you going for vacation or business?"

"Vacation. We're both so burned out. We needed a little time to ourselves."

He smiled his understanding, "If you don't mind, may I ask you a question?" Shifting his weight from one leg to the other, he rested his hand on his hip.

"Sure," Shelia answered, giving her full attention to the slightly built flight attendant, noting his gay demeanor. His name tag read "Simon." She looked him up and down, trying to decipher his body language.

"Your husband?" Simon whispered, as if he was telling her a secret. "Is he the singer, Charles Avery?"

"Yes, he is Charles Avery." She watched his eyes light up. A second later, they turned dark and were accompanied by a mischievous grin.

"But he's not my husband," she added, lifting her chin and meeting his gaze straight on before she continued. "He's my boyfriend." Hearing herself say the words caused her some disquiet, but she kept all expression out of her voice.

"Oh, I apologize," he quickly amended. "I just thought—"

"I know what you thought," she quickly interrupted. She had no idea what he was thinking. She just didn't like the way he was thinking it. "That will be all." There was enough criticism in her tone to discourage further comments or questions. Maybe he was after her man. Maybe he was just trying to spy. Whatever it was, she didn't want any part of it.

Now that he allegedly had a girlfriend *and* a mistress, Charles had become unbelievably sought after. Everyone was trying to break the story, even though there wasn't a story to tell. His record sales were rising again and Everett, his manager and agent, couldn't have been happier. Shelia assumed that he probably didn't want to set the record straight. If it weren't for her dad, Shelia would have already corrected the misinformation. The rumors of other women were becoming wilder by the minute, and there was nothing she could do or say.

She turned around in her swivel recliner, faced the window and dismissed all thoughts of him. As she leaned closer to the window, trying to see the archipelago that was the Bahamas, Charles stirred in his chair.

"You handled that pretty well. I think that I better keep an eye on you. I was about to get up and handle him for you, but you got chops."

"And you better know it. So, did you sleep well?"

"Yes, it was much needed. Now I'm revived and ready to get on with our vacation. You didn't sleep?"

"No, I'm too excited." Again, she turned her head and looked out the window. "Which island is ours? Harbor Island?"

He reached across her, looking out the window. "I don't know. They all look the same to me. It's beautiful, isn't it?"

"I can't wait!" Her excitement was overflowing.

"Calm down, baby," he joked. "You'll pass out before we get off the plane."

Shelia walked through the lobby of the Pink Sands, awestruck. She had been given a description of the grounds when making the reservations, but she had not imagined anything close to the sights before her. Through the open pavilion, the azure water could be seen stretching for miles. Beautiful, tranquil, clear and relaxing, the inviting seas beckoned to her as she walked to the open patio doors.

"Mr. Avery, your room is ready, sir," the bellman said cheerfully as he pulled their luggage behind him and led them along the broken cement pathway to their cottage on the beach.

"Thank you," Charles replied, placing a hand on Shelia's back to guide her along the walkway.

Shelia became newly bug-eyed with each new discovery. She gasped when she saw the breathtaking stretch of pink sand beach and again as they walked through the tropical garden leading to their cottage. She had a wonderful, almost childlike, appreciation for new experiences.

"I love it," she exclaimed, twirling around the room before finally collapsing on their queen-size bed. "Isn't it beautiful?" she asked, jumping back up and walking toward the outside.

"It's not as beautiful as you are, baby," he said, coming up behind her and putting his arm around her waist. Nibbling on her neck, he whispered softly, "We could do something to take your mind off the view."

"I know what you want to do." She turned, offering her lips to him. "But we just got here. Don't you want to go explore some first?"

"I'd rather explore you."

"Come on, let's go sightseeing before lunch." Dragging Charles behind her, Shelia's energy bounced off the wall as she scurried around the room gathering items she thought that she might need on her sight-seeing trip. Giggling like a little girl, she stuffed her camera, sunglasses, straw hat, and sunscreen into her straw bag.

Charles and Shelia enjoyed the afternoon, shopping at the local market for gifts to take home and going on a historical walking tour. Instead of stopping for lunch, they snacked along the way, buying fruits and drinking water from local vendors.

"Baby, let me try to do it," Charles said, removing his shades to attempt using a machete to carve a pineapple as efficiently as the fruit vendor had just demonstrated.

"Maybe, ooh…," Shelia moved out of the way as he bought the sharp instrument down, completely missing his target. "Maybe you should leave this to the professionals."

"I got it, baby," he said, trying again. Instead of missing the pineapple, he hit it at such an angle it flew through the air and landed near a pail of fish in the next vending area. Defeated, he handed the machete back to the vendor, grabbing her hand and leading her down the lane.

"What else do you want to do?" she asked, trying to stifle the laugh that threatened to break out.

"I'm ready to go back to the cottage and rest before dinner. Aren't you tired yet? We've been out here all morning. With all that you have scheduled for us tomorrow, I think we need to stay close to the resort."

"Okay, if you say so. How long do we have before dinner?" she asked, reaching for his free hand.

"We have a couple of hours to relax before dinner. I only hope I make it back to the resort with all these bags I'm toting."

"If you make it back to the cottage, I'll give you a big surprise," she laughed, playing along with his game. "Hey, slow down," she urged as Charles quickened his pace.

After a meal of lobster, steak, and mixed vegetables, Charles and Shelia sat at their table in the resort restaurant listening to the soft calypso music being played by a lively Caribbean band. A calm breeze circulated through the room, helped by numerous ceiling fans and having a hypnotically soothing effect on the small crowd of patrons.

"Do you want to dance, baby?" Charles asked, reaching for her hand across the small table.

"I'm so full right now. I think I ate a little bit too much," she giggled.

"Are you tipsy?" he asked, bending down slightly to look into her half-closed eyes.

Her smile told him everything he needed to know as she struggled to focus on his face. "I think that I might have had just a little too much."

"Are you okay? Do you want to go back to the cottage?" Concern wrinkled his brow as he reached into his wallet for his platinum Visa card. He signaled for their waitress. "Could you please handle this as quickly as possible?" He turned back to his wife. "Hold on for a second, baby, and we'll be out of here."

"I don't want to go back to the cottage. It's such a beautiful night, and who knows when we'll get a chance to be alone like this again. I don't want it to end. Let's walk along the beach."

"If that's what you want to do. Are you sure you'll be okay?"

"I'll be fine," she replied. Teasing him with her eyes, she lifted his hand to her mouth for a sensual kiss.

Charles brow formed an unspoken question. "Don't start some—"

"Here you go, sir," the waitress interrupted. "I just need your signature. Thank you very much. Enjoy the rest of your evening."

"Thank you. Come on, my beautiful little drunk. I swear, I can't take you anywhere," he joked, taking her by the elbow and leading her out of the restaurant as gracefully as possible.

It was lovely along the beach, just after dusk. In the horizon, the moon left shimmering images on the water. Waves from far away came crashing onto the never-ending coastline.

Shelia lifted up her ankle-length orange-burst sundress and dipped her feet into the cool water. She was soon splashing around like a school kid.

"Come join me, Charles," she called to him as he stood on the shore watching her enjoy herself.

At once, he reached down and removed his loafers and rolled up his tan Dockers. Keeping his eyes on her as he waded in, Charles felt an onrush of emotion as he joined her in the surf.

"Shelia, baby, you are so beautiful," he crooned, taking her in his arms and whirling her around.

"Thank you," she said, lifting her head and waiting patiently for his lips to touch hers. "Charles, don't you just love it here?"

"Yes, baby, it's very nice. I'm glad that you're loving it."

"I'm so glad that we don't have to deal with all that hiding and sneaking here. I don't ever want to leave. It's so peaceful." She put her arms around his neck.

"If you want, I'll talk to the folks when we get home."

"No. I'm a grown woman, Charles. I don't have to explain everything to them."

Charles sensed quickly that the one glass of wine she had with her dinner was doing most of the talking for her.

"In fact," she continued, "I didn't even tell them that I was coming here with you."

"You what?" He stopped their movements, suddenly holding her by both arms and bending to look at her directly. "You what?"

"I didn't tell them that I was going away. I don't have to tell them everything."

"Shelia, why would you do that? You know that they're probably worried out of their skulls by now." He released her, walking back to the sand, his hands on his hips. "I don't think that was smart."

"What do you mean by that, Charles?" She marched up behind him.

"You keep saying that you want to be treated like an adult by your parents, but then you do this. This isn't something an adult would do. What are you trying to prove here?"

"I want to be treated like an adult by my parents, and by my husband."

"Then start acting like one. First thing in the morning, you're going to call home and tell them where you are."

"I'm sure they know by now. Your parents know, right?"

"Yes, they know because I'm not selfish enough to go away for a weekend and not tell them. Remember, I came home to visit my family."

"That was a low blow." Shelia stalked off, heading toward their cottage, kicking up sand with each step. Her hands were balled into fists as she seethed over what had amounted to be a reprimand.

Letting out a low sigh, Charles followed her, wondering if he had been too hard on her.

Sylvia Daniels put the last dish in the drain, and then rinsed her chrome sink and wiped her hands on the apron around her narrow waist. It was not yet eight in the morning.

Pulling the vacuum cleaner out of the hall closet, she pushed it into the living room, then returned to the kitchen to finish her second cup of coffee. She had been up since five-thirty cleaning house. It was her favorite tension-reliever when she was mad or upset. Right now, she was both. But she wasn't sure if she was madder at herself for being too over-protective or at her daughter for her deceit.

Her daughter had her on pins and needles wondering where in the world she had disappeared to. Until late last night when she talked to Brenda Avery, she hadn't a clue. Her heart ached as she realized that her relationship with her daughter was changing.

Shelia wasn't trying to be, and didn't want to be, her little girl anymore. Her daughter had told her enough times, but she wasn't willing to listen. And as much as it hurt her that Shelia had kept them out of a part of her life, she realized that she and her husband had pushed her to do so.

Once again, they had interfered far too much in one of their children's lives, something they had promised themselves that they would never do again.

The phone made her jump, catching her off guard by the suddenness of its ring.

"Hello. Good morning," she spoke hurriedly into the mouthpiece.

"Hello…Mom," Shelia cleared her throat hesitantly. "Mom, I was just calling to let you know that I…I, me and Charles are in the Bahamas."

"Yeah, I heard that from Brenda last night." Sylvia sat quietly, unsure for the first time in a long time how she should handle a situation with her daughter.

"Um…I know that you're pretty mad at me for not telling you that I was going away. I, um…"

"Shelia, you don't owe me an explanation. You're a grown woman." Sylvia stood up and walked over to over to the sink, looking out the back window. She remembered Shelia as a young girl, remembered the pain of losing her eldest child Brian, and the joy of having Jeff return to the fold after reconciling with his father. Determined not to lose her daughter, she finished, "I think that I owe you an apology. Shelia, you have always been our baby. After Brian left, we held onto you so tightly, you and Jeff, but especially you because you were the girl. But I don't want to lose another child."

"Mom, you haven't lost me. I love you." Shelia absently wiped the stray tear falling from her eye. "I just need to be able to be me, Shelia Daniels, not Mommy's little girl."

"I understand, baby. And I love you, too." A sniffle escaped her open lips as she continued, "But just because I'm willing to give this a try, doesn't mean your father is going to be so easy. He was very upset when he found out that you had left. As soon as you get back home, I suggest you have a heart to heart with him."

"I will, Mom."

"Tell Charles that I said hello, and enjoy yourself."

"I will. I love you, Mom."

"I love you, too, baby."

Shelia hung up the phone feeling much better about herself and about her relationship with her mother, but she was still not ready to expose her deepest secret. Her dad would be a much different story. Instead of listening to her, he will probably rant and rave for an hour.

Listening to the constant waterfall in the shower, she decided that she should make up for her ill behavior the night before. She owed her husband an apology, a big-time apology, she thought, as she opened the bathroom door and tip-toed into the room.

CHAPTER 15

After sharing a cool shower, Shelia and Charles ate a quick breakfast and set out for their scheduled tour of the island. She had come to regard this brief vacation as the honeymoon they weren't able to have immediately after their wedding.

"On the way back, I need to pick up a couple of more things," she said as they walked through the crowded marketplace.

"I thought we did all the shopping yesterday." Charles was excited about the island excursion he had booked for the day.

"I just saw something on that little stand right there." She pointed to a table covered with jewelry made of colored beads.

"Let's hurry up before all the equipment is gone. I can't believe you've never been parasailing," he said as they headed to the dock.

"I've never been, and I might not be going this time. We'll see how my nerves hold up once I get there," Shelia hedged, already having made up her mind that she was not going to parasail.

Once they were there, Shelia watched comfortably from the sailboat as Charles flew high into the sky with the assistance of a parachute.

"You need to try this," he yelled, as the sailboat pulled him through the air. "It's really exhilarating. Whee…Shelia, I love you."

"You're crazy, you know that," she laughed.

"Crazy in love, baby, crazy in love," he said, blowing her a kiss.

They had rented the sailboat and guide for two hours. After Charles finished his ride, they took a scenic tour of some of the other islands that make up the Bahamas.

Enjoying the water, although leery of the possible appearance of sharks, Shelia agreed to one day learn how to jet ski. But she never ventured too far out into the water.

Back on solid ground, Shelia finished her shopping, and then they headed back to the cottage to rest before dinner.

"Are you hungry?" she asked, feeling gurgling in the pit of her stomach.

"Not for food. Honestly, I'm exhausted. I think vacation takes more out of you than work does." Pulling her close, he fell back onto the bed, with her collapsing on top of him. He gently rubbed her back, untying the string to the bikini top she wore with a pair of jean shorts.

Shelia eased over him, kissing his face and lips. She sighed as he gently stroked the fire growing within her. She steadily kissed him, his eyes, his nose, his cheeks—until she heard his soft snoring.

"I guess you were more tired than you knew." She caressed his forehead before rolling off him. While he slept, she began packing. One suitcase for dirty clothes, one suitcase for clean clothes, and a large bag of gifts for their families. She suddenly felt sad because tonight was their last night alone, their last night in paradise.

That night, after leaving a party at the resorts restaurant, they took off their shoes and walked along the beach, letting the wet sand massage their toes.

The party had been very festive and lively, and Shelia and Charles had joined in dancing to reggae and other Caribbean music. They also played many of the party games. It felt good to go somewhere and be able to relax, free of life's little burdens. This time allowed Charles to just be himself. But they wanted to spend their last few hours together alone.

They walked until they ended up near a deserted pier. The music from the resort could be heard faintly as they stood wrapped in each other's arms.

"Thank you, Charles, for this weekend. I had a good time. This was really nice," she said between kisses.

"I'm glad you had a good time, and I'm glad that we came. I love you, Shelia."

"I love you, too." She looked him in the eye, sending a silent message of seduction. "Do you really want to go back to the room?"

Charles got the double meaning of her question—the question behind the question. "No, I don't," he said, allowing her to guide him down to lie next to her on the wet sand.

Waves of water clashed with waves of passion as they unveiled themselves to each other under the moonlight in the seclusion of darkness, expressing their love as sounds of two lovers filled the air.

On Sunday, they walked hand in hand through the crowded island airport, having actually forgotten about Charles' celebrity because of their two days of total freedom on the island. Blissfully engrossed in each another, surprise drained the blood from their faces when a light flashed in front of their eyes. Charles only had time to grab Shelia's arm and pull her closer.

Taken completely by surprise, neither of them had time to react when a heavy-set young lady wearing colorful pastel capris and a bright pink halter top with matching high-heeled sandals screamed at the top of her voice, holding a hand to her chest. There were three other young ladies also dressed in colorful outfits.

"I told y'all," the first one sputtered, struggling to catch her breath. "I told y'all it was him." Prancing back and forth, trying to contain her excitement, she exclaimed, "A-ar-aren't you Charles Avery?"

Just that fast they had gotten used to being out and about—completely unguarded. Charles accepted defeat and the inevitable. Reality had intruded on their private time.

"I'm sorry, baby," he whispered to Shelia, grimacing.

"I understand." She squeezed his arm, trying to ease his despair.

The lady stood there digging in her purse. "Please, can I have your autograph?" Two of her friends already had their papers out. "Oh, my God. Are you Shelia, the girlfriend?" she asked, extending her hand to Shelia.

A knot caught in Shelia's throat as she accepted the woman's hand. This was the second time on this trip that she had accepted that title. She didn't like it, but it was her own fault. All she had to do was come out of the closet-so to speak. Instead, she smiled at the women and waited for Charles to finish his duty, praying that the small crowd gathering wouldn't cause too much of a commotion.

Charles tried to draw the woman's attention away from Shelia and back on him, but her screeching friends only compounded the situation. The small crowd grew larger as other vacationers recognized the recording artist and asked for autographs. Airport security finally arrived to clear the area and escort them to the waiting jet.

"Shelia, what's wrong, baby?" Charles asked after they were settled in for take off.

"I'm just going to miss it, that's all," she confessed sadly, a single tear clinging to her long eyelash.

"Oh, don't cry, baby," he whispered, unable to undo his seatbelt and go to her. He reached for her hand. "We'll come back, and also visit so many other places. I promise you."

"I know. It's kind of silly for me to even be this upset, but it's like…I don't know…like that's how our lives are supposed to be. We should be together all the time, enjoying each other."

"Shelia, what do you want me to do? I'm trying as much as I can to make this work between us. We just have to wait a few more months. But if you want, as I said, I will talk to our parents and tell them the whole truth."

"No, baby, it's all right. I'm just going through some emotional stuff, that's all." She squeezed his hand reassuringly. "Don't worry, I'll be all right."

"It was perfect, wasn't it?"

"Yes, it was. But at least I still have the memories. So, when I'm back at school freezing in my bedroom, I can think of the Bahamas and warm right up. We can come back?"

"As often as you like; just make the reservations."

Who would have thought that she would ever be able to just pick up the phone at any time and travel to the islands for a weekend? It was crazy, but it was fun. Though she still had some reservations as far as the money was concerned, she knew that Charles was very sincere and adamant about her getting used to it. As the plane took off, another thought intruded on her pleasant weekend memories. Her father would be waiting for her.

Shelia opened the door to her parents' house, trying to make as little noise as possible. After convincing Charles that she should handle the situation alone, he agreed to go to his parents' home and wait for her phone call.

As expected, Edward and Sylvia Daniels were sitting at the kitchen table enjoying a hearty dinner of salad, vegetables, and skinless chicken breast.

"Hello," she sang as she walked into the room. A bright smile on her face, Shelia was determined to face her parents on an even level.

"Hello, Shelia," her mother said, coming around the table with her arms opened for a warm embrace. "I'm so glad you're back. Oh, Shelia," her mother paused to take a good look at her. "Girl, you must have had a great time down there. You're positively glowing. Look at your skin." She placed a hand on the side of Shelia's face.

"I had a great time. I bought you something." Reaching deep into her bag, she pulled out a gift box wrapped in colorful pastel paper.

Her mother opened the box excitedly, giving Shelia a look that said it was time to have that talk. Shelia simply nodded.

"Oh, Shelia. It's beautiful," she said, pulling out a crystal globe filled with colorful stones that sparkled in the sunlight.

"I'm glad you like it."

"I'm going to go right now and find the perfect place for it." Acknowledging Shelia's silent protest, she placed her hand on her daughter's and moved past her.

"Hi, Dad," Shelia said, after hesitating for a split second. She rounded the table so that they would be face to face.

He didn't answer her. He just sat there with his fork paused in mid air. Then the fork hit the plate, making a clanking sound that made Shelia jump involuntarily.

"You got something to say to me, young lady?" he asked, sitting back in his chair and crossing his arms across his chest.

"I brought you back something."

"I don't want it. I want to know why you felt the need to deceive your mother and me and run off with that boy."

"Dad, listen to yourself. Do you really have to ask that question?" Shelia allowed her temper to match his. "That boy is Charles Avery. You've known him practically all his life. He's my boyfriend, Dad. He's Jeff's best friend, not some complete stranger. Why are you acting like this?" She sat down at the kitchen table, trying to meet him grimace for grimace. Realizing it was a useless battle, she decided to speak from the heart. "Dad, look at me. I know it's hard for you to accept, but I'm not a kid anymore. Dad, I'm not your little girl. I'm Shelia. I'm a grown woman. I don't have to tell you my every move. Out of consideration, maybe I should, but I don't have to."

Edward didn't want to look at her and see a grown woman. He saw his Shelia. Shelia with the pigtails running after her two older brothers in her Sunday best. Shelia sitting in front of her mother's vanity table, putting on lipstick and fixing her hair. "I'm sorry, baby girl. You'll always be my baby girl. I can't help it." He stubbornly sat at the table, unwilling to give up the past and confused about the future. "I talked to Charles, and I told him that I was okay with you two dating. I was going to work on it, but then, you do something like this. You didn't have to keep it a secret that you were going away with him. That was inconsiderate and immature."

"Well, I'm sorry about that, but Dad, even though you can't give up your baby girl, I can't be her for you anymore." Shelia stood up from the table, dug in the heavy straw bag and placed his gift on the table before walking to the steps and taking them two at a time up to her room. Charles had wanted her to tell her father the truth, but after their conversation, Shelia was sure she made the right decision keeping their marriage secret.

Edward stared at the tall wrapping, unsure if he wanted to open it. But curiosity got the best of him. He ripped the brown paper from around the package and found a lovely statue of an African woman standing with her head raised high as she looked to the sky. Pride and strength showed in her face. Around the bottom of her skirt, children stood looking up at her. The base of the statue read, "As She Grows So Does Her Worth."

Sitting back in his chair, Edward pushed his plate away and placed his hands behind his head. He knew his wife was standing behind him. Just as he knew his daughter was right. But knowing it was right didn't make it any easier.

New Year's came in with a bang. As was the case every year, *Chauncey's* was overcrowded with revelers. A live band performed songs from the eighties and nineties. Wearing party hats and carrying noise-makers, people danced nonstop.

Tia and Denise, both about six months pregnant, sat with Shelia at a table toward the front of the club.

"So, tell us all about the trip," Denise said, sipping a glass of apple juice. She wore a long black spaghetti-strap sequined dress. "Was it beautiful down there, or what?"

Shelia placed her hand over her heart and let thoughts of her romantic getaway flow over her. "It was wonderful," she said dreamily. "We had a good time."

"It's romantic, isn't it?" Tia piped up, remembering her own trip to the Caribbean.

"Very romantic. I can't wait to go back." She smiled at the two expectant mothers. "But enough about that. How are your pregnancies coming along?"

"Good," Denise allowed, her infectious grin setting a positive. "We are enjoying it so much, being best friends and all. But Chauncey is having more fun than I am. Everyday he comes home with a gift, a stuffed animal, a little toy. Yesterday he brought a pair of baby Nikes home. He swears it's going to be a boy."

"Well, what do you want?" Shelia asked curiously.

"I don't care what I have. I just want a healthy baby. Men are the ones wrapped up in the sex of the baby. I bet Jeff wants a boy, doesn't he, Tia?"

"You know it, girl. He says that it's time for the men of the house to pull rank. Right now, the score is tied. Two boys, him and Kevin, and two girls, me and Kayla." Lifting her glass of juice, she watched her husband at the bar, restocking the shelves. "They seem to be doing pretty well tonight."

"Yep. The other two clubs are open, too. I told Chauncey the other day that he needed to hire another manager so that he and Jeff could lie back and rest a bit," Denise complained.

Shelia knew that Jeff and Chauncey were working a lot of hours running three popular nightclubs, two of which also had restaurants. But surely they weren't trying to do it all by themselves. "I'm sure they're trying to hire someone, but you know, it's hard to find reliable people. By the time the babies come, they'll both be able to take some time off. They'll have somebody by then."

"Well, I hope you're right," Tia said, raising her glass high, as did Denise. "Oh, don't look now, Shelia, but somebody's stopping your man."

Charles was enjoying the evening, enjoying being with his family and friends for the last few days of his vacation. Having left both his brothers back near the pool table, he decided to see what Shelia was up to. He spotted her and his sister and Denise at the same round table they had been at earlier, sipping on juice. Intending to ask her to dance, he made his way to the table.

"Excuse me."

Charles turned his head in the direction of the voice, knowing the sensual tone was meant for him; it was attached to the thin feminine hand that rested on the sleeve of his suit jacket.

"Excuse me. Are you Charles Avery?"

"Um...yes. Can I help you?" he asked, trying to ignore the faint smell of the honeysuckle perfume she wore.

She took a step closer, the thin material of her red dress swaying with every movement. Smiling seductively, she asked, "You don't remember me, do you?"

Charles looked at the beautiful lady, not recalling her face or figure from anywhere.

"It's me. Judie Miller."

"Judie Miller? Judie Miller from school? No way," he said, surprised when she pulled him into an overly familiar embrace. Judie Miller had been a math nerd in school. He had flirted with her more than once to get her help studying for a test or completing an assignment. But the Judie Miller he remembered wore glasses and had braces.

This woman didn't have a single blemish on her caramel smooth skin, set off by her perfectly defined nose and high cheekbones. Her hair was in afro-puffs, but slicked back from her forehead and falling over her shoulders like a waterfall. And her body, her body...

Charles stepped back, becoming increasingly uneasy under the scrutiny of the ladies at the far table.

"So, how have you been, Charles?" she asked when he turned back to her.

"Oh, I'm good. Real good."

"I've been hearing your music everywhere. Congratulations."

"Thanks, Judie. Listen, I got to get over to my table. Um, it was nice to see you again."

Before he could walk away she grabbed a hold of his arm again. "Do you think Shelia would mind one dance for old time's sake?"

"Oh, you know about me and Shelia?" Glancing down, he noticed the way she moved her head to the side, exposing a span of welcoming neck.

"I don't think she would mind, but how about later?"

"I'm leaving in a few minutes." Grabbing his hand, she led him past Shelia's table and out onto the dance floor.

As he walked past, Charles shot a helpless look over his shoulders at Shelia's pensive face, trying to let her know that this was not his doing.

"Who's that?" Shelia asked.

"I don't know," Tia answered, studying the woman intently. "She looks like...nah, it couldn't be."

"If I didn't know better, I would say that was Judie Miller," Denise insisted. "Doesn't she look like Judie Miller, Tia?"

"That's what I was about to say, but Judie Miller couldn't have turned out looking that good. That chick is breathtaking."

Well, whoever this Judie Miller is, Shelia thought, *she's dancing too close to my man.* Jealousy wasn't one of her usual impulses, but lately, she had been unable to control herself. She was very secure in Charles' feelings for her, but she still didn't like having a bunch of hoochie mamas after him.

For the third time, Charles took a step back from Judie. He couldn't wait for the song to be over. She looked good enough to be a supermodel. She was dancing like a professional, but as fine as she was, she wasn't Shelia. All he wanted to do was go back to the hotel with his wife. They had been back in town only a day from their Bahamas getaway, and had decided that for the next couple of days they would stay together. Even as boyfriend and girlfriend, no one could say anything about that.

Shelia had to leave Thursday, and so did he. He had a four-month tour of the United States starting next week, and he still had to go over a million last-minute details. Looking over at the table, he could see her watching them dance, and a smile spread on his face.

The instant she saw him watching her, Shelia looked away.

Charles glanced down at his watch. It was almost midnight. He abruptly stopped dancing. "I apologize, Judie, but I have to get back to Shelia now. You have a happy New Year." Hesitantly, he hugged her loosely.

"It's too bad you have to go, Charles. You know I've had a crush on you since high school."

"Yes, but I've had a crush on Shelia since high school. You enjoy the rest of the night." He turned toward the table and smiled when he saw Shelia looking in his direction.

"You do the same," she yelled after him, fully aware that he hadn't heard a word.

Shelia stood as he neared the table, her hands crossed in front of her. "Let me guess, another number one fan."

Ignoring her fake annoyance, he pulled her into his arms. "Oh, jealous, are we?"

"Hell, no, I'm not jealous. I knew you'd be back over here before the New Year came in." She kissed him roughly on the lips.

Although aroused by her mood, he decided he could wait the five minutes it would take to bring in the New Year before they rushed back to the hotel to make love.

"Five...four...three...two...one. Happy New Year."

Chauncey's erupted into loud cheers, with much hugging and kissing all around. When the New Year came in, Charles turned his wife to him and kissed her over and over on the face, lips, and neck.

"Baby, Happy New Year."

Shelia wound her arms around him and pulled him closer, her earlier thoughts about hoochies forgotten. "Happy New Year, love." It felt good to be held by him.

"Okay, let's go," he whispered into her ear, huskily. "Family, happy New Year," he said to those family members standing near. "We love you all, but it's time for us to go."

"Oh, still a little tired from all the traveling, huh?" Troy teased.

Charles smiled at his big brother, his backup man, "Yeah, something like that." Everyone laughed, saying their good-byes as they watched the couple leave.

The hotel room was nice and warm when they entered. Shelia could hardly keep her eyes open. She wanted to talk to Charles, but as soon as her head hit the pillow, all thoughts left her.

She woke in Charles' arms. He was warm, and she moved deeper into him. Because her back was to him, she didn't see the smile that spread across his face. She thought he was asleep, but how could he sleep with her lying almost beneath him like this? As if calculating his movements, he brought his arm in closer to her body. His hand covered one breast. He tried to keep his breathing even, but it was difficult.

Slowly, he massaged her breast until she began to moan. She could feel the hardness against her buttocks and pushed still closer to him. Charles was biting her neck and shoulders. He pinched her nipples and then ran his hand up and down her body. Lifting one of her legs, he placed himself between them and put her leg back down. Shelia spontaneously started moving her hips over him.

"Oh, Shelia," Charles whispered into her ear.

She could feel herself getting excited and wetter when he slid his hand between her thighs. Using his fingers, Charles played with her sweet essence. An essence, he thought, that was all his, and only his. He couldn't wait any longer; he had to be inside her. A soft moan escaped her lips as he slowly filled her with his erection. Charles kept still, allowing her to adjust to him. When he felt her muscles convulse, he groaned and began to move inside her. The rhythm they set was long and slow. Each wanted to enjoy this last time together. They wanted to make it last.

But, their pleasure was mounting more rapidly than they had wished. The forces were pulling them fast into a tight knot. As their pace increased, Charles moved with Shelia until she was on her stomach. He spread her legs far apart and raised her hips.

"Oh, God," Shelia screamed.

Charles fought to control himself and forced his brain to command his hips to slow down. He didn't know if he had hurt her or if she was enjoying it.

"Don't stop, Charles...don't stop." Shelia moved her hips, pulling him in and out of her.

Charles gritted his teeth and plunged deep into her. She screamed and he moaned, but the pace never slowed. He licked her back, kissed her neck and shoulder, and slapped her backside before finally grabbing hold of her hips and driving into her with all his might until he was over the threshold.

"Oh, baby...Shelia, God...I love you, baby." Charles was trying to catch his breath and talk at the same time. It wasn't working. He didn't even know if he was making sense. But she made him feel so good that he had to express himself, had to let her know.

Shelia lay beneath him, still quaking from the aftereffects of her own orgasm. She didn't want to move or talk. Her orgasm had been so strong that it had scared her a little. This man of hers was showing her new things. Every time she thought she knew it all, he opened her up to yet a new experience. It was a little more painful this time, and she knew she would be sore afterwards, but as she lifted her hand to his head, she thought about how she had enjoyed it and how much she loved him. She couldn't wait for her next lesson.

CHAPTER 16

Shelia lay in bed her first night back on campus, reliving the great time she had during her holiday break. She was relieved it had gone so well. Their families were amazing. The matter of the pictures was never bought up. It was as if they had all decided it must be a lie. Their love and support, expressed and unexpressed, only made her guilt more intense. She had been more than ready to leave when the time came just to get away from that guilt.

Now all she had to do was wait out the next five months, and she would be home free. She considered changing her mind and having a second wedding just so she wouldn't have to tell her parents the truth. But that would only compound the lie that was causing her such grief. She didn't want the truth to come out later and have the two families thinking they been betrayed twice. When the time came to tell them the truth, she would just have to pray for their understanding. Meantime, she figured it wouldn't hurt to pray for divine intervention now.

Things were falling into place for Shelia. She had a beautiful house back in Chicago. After this last tour, Charles planned to take a break to finalize his relocation to Chicago. Her studies were going well. She was still receiving honors and preparing to take the last of her elective classes, pediatric surgery. She chose to make this particular elective her last of the year because, although her workload was full, it was more flexible in the spring. She liked being able to spend extra time with the children.

Her schedule had no down time, which suited Sheila fine. Her day started at four-thirty in the morning when she showered and ate a quick breakfast. Then, she met her instructor and student-partner at Howard University Hospital for the morning conference. Afterwards, she would do her rounds with the surgical team and attending physicians, making sure she took specific notes, assisted in patient work-up, preoperative, operative, and postoperative care. Then, she sat in discussion with residents on a variety of surgical topics.

If she could squeeze in a lunch, Shelia would, right before attending her scheduled lectures. These she loved as the professors, usually doctors of the hospital, would ask for input of procedure and treatment on hypothetical medical cases. She always tried to make it to the library to study after a quick dinner. And, when she needed a break from all the monotony, she might head to the student center, but that was a rare occasion. Around ten in the evening, she fell into bed.

Charles called every night without fail at midnight, always from a different city. Some nights, he had just finished a concert; other times he was on a bus or plane heading for the next venue. They missed being together, but focusing on their plans for the future kept them grounded.

A few of her friends had warned her that her grueling new schedule was taking its toll. Shelia didn't listen.

She was rushed to the hospital on a Monday morning in early February after fainting in the dining room just after dinner.

When she came to, Shelia was mortified to find herself being rolled through the hospital on a stretcher. She tried to sit up and tell the technician that she was all right, but strong hands held her down. She should have known better. She was paying a price for all her running around. Exhaustion had crept up on her.

In the emergency room, Shelia learned that she was dehydrated, that she would be spending a couple of days in the hospital, and that she was pregnant.

No way, Shelia thought, as they wheeled her into her room. But then, she thought back to the last time she and Charles had been together. They had not used protection.

Now they had really done it. There was no way she was going to be able to hide this. But why should she try to hide it? Who could say anything to her? In three months, she would be done with school and starting her internship.

So many questions filled her head that night, with each leading to another, more vexing, question. What would her parents say? What would Charles think? Would she be a good mother? Was she ready for motherhood? She had always said she wanted to quit before starting a family, but now that it was out of her hands, what was she to do? Money was no longer a concern, but she had wanted her career to be off the ground first. The majority of her life had been expressly put aside with one goal in mind—becoming a general surgeon. That goal couldn't just be cast aside.

Shelia was even more tired the next morning. She hadn't slept well, and her nerves were fraying. And time was running out. She would soon have to call her family and let them know what was happening.

It felt as if she had fitted a lifetime into the last seven months. It takes some people ten years or more to meet a soulmate, fall hopelessly in love, marry, and start a family. Shelia ran a hand through her hair. She must truly be in love, she thought.

Charles was a total wreck himself by the time he got through to Shelia at the hospital. Since the night before, her dorm advisor had been trying to reassure him that she was all right, that she just had to stay in the hospital for a couple of days. He didn't want to hear that; he wanted to know what was wrong with her. All morning long, he had been snapping at everyone, from his personal assistant to the wardrobe woman.

When he called the hospital, the operator answered and informed him that Shelia Daniels was there, but it was after hours. She asked him to call in the morning. In the morning, the lines were busy. He was going frantic with worry.

Still feeling the effects of sedation, Sheila sounded groggy when she answered the telephone.

"Shelia, baby, is that you?" Charles asked.

"Charles…yes, it's me. Where are you?"

"Baby, I'm still in New Orleans. How are you doing? What happened?"

"Um…huh?" she mumbled, trying to fight sleep.

"Shelia, are you all right?"

"Yeah, I'm fighting this medicine they gave me to help me relax."

"Baby, are you all right?"

"No, I'm not all right. I'm pregnant." Shelia wasn't making sense even to herself. She kept drifting off.

"What? Shelia, what did you say?"

"Huh? Charles, I'm sorry. I didn't mean for this to happen. Charles…Charles…Can you hear me?" Her words were slurred, but she was fighting to focus long enough to finish the conversation.

"Shelia, did you say you were pregnant?"

"Charles, the doctor said that I was dehydrated… Charles."

"Shelia, did you say you were pregnant?" Charles could tell that it was no use. He was going to have to wait until she came out of whatever they had her on. "Baby, I love you. I'll call you back later…Shelia? Shelia?"

Charles listened to her shallow breathing for a few minutes before hanging up. A completely different Charles walked away from the phone. A smile was on his face, a little hop in his step. Certain he had heard her right, Charles was more determined than ever to finish this tour and go home to his family. He met with his manager to see if any of the concert dates for the last month could be moved closer together. How in the world was he supposed to not see her for three more months when she was carrying his baby? A baby. His baby. Their baby. Cloud nine was not high enough for Charles the rest of the day; he was in heaven.

That coming Saturday, Charles had a Valentine's Day concert scheduled for New York City. They had already made plans to meet there for the weekend. He hoped that she would feel up to it. It would be perfect. He would make it perfect. Everything was going to be all right.

CHAPTER 17

Her mother called her Thursday, when she left the hospital, to check on her. Shelia was lying in bed. After her friends Sarah and Ronette were satisfied she was comfortable, she left her room dark so she could relax. Her mother always knew when something was going on with her daughter's body. Tears coursed down her face as she told her mother the news.

"Oh, baby. That's wonderful. I'm so excited. Why didn't you call to tell us you've been in the hospital? I called the dorm twice, somebody answered and told me you were in class."

"Because I asked them to tell you that, Mom. I knew that you would have taken the next flight out of Chicago. And it was just a little dehydration."

"Of course, I would have flown to you. As grown as you think you are, you're still my daughter. Baby, you're pregnant. You don't need to be in Washington all alone. I can still come down and stay for a while. Help you out."

"Mom, I'm okay. You talk as if the baby's already here."

Shelia needed support. What else could she give her but that? Shelia was a grown woman and a good daughter. She had never given her any worries. With a good head on her shoulders and a strong man behind her, her life would not be as hard as she might be thinking now. "Shelia, all I have to say is that I love you, and I will help you out in any way that I can."

"Thanks, Mom. I know. I'm just so...I don't know. I can't explain it."

"One good thing is you'll be out of there in a few more months. Are you getting sick?"

"No. I've made a vow to take much better care of myself. I really do want this baby, in a weird kind of way, you know?"

"That's the motherly way, baby." Sylvia's could hardly contain her emotions. "Did you talk to Charles?"

"Yes, he's thrilled, of course. Mom, I know you're dying to tell Mrs. Avery, so why don't we call her together on your three-way."

"Oh, Shelia, you don't mind?" Sylvia asked.

"No, Charles told me that I should tell you two together. With his schedule, he didn't think he would be able to get to his parents until very late at night, and he didn't want to do that. He thought it would worry them. Umm…where's dad?"

"Girl, you know you got yourself a good man. And one of these days, he's going to make a wonderful husband. Don't worry about your father. I'll talk to him. He'll be mad for sure, but I got a way with that old softy. You just let me worry about my husband. He'll be all right. He'll get over it. Does this mean we will be hearing wedding bells in the near future?"

Shelia didn't trust herself to even attempt a response.

"Mom, dial the number."

"Hello, Brenda."

"Yes?" Mrs. Avery replied.

"Girl, this is Sylvia."

"Sylvia, what are you up to? I just hung up from you. What's wrong? It's not Edward, is it? Is he not taking his medicine again? Is it the kids?"

"Nothing. Everything is just fine. I have Shelia on the line with me."

"Hi, Mrs. Avery."

"Well, isn't this a surprise? Hello, dear. How are things at that big school of yours?"

"Just fine, Mrs. Avery."

"Shelia, you're really too polite. Ms. Brenda will do. I feel so old when people call me Mrs. Avery."

"I'm sorry," Shelia said.

"So, do tell, Sylvia, to what do I owe this pleasure?"

"Brenda, are you sitting down?"

"No. Do I need to be?"

"Well, you might want to."

"Okay, I'm sitting," Brenda lied.

"Brenda, Shelia is pregnant!" Sylvia yelled.

"Oh, my God. Praise the Lord." Brenda jumped around, shrieking, before calming herself down. "Are you sure? Of course you are. Oh, Shelia, baby, that's wonderful. Oh, thank you for sharing this with me. Does Charles know?"

"Yes, I talked to him yesterday. He's very happy."

"Well, of course, he is. He loves you very much. Lord, I have to tell the family. That is okay, isn't it?"

"Yes, of course," Shelia answered, smiling with relief.

"Maybe soon there will be another wedding in our families, huh, Sylvia?"

"I'll pray on it, Brenda."

"I'll talk to you later. I love you both." Brenda hung up the phone and ran to find her husband, who was in the basement organizing his tools.

"That's good, dear." John kept on working. He was used to hearing that kind of news. "I'll try to give Charles a call as soon as I finish up down here."

By seven o'clock Thursday, Shelia was worn out. She was supposed to pack her bags for her weekend trip to New York, but after having talked to everyone in the family, sleep was the last thing she had energy for. It seemed foolish that she had not told her mother the truth earlier when she had her on the phone, but she just couldn't hurt her feelings after her reaction to the pregnancy.

They had been so happy that she and Charles had made this life growing inside her. Even her brother, Jeff, was pleased. Teasing, she told him that now he didn't have to be so protective of her. But he said that now he had to be even more protective.

That Friday she boarded a plane for New York City to join her husband for Valentine's Day. They would have only two days together because he wouldn't arrive until four that afternoon and was scheduled to leave Sunday morning around ten. Shelia was in a positive mood, determined to make their first Valentine's Day together special.

Shelia walked off the plane at LaGuardia Airport in New York. She was met by a very friendly woman dressed in a navy blue business suit and escorted to the President's Club.

Despite having had a full breakfast, Shelia was already hungry. But as she entered the President's Club, all thoughts of hunger disappeared when she spied Charles sitting at a table with some of his associates. He looked up at her as she entered the plush lounge, and all her desires doubled. She couldn't get to him fast enough. People were watching, but she didn't care.

Shelia dropped her bag and ran into his waiting arms. It had been a month since she last saw him. He looked so damn good in his khaki chinos and a dark brown turtleneck sweater. He let his beard thicken, and it had been freshly cut and shaped-up. He was sexy, and he was hers.

All but knocking him over when she reached him, Shelia hugged and kissed him until the good-natured giggles of the onlookers finally sank into her brain. Making an effort to calm down, she stood beside her husband, holding his hand tightly.

"Okay, everyone, if you haven't already figured it out, this is my girl, Shelia," Charles announced, not in the least embarrassed by her public display of affection. On the contrary, he was flattered. It made him feel good to know that she had missed him just as much as he had missed her. "Shelia, this is everybody. They'll all get around to meeting you later. Right now, we need to get out of here." He motioned to a slim man dressed in an expensive double-breasted suit. "Jacob is my personal assistant. He keeps track of my appointments, etc. He's also good with the press. Believe me, there are going to be a lot of them out there; that's why we came in early. They know that I was due in at four."

Shelia snuggled closer to Charles when she felt his arm around her waist tighten. He placed his other arm across her abdomen. By all appearances, Charles was simply embracing his woman. Only Shelia knew that he was acknowledging his unborn child. His fingers flexing against her belly made it hard for her to concentrate on Jacob's briefing.

"Hi, Shelia," Jacob began, his voice unexpectedly deep and soothing. He had a calming effect on her as he spoke, but not as calming as Charles' gentle touch. "Listen," he said, "for right now, all we need you to do is stay right next to Charles." *Not a problem,* she thought. "Make sure you keep hold of his hand, and when we encounter any press, just look straight ahead and focus on getting through the crowd. Aside from the press, there will be fans coming at you from every direction. Not to worry though, there will be bodyguards surrounding you. Just keep moving, and they will quickly and safely push you through. Any questions?"

"No, I'm ready." He patted her arm reassuringly. She was ready to begin this wonderful weekend with the man of her dreams. Shelia looked at her left hand and was about to remove her wedding band.

But Charles took her hands to stop her. "I'll hold that hand, baby."

"But..."

"Uh, uh," he whispered, kissing her on the cheek. "Keep it there." He didn't want her to take the ring off in front of him. Charles wished he had never agreed to go along with this hoax. She was his wife, for

God's sake. Besides, she would have drawn attention to herself. Very few of the people he dealt with even knew they were married. Right now, all eyes were on them.

Once they were safely in the stretch limousine parked in front of the airport, Shelia breathed easier. Jacob had briefed her well. From the minute they stepped out of the President's Club until they reached the car, crowds of people came running up asking for autographs and snapping pictures. She knew Charles regretted not being able to talk to his fans, but if he stopped and talked to everybody who wanted to talk to him, he would never get out of the airport. Instead, he kept her close to his side, smiling and waving, but maintaining a steady path toward the exit doors.

The car pulled away from the curb, and they were on their way to the hotel. During the ride, Charles relaxed and took her into his arms.

"Sorry, love. That's the way things usually go around here."

"It's okay. I'm just glad to be with you again." Shelia leaned over and kissed him on the cheek.

"How have you been? No morning sickness or dizziness?" His hand was once again resting on Shelia's stomach, gently, massaging it with circular motions.

"Nope, not since I left the hospital. I'm taking good care of myself. I've just been hungry, very hungry."

He laughed, kissing her forehead, "Well, that's good. A healthy appetite means a healthy baby. Shelia, you know this is a good thing that's happening, don't you? I mean, you're okay with this, right?"

"Charles, I'm very happy about this baby. It's me and you together. How could I not want this?"

"Good, because I can't wait to hold this little boy."

"Little boy? Charles, you might be holding a girl."

"Nah, baby…it's a boy. I know. I love you."

"I love you, too. How are you doing with all this touring?"

"I haven't been able to keep my eyes open for longer than two hours at a time. At first, I thought I was overdoing it, but I saw the doctor Wednesday and told him that I had a baby on the way, he said that was probably the reason. Isn't that weird?"

"Well, I think it's great. At least I'm not going through this alone. You know I was a little scared at first, but it's going to be okay."

"Of course, it is. We'll make it okay together." He looked at her. "I spoke to Mom and Dad the other day. She says that everybody back home is excited about the baby."

"I know. Even my Dad is anticipating the sound of another pair of little feet around the house. Mom said he fussed and argued when she first told him, then he broke down and cried, but now everything is all right. He's talking about the baby more and more."

"You know they've been asking me when we are going to get married." Charles paused, looking at her hopefully. Might she finally be ready to come clean?

"Yeah, me, too." Shelia breathed out, and then changed the subject. "Tia had told me that I could go into the delivery room with her. I told her no before I became pregnant. But now I'm thinking maybe I should."

Charles pulled her close, "I love you." He put his hand back on her stomach. "Whatever you decide, I'm with you, but maybe it's time for us to tell our families the truth." He had decided to return to the subject she was avoiding.

"I know. I love you, too. I just can't yet, Charles."

"Okay, if that's how you want." With nothing left to say, Charles relaxed and closed his eyes. He had no choice but to honor her wishes even though he was beginning to have doubts as to the wisdom of the original plan. Part of the blame was on his shoulders, as they had come up with the idea together, so they were in it together.

Shelia opened the door to a large, beautiful room filled with roses of every color conceivable. Vase after vase of roses; it was spectacular.

"Oh, Charles, you didn't have to do this." Clasping her hands over her mouth, she looked around in wonderment.

"Yes, I did. Tomorrow is Valentine's Day, and I wanted you to wake up in the morning to the smell of flowers and a reminder of my love."

Reaching for him, she said, "Charles, you are too good for me. If you aren't careful, you'll spoil me rotten."

"That's the plan. For all of our days, I want to spoil you in every way possible." They rocked back and forth in each other's arms as he planted small kisses on her forehead and face. "So, what do you want to do for the rest of the evening? I have an open calendar. I'm all yours."

"I like the sound of that. Our time together is short, so I just want to be alone with you. That's all. We can order some room service and keep each other company."

"Sounds great. I'll call Jacob and tell him not to disturb me until tomorrow's rehearsal."

"Okay. I'm going to the bedroom to unpack a few things." Shelia walked across the suite to the double-bedroom doors, which opened to a magnificent king-size mahogany bed with matching dressers, a lovely brass vanity table and stool, and a lounging sofa covered with the same material as the comforter on the bed. She picked up her suitcase, intending to begin unpacking, but it was practically weightless; it was empty. "Charles," she called out, "all of my things are missing."

"Wait…I can't hear you," he called back, walking into the room with his hand over the phone's mouthpiece. "What's wrong, baby?"

"My stuff is gone." She stood with her hands on her hips.

Charles laughed. "Baby, check the closet. They probably already unpacked our stuff." He turned to finish his call.

The closet did indeed contain clothes—more than enough for a weekend. She saw four suits, two pairs of jeans, and a lot of sweaters and shirts, which she assumed were for Charles. The other end of the closet had three dresses, three pairs of jeans, a dress suit, and many women's sweaters and shirts—for her, she assumed. And they were all the right sizes.

Charles walked up behind her and put his arms around her waist. She turned to face him.

"I didn't bring any of these clothes with me. Where did they come from?"

"Jacob probably had somebody buy them. He gets paid to think of the little things that I might not think of. Do you think I actually went out and bought any of those suits?"

Shelia again looked at her clothes and said, "I like him."

"I went ahead and ordered dinner. How does roast chicken, yams, greens, macaroni and cheese, and biscuits sound?"

"Sounds real good. I hope you ordered enough. I could probably eat a whole horse right about now." She laughed and hit him on the arm after he gave her a look. "Don't worry. I won't gain that much weight."

"Honey, you could get as big as a house. I would still love you."

"Yeah, you say that now…What's for dessert?"

"Um…I didn't order any, but if you want it, you got it, baby," Charles laughed, as he put his hand on her stomach and felt for the life that he longed to hold in his arms. "I love you, Shelia." Turning her face towards him, he slowly dropped his head until his lips met hers. Kissing the corners of her mouth before taking hold of her full lips, his tongue softly caressed the slit between her lips until they opened. He moaned, "Can we have dessert before dinner?"

"No…but I'll make it up to you later. Right now, I want to shower and change before the food comes. I love you, too." With one last kiss, she went to the dressers to find her underclothes and the lounging set that he had bought her during their trip to the islands. "I'll only be a minute."

"Maybe I should join you…I'm very dirty."

"That you are. I'll be out in a minute." Shutting the door behind her, Shelia smiled at herself in the mirror. In the privacy of the bathroom, she did a little jig trying to release some of the energy suddenly overwhelming her. She was so happy. A bang on the door interrupted the tranquil atmosphere that the steam from the hot water had created in the bathroom.

"Dinner's here, Shelia. Come on before it gets cold."

"I'll be right out," she yelled back, feeling as if all her energy had drained out just as quickly as it had arisen.

"Oh, Charles, that feels so good," Shelia whispered, moving her head from side to side as he used his mouth to bring her closer and closer to heaven. He kissed her along the inside of her thighs then ran his tongue back across her sweetness. She squirmed when she felt his tongue graze the side of her abdomen as Charles retraced his path back up her body. He licked across her belly until he was at the valley between her breasts.

"Shelia, I missed you so much." His hands held her breasts as he stroked each nipple before pulling it inside his mouth.

"I can tell that you have," Shelia replied, reaching down to stroke him.

Charles was ready for her. He wanted to be inside her, to feel her around him, to be where he was when they created the life now growing in her. Then he moved down and kissed her stomach, keeping his head there for a moment. "Shelia, I don't want to hurt the baby. We don't have to…you know that sometimes I get carried away."

"Charles, you don't have to worry about that. You won't hurt the baby." She put her hand behind his head and rubbed him, touched that he cared enough to be careful with her. "Don't worry; nothing is going to happen to our baby."

Charles looked at her uncertainly, kissing her stomach one more time. "I'll be careful." He kissed her softly, tenderly as he used his knee to spread her legs apart.

Shelia wanted this more than anything. She wanted to be as one with her husband, to be loved by him. She was ready for him as she arched her back and jerked her hips forward as he entered her.

Shelia helped him bring them both to a completely satisfying leap over the edge. When he pulled up her leg, she lifted the other one. When he grabbed her behind and lifted her further into the air, she grabbed him, massaging his backside. When his strokes deepened, she tightened her muscles, working with him to stimulate both of their demands for release.

Afterwards, he held her in his arms, showering her with light kisses until she fell asleep.

When she rolled over, the sound of paper crinkling caused Shelia to open her eye. She picked up the note and crushed rose from the bed.

Baby, didn't want to wake you. Went to rehearsal.
Should be back by one p.m. Don't eat. We'll go out.
Love,
Charles

She had slept very late; it was almost noon. Shelia hopped out of the bed, intending to shower, fix her hair and makeup, and do her nails before her husband returned. Today, she wanted to look good for Charles.

At precisely one, Charles strolled into the room, followed by Jacob, who was talking a mile a minute.

"Just make sure that you are down in the lobby and ready to move by seven p.m. sharp. Of course, Mrs. Avery will have a seat available to her backstage. Everett called to say that Essence magazine would like to do a cover story on you and 'Ms. Daniels.' I told him you would call him yourself on that matter."

"Thank you, Jacob. Will that be all?" Charles asked impatiently.

"Yes, except, did you stop by wardrobe while you were at the hall?"

"Yes, I did." Charles smiled, having thought of something before Jacob reminded him.

"Very well, then, that's all. Enjoy the rest of your day…until seven p.m."

"Good-bye, Jacob." Charles shut the door and shook his head. *Jacob was a good, loyal, and hard worker,* he thought, *but the guy needed a life.*

Turning around, Charles saw Shelia standing in the bedroom doorway, and thoughts of the night before came rushing back. They had talked about their baby and the room to be decorated in their new house. Their lives would be very different once they were settled in Chicago with a baby.

And he had made love to his wife. He loved the way she screamed out his name and held onto him as he pleased her. She had no idea how good she was for him, how she humbled him and made him stay focused. She had no idea how much it pleased him to know that she was there for him and had given her heart and love to him.

He wanted nothing more than to take her into his arms and make wild, passionate love to her forever, or at least, right now. But he had written her that he would take her out, and she was probably looking forward to it.

She saw the look in his eyes, and knew what it meant. He wanted her. Goose bumps appeared on her arms, and a familiar tingling ran up her back. *Lord, she would never get enough of this overwhelming love he had inside of him.* Smiling, she raised her hand and pointed at him. Then she turned her hand and beckoned him with her finger.

Charles all but leaped over the sofa in the living room trying to get to her. He wanted to take things slow—that's what his mind was saying—because she would be leaving in the morning, but sometimes it was difficult to hold back.

They rolled around together on the king-size bed pulling off clothing until they were both completely bare. That was enough fore-play for him. He quickly spread her legs apart and drove himself into her. He was in to the hilt, and although she cried out in a little pain,

Shelia wrapped her legs around his hips and pulled him closer. Neither held back as they moved together at a fast pace. Shelia met him stroke for stroke, groan for groan, and murmur for murmur.

"Oh, Shelia, I'm comin…"

"Hold me, Charles, hold me…"

"I love you-u-u…"

"Oh…oh…Charles…oh, God…Charles…"

Once they were both satisfied, Charles collapsed on top of her, kissing her face and hair. Then he realized he couldn't stay like that and he quickly moved to his side, pulling her close.

"I didn't hurt the baby, did I?"

She was about to tell him to stop being silly until she saw the concern on his face. She placed a hand on his cheek. "Charles, everything is fine." She kissed his nose.

"Okay, I love you, Shelia."

"I love you, too, Charles." Seeing how vulnerable he was where the baby was concerned, she hugged him to her.

They drifted into a restful sleep, but soon after, Shelia was awakened by a rumbling in her stomach. She got out of bed and ordered lunch, then woke Charles so they could eat together.

After lunch, they took a walk through Central Park, bought a bagel, which Shelia didn't find too appealing, and stopped by a toy store so the soon-to-be father could buy a stuffed animal for mother and baby. They got back to the hotel just in time for Charles to meet his ride to the music hall.

Charles sang beautifully. Tears came to Shelia's eyes as she listened to him mesmerize the audience. His songs did that to people. The words were strong and meaningful. And that voice. It held you captive with every note, every syllable. You felt his pain and heartache, his joy and happiness. If Charles' songs made him famous, his performances made him unforgettable.

Halfway through the show, Charles talked to the audience about love and commitment, and about family in general. Because it was Valentine's Day, he asked everyone who was there with his or her valentine to stand. Almost everyone was coupled.

Men and women dressed in red and pink jumpsuits ran down the aisles handing every couple a gift of two roses with a gift certificate attached for dinner to a trendy restaurant. Appreciative cheers and filled the arena.

"Before I sing the next song," Charles began, walking up and down the stage. "I want to tell you about my own valentine. About ten years ago, I found myself falling in love with a beautiful young lady. I was a teenager, and her brother was my best friend. But because she was so young and out of respect for her brother, I never acted on this love. However, deep in my heart, I knew that one day I would make her mine.

"Well, last year, I was home for the wedding of her brother, who, incidentally, was marrying one of my sisters, and I saw her again. This time I saw a beautiful, mature woman. And this time, I couldn't let her go." He looked at her sitting off stage. "She's been a part of my life since that day. You've probably have seen the tabloids and television stories, but you can't believe everything you see or hear. About a week ago, my lady gave me some really wonderful news."

Shelia's mouth popped open as she prayed that he wouldn't say any more. His fans applauded loudly in preparation for his announcement. The support and love they showed amazed him.

Charles raised his hand to quiet the crowd, "Well, tonight, I want you to meet the love of my life." He reached his hand out to her. "Come on out here, baby."

Shelia was petrified. No wonder he had asked her to wear this particular gown. It was his favorite, showing off her slim waist and wide hips. The strapless, full-length red gown had a sheer overlay from the high waist down. She had to admit that it flattered her body well. But this meant that he had planned this whole thing. Just wait until she had him alone.

"Come on, baby," Charles repeated, urging her on stage.

The applause was already loud, but when Shelia finally came out from behind the curtain and shyly walked across the stage, it became deafening. Shelia just kept her eyes focused on him and concentrated on reaching him without becoming ill. Stage fright was just a heartbeat away.

"I can't believe you did this," she mouthed to him when she reached him.

"Just enjoy it, baby," he said, kissing her on the cheek. Turning back to the audience, Charles spoke into the microphone: "Everyone, I would like you to meet my lady. This is Shelia." He didn't want to say Daniels and knew that he couldn't say Avery. Looking down at her, he continued, "Shelia, I wanted to bring you out here today to ask you to spend the rest of your life with me as my wife." The crowd became so loud that he had to wait for them to calm down before finishing. "To raise our children together and to grow old together. I love you, and I need you to stay a part of my life."

Charles didn't ask her to marry him because they were already married, and to do so would have meant he was deceiving his fans and family. Instead, he asked her to be all of the things he needed her to be and let people think whatever they wanted to think.

She reached up and put her arms around his neck and held onto him. Her makeup was ruined, thanks to the tears coursing down her face, but she didn't care. Shelia didn't have the strength to keep her emotions in check. She pulled him down to her and opened her mouth to receive his kiss.

"I love you, Charles. I will always be a part of your life."

Charles held her to him and tucked his face into her neck. Sometimes a man needed to be hugged and held more than a woman did.

A lot of the women in the crowd were in tears, so taken were they by the display of love onstage. Couples were hugging and professing their love for one another. It was truly a magical night. And Charles had made it so.

Shelia left the stage and Charles continued his concert. The makeup woman came and asked Shelia if she wanted her makeup repaired before the show was over. Shelia declined at first, but when the lady mentioned pictures, she quickly changed her mind. She didn't want to embarrass Charles by looking a terrible sight alongside him.

Shelia woke the next morning to the smell of bacon, ham, and toast. Although she was still tired, her belly, or the baby, forced her to get up and investigate the aromas coming from the living room.

Charles sat at the table reading a newspaper article about his concert the night before. According to the paper, the concert had been a success.

"Morning, love. Did you sleep well?"

"Yes. If I weren't so hungry, I would still be sleeping."

"I was going to wake you in a minute, anyway. We only have four hours until your flight. We have to start getting you ready."

"I know…I know. God, I hate the leaving part so much."

"Baby, don't worry. We only have a few months left before you're finished with school. Everything's going perfectly. The baby, our marriage. Just think, we've practically made it through the tough part of our marriage. Most of the first year has been spent on totally oppo-site sides of the country. The pressures of your education, my career. Baby, we've made it." Pushing his chair back, he pulled her onto his lap and held her close.

"You're right, baby. We did make it."

They were standing in the small terminal reserved for private aircraft waiting for Shelia's rented plane to leave for Washington, D.C. Charles' plane was headed to Boston, where he was to perform the following night.

ONE OF THESE DAYS

The small group traveling with Charles left them alone to say their good-byes privately.

To Shelia the final hugs and kisses only made her departure harder, but she took relief in the knowledge that this would hopefully be their last good-bye for a while.

CHAPTER 18

Trying to ignore the sting of the sharp wind against her face, Shelia hailed a cab as soon as she walked out of the Ronald Reagan International Airport arriving-flights terminal. Luckily, her plane took off from New York before they had begun canceling their departing flights due to the snow storm moving into the region. She only hoped that Charles was able to leave as well.

The heavy snowfall made it hard for her to see as snowflakes, propelled by the wind, flew into her face full-force. She made her way through the crowd of fellow travelers to the curb, where a burly man stood beside a waiting taxi. He put her luggage into the trunk and then opened the door her.

"Where to, lady?" His voice was rough, probably due to a long day of work, made harder by the bad weather.

"Howard University, please," Shelia replied almost as roughly. She wasn't the cause of his problems. "And I'm not in a rush," she said, as he pulled sharply into the flow of traffic.

"New?"

"No."

"Student?"

"Yes." Conversation was pointless. They were both obviously tired, both ready to bring a hectic day to a close.

Weaving in and out of traffic on the busy interstate seemed second nature to the driver, but it did nothing for Shelia's nerves.

"Could you slow down, please?"

"Come on, lady. You're my last fare. I'm trying to get home, too, you know," he retorted, turning sideways to give her a stern look.

"Stop!!" Shelia screamed, instinctively putting her hands up to protect her face. The cabbie quickly turned, but it was too late to avoid the car that had slowed down ahead of them.

The impact pushed her hard against the plastic window that divided the driver from the passenger. She was stuck between the hard plastic and the back of the cab. Her luggage had been pushed through the back seat by the car behind them, the driver of which had been following the cab too closely.

Excited voices, though unclear, let her know she was alive. Although she couldn't focus in on the faces connected to the voices, she strained to hold onto them. Then she passed out.

Shelia opened her eyes slowly, then shut them tightly against a blinding light. Her head was throbbing. The medical terminology she heard told her where she was, but she didn't know why. Someone was calling her name.

With all the strength she could muster, Shelia opened her eyes again and focused on the face hovering over hers. It was Nathan Adams, a doctor at the university's medical center. He had taught a couple of her courses.

"Shelia, can you hear me?" he asked quietly, his body betraying tension.

She tried to talk, but there was something in her mouth.

"It's okay. Just relax. Pull that tube—carefully." Moving her head slightly, she realized there were other people in the room.

Shelia felt the burning sensation as the technician slowly removed the long plastic tube that had been placed down her throat. *What in the world was happening to her?*

Feeling a chill, Shelia realized she was only half covered. She saw blood and panicked.

"Calm down, Shelia. Listen to me." Dr. Adams took her hand after seeing the look of horror on her face. "Look at me, Shelia. Listen. The cab you took from the airport had a little accident. It collided with another vehicle on the interstate." He paused. "Do you understand me so far?"

"Yes," she whispered hoarsely, her throat causing her eyes to water.

"It's five-thirty. You've been unconscious for almost three hours. You have a concussion, some abrasions and cuts, and a very badly broken leg. It has already been set; a cast is being put on now. We've given you an epidural and a mild sedative. We had suspected some internal bleeding, but there is no evidence of that." Nathan paused, finding it hard to be professional with someone he knew personally. Looking into her eyes and holding her hand, he lowered his voice. "Shelia, about the baby."

"No...no," she whispered. Tears fell on the pillow as he told her what she already knew.

"Shelia, you miscarried. I'm sorry," he said, making sure she understood him.

She couldn't say anything; she just closed her eyes and turned her head away. She wondered how she was going to tell Charles that she had lost their baby. He had been so happy. She had been so happy. Only hours earlier, she had been thinking about buying baby clothes and furniture. They had already discussed baby names. *Lord, how much more of this roller-coaster ride that has been my life for these past few months can I take?*

As tears slid down her face, Shelia was oblivious to all sounds, as well as to the slight discomfort she felt while they put the cast on her leg. She was barely aware of being cleaned. All she felt was the pain and grief of losing her baby.

"Shelia, baby, wake up." Charles was visibly upset and anxious to make sure that she was fine. He had received a call from his mother while en route to his next stop. He immediately contacted the pilot and demanded that he turn around and fly him to D.C.

His mom had tried to assure him that Shelia was okay, but Charles had to see for himself. He called Shelia's brother, Jeff, who told him that some of the family planned to fly down to Washington to be with her. The children where being left with Charles' oldest sister and her husband. Before hanging up, Charles told Jeff that Jacob would be calling him back with the number and flight time of the next available plane with enough seats for everyone. What Jacob actually did was rent a private jet from the airport in Chicago. It was ready for departure within two hours. A shuttle bus was waiting at the airport to drive them to the right terminal.

"Shelia, I'm here, baby," he said, hoping for a response from her. As long as she was okay, he could handle anything.

"Charles…"

"Yes, baby, I'm here."

"Charles," she said, a slight whine in her voice. She still wasn't fully awake, "Charles, I lost…"

"Shh…baby, I know. It's all right. Everything is going to be all right." He kissed her cheeks, happy she was awake and okay.

She looked at him. He was a mess. Worry lines criss-crossed his handsome face, and she could tell he had been crying. His eyes were blood red. She put a hand on his cheek, and he leaned closer.

"Charles, I'm sorry. I lost the baby," she said sadly.

Charles held her and kissed her tears. "Shelia, I love you. I don't know what I would do if you weren't all right."

She didn't know why she felt the way she did, and didn't care. Shelia was suddenly mad at him because he seemed not to be listening to her.

"Charles, did you hear what I said? I lost our baby."

"I heard you. Shelia, that doesn't matter as long as you're all right. I just—"

"It doesn't matter? What do you mean it doesn't matter?"

"Shelia, why are you getting so upset?" Truly perplexed, he straightened up to look directly at her. Charles didn't understand.

"Charles, look at me. Do you understand what I said? I lost *our* baby."

"We can have more babies, Shelia. Please calm down. This can't be good for you. Do you want me to get the doctor or something?"

Shelia became really upset. How could he just brush it off like that? Didn't he realize what she was going through? A life, a beautiful little life that they had created together, was now gone, just like that. It was her fault; she had done it. She should have taken better care of herself to protect the baby. This was some sort of punishment. She was being punished for her deceits. Irrational thoughts had made their way into the mind of this usually intelligent woman. Guilt for her secrets, compounded by the guilt of losing the baby, was eating away at her.

Charles *was* upset about the baby. He had really wanted this child with her, but he wanted her to understand that she was the most important thing to him right now. The love he had for her was the strongest it had ever been. And that love would give them more children. It just wasn't meant to be now, that's all. Maybe the Lord was trying to tell them to slow down and get their lives back on track before bringing children into the picture. They would just wait.

The argument he was trying to avoid came to a head, with her screaming that she hated him and him walking out of the room, slamming the heavy door behind him.

Ten minutes after he was gone, she wanted him back. She tried to get a grip on her emotions. Shelia knew she was being silly and that her hormones were controlling her. The shock to her body due to the loss of the baby and blood had her hormones swirling. As a fourth-year medical student, she should have known this would happen.

Shelia hoped he would come back so she could apologize. She knew he was having the same sense of loss. His eyes showed her that. *Oh, Lord, why did I do that?* She decided to give him a little time to cool off and then call him on his cell phone. They would talk this out as they did everything else and get through it together.

She was administered more pain medication, and, mercifully, fell asleep almost instantly.

Charles was still mad when he returned to his hotel. She wouldn't listen to him. He knew her emotions were playing a big part in this whole thing, but he couldn't take the things she had said to him. Only the day before they had been wrapped in each other's arms making love, and now she didn't believe he loved her at all. He could feel his temper rising fast as the memory of their argument filled his mind. She wanted to be away from him. He had lost a child, too. The pain of the experience wasn't only hers. He started thinking that if he hadn't asked her to come to New York in the first place that she wouldn't have been in an accident.

But common sense had stepped in before that line of thinking took hold. He couldn't have controlled the other drivers anymore than he could have controlled the freezing weather that raced up and down the East Coast in recent weeks.

Charles felt terrible, and the longer he stayed in the hotel, the worse he felt. It was time for him to go. He had left a note at the hospital's nurses' station for his mother to call him when she arrived. If Shelia didn't want to be bothered by him, he wouldn't bother her. He had done the right thing by rushing to his wife's side, and she was obviously all right. Although he wanted to stay, she needed this time alone. He would give it to her.

Jacob was ready to quit by the time they boarded the plane for the flight to Cleveland. After missing the Boston concert, they headed for the next scheduled venue. Charles was in a foul mood. He griped about things he would normally overlook. Something had gone seriously wrong for his boss to be acting like this. It had been a long time since he had seen him in this grim a mood. He knew firsthand how hard Charles had worked to keep his dark side at bay, because he was the one who scheduled the anger-management classes that he had been attending.

Jacob took care of last-minute details, making sure the rest of the small entourage was aboard. Only Charles' stylist and barber flew with them on the private jet.

When Shelia woke, she expected to see Charles standing in the doorway, but he was not there. She was feeling better and was definitely in a better frame of mind, having rationalized her loss. If God took her baby from her, He did it for a reason. Although the pain of the loss was still raw, she should be thankful that she could still have children. Charles had told her as much. Her mother would have told her to consider herself blessed that she was still alive.

The commotion in the hallway told her that her family had arrived. She automatically checked her ring finger to make sure only the engagement ring was there. She had to call Charles as soon as possible.

The door opened, and her mother and father rushed in, and she was instantly wrapped in two pairs of arms. When the tears stopped and they calmed down, Shelia put her head back on the pillow, feeling weak from overexertion. Her mother began to fluff the pillows and straighten the sheets.

"Mom, I'm all right. You don't have to do that," she said, reaching for her mother's hand.

Her father looked at her. "Shelia, you know this is what your mother needs to do."

"I know, Dad. I'm sorry. I guess I had you kind of worried, huh?"

"Just a little, dear," Sylvia answered, putting a hand to her daughter's cheek. "But it's going to be all right. You just have faith. God, doesn't put more on you than you can handle."

Shelia reached both her parents' hands. "I'm glad you came. I want to apologize for the way I've been behaving lately. I didn't mean to make it hard on you guys, especially you, Dad."

"Baby girl," her father began, squeezing her hand, "I'm the one who needs to apologize."

"No, Dad…"

"Baby girl, let me finish. I'm sorry for trying to smother you. I know you have grown up. I just never wanted you to. You're the last of our babies, and I didn't want to lose you."

"It's okay, Daddy."

"No, it's not. Your mother and I talked long and hard about this. I don't know how well I'll do, but I promise to try to start treating you like the adult you are." He raised her hand to his mouth and kissed it.

"Did you go to the hotel first?" she asked, quickly changing the subject.

"Yes, Charles sent a plane for us and had a bus waiting. Even had our hotel rooms ready. That's a very considerate and loving man you have, Shelia." Then her mother realized she hadn't seen him. "Where is Charles, anyway?"

Her tears brimmed. "We had a little argument. It was all my fault. I was so hard on him; I just couldn't control myself. It was terrible. I said such mean things. I really need to call him. Mom, can you please dial this number?"

After dialing Charles' private number, Sylvia let the phone ring ten times before hanging up. "He's not answering the phone, Shelia. It rang ten times. Maybe he's on his way back here."

"Yeah, I guess you're right," Shelia agreed, but she didn't believe it. *He must really be mad, or he would have answered the phone no matter where he was.*

Troy walked into the room, accompanied by Nathan Adams. When Nathan saw that Shelia was awake and in better spirits, he permitted the rest of the family to come in to her room for brief periods of time. Although it was hard to do, they all agreed to be as quiet as possible. It was a good thing that she had a relatively large private room.

Charles' parents, Elizabeth, Jeff and Tia, and Troy and his wife took turns trying to make her laugh. Nobody mentioned the baby, which was a good thing, because if someone had, she would just fall apart. She didn't know how long she could keep up this pretense of being "just fine." The love these people offered her was wonderful, but there was one person's love she wanted, and he wasn't there.

She hadn't noticed that Charles had signed her cast until they pulled back the blanket and took take turns passing the marker. It was beautiful—a red heart with roses around the top left corner and an arrow passing through it. It simply read, "My love; my life."

"Here, squirt, clean your face," Jeff said, passing her a tissue.

"Thanks, Jeff. You always know just what I need."

"Hey, I got your back, always." He was about to hit her on the forehead as he usually did, but stopped in midair, bending down to kiss her there instead. It was a welcome change. He had been hitting her on the forehead—his so-called love taps—since she could remember. She believed that the slight indent between her eyes was possibly a direct result of Jeff's love.

"Girl, I'm glad you're here. I haven't talked to you in a while."

"Hey, I almost didn't make it. But when your mom told me that Charles had a private jet waiting; I grabbed my bags and hitched a ride.

I love you, girl, and…" Elizabeth grabbed her hand instead of finishing her statement.

She was still talking to Elizabeth while everyone else finished signing her cast when she looked at the screen and saw the news flash about a plane crash at the airport. She didn't really pay it any attention at first.

Then she let out an anguished scream, "Oh, my God! Oh, no, God, no!" Shelia lifted herself up and tried to get off the bed. She didn't know how she was going to do it or where she was going, but she had to go. She was hysterical.

Troy, who had been watching the television, too, reached for the volume switch.

"Once again, a private jet carrying recording artist Charles Avery and several members of his entourage has reportedly crashed during a scheduled take off from the Ronald Reagan Washington International Airport located just south of Washington, D.C. The crash occurred about two hours ago, and as you can see, rescue personnel are still on the scene. No word as to the extent of injuries to the passengers and crew. The singer/songwriter was apparently in the city visiting his girl-friend, Shelia Daniels of Chicago, Illinois, Mr. Avery's hometown. We've just learned that Ms. Daniels is a patient at Howard University Hospital due to injuries sustained in a car accident just yesterday. There is no information on the extent of Ms. Daniels' injuries. Please stay tuned for further details on this breaking story."

The room erupted. Sylvia and Edward tried to calm down Shelia, who was still screaming and trying to get out of bed. Brenda had fainted. Troy and John Sr. were trying to get her up and awake. Jeff was dealing tissue out of a box and helping his wife, while her sisters were being helped by their husbands.

Once his mother was revived, Troy turned his attention to Shelia, who was still hysterical.

"Shelia, listen to me. Listen to me. Is there a hospital closer to the airport?"

"No. I don't know. I have to get up. Troy, help me," she pleaded, tears running down her face. "Charles needs me." When he tried to hold her down, she fought harder. It took Troy and Jeff to keep her still while her father went to summon the doctor.

"Nathan, if you can, please give her something very mild." Troy pulled Dr. Adams into the hallway and explained what was going on.

"Oh, Troy, I should have known by the last name that there could be some relation. I'm sorry, man. Your brother was taken to St. Elizabeth's Hospital and then transported here because his injuries are so extensive. He was brought into emergency a little over an hour ago. He's in surgery right now."

"Do you know what his condition is?"

"Well, between you and me, he's in very serious condition." They walked over to the nurses' station for more privacy. "His collarbone and left arm are broken. They operated to remove his spleen, which had ruptured. He has a couple of broken ribs, and a head injury. On top of that, he has some deep cuts and punctures caused by debris from the plane. As you know, none of the injuries are life-threatening alone, but compounded, the healing process can be very slow. He was unconscious when they brought him in, but he should be out of surgery shortly."

"Can you do something for me?"

"Say no more. I'll speak to the chief of staff and see about you going in once he's in recovery. Oh, and someone named Everett called and left a message for someone in the family to get in contact with him. The number is over at the nurses' station. I told him I would have someone call him as soon as possible."

"Thanks, Nathan. I owe you."

Jeff was still holding a surprisingly strong Shelia in place when Troy walked back into the room. He sat down on the bed beside her and filled her IV with the medicine that Nathan had given him. Slowly, the medicine took effect, and her brother let her fall back onto the bed. Troy waited until he had the full attention of everyone in the room.

"Okay, here's what we got," Troy began. "Charles was brought into this hospital almost an hour and a half ago. He's in surgery, but he should be out soon. They'll take him to recovery for another hour. When he came in, he was unconscious."

He looked around the room at his parents and decided to get it over with. His wife was trying to help his mother and father. Elizabeth and Tia was standing with Mr. and Mrs. Daniels, and Jeff was trying to console Shelia.

"He was beat up pretty bad." Troy focused on Shelia and plowed ahead. "He has a broken collarbone and arm, a couple of broken ribs, head trauma, and some deep cuts and punctures. I won't know where until I see him. They are operating to remove his spleen, which was ruptured." Shelia began to shake, but he pressed on. "It's really not that bad. Right now, the most serious thing is that he hadn't regained consciousness before they operated. Shelia, listen, don't you fall apart on us now. Charles needs you to be strong more than anything. Remember your studies. You know these wounds aren't life-threatening."

Turning to the others, he said, "We all need to keep it together for Charles' sake. As soon as I see him, I'll come back to let you know something." Troy kissed Shelia on the cheek and handed her tissues to Elizabeth. He walked over to his mother and kissed her forehead. Then he left the room and slowly took the long walk to the men's bathroom at the far end of the hall.

His wife followed him. Stephanie knew her husband very well. He would put up a strong front because his profession required it, and his family needed him to, but his love for his younger brother and his need to worry unobserved would soon come to the surface. When she found him, it broke her heart.

Troy was hovering over the bathroom sink, his head down, his arms braced against the sides of the wall mirror. He was tense and struggling hard to get control of his feelings. But Stephanie knew that when the pain and stress got to be too much, you had to release it in order to function. She had been dealing with Troy's pains for a long time now. So, she gave him the release he needed.

Stephanie put her arms around him and pulled him close. She talked to him and consoled him until all of his frustrations and feelings of helplessness poured onto her shoulder as he held her and cried. He cried like a man, a proud man, hard and long. And when he got himself together, she looked into the face of the man she had fallen in love with so many years ago. He was a strong man, always ready to shoulder his family's burdens and hardships. He was a man filled with love. And she still loved him as much as she had at the beginning of their relationship for those same reasons. Afterwards, Stephanie rejoined the family to wait for word from her husband that Charles would be okay.

CHAPTER 19

It was taking far too long for Troy to return, and Shelia's anxiety was growing with every passing second. She had already bitten off the last of her short nails, much to her mother's dismay. She was now twisting the edge of her bed sheet.

Shelia had to keep herself focused on something, for she feared she would leap out of bed and make a run for the door. It wouldn't do her any good; she knew that, but she felt she would soon have no choice but to risk it. If word didn't come soon, her next stop would be the mental ward. She was going crazy just sitting there while her husband was suffering.

They learned from news reports that the plane had hit a patch of ice on the runway during takeoff. A damn ice patch—an ice patch that should not have been there. Two of the people in the plane had been killed. Pictures of Jacob and Thomas, who she knew to be Charles' stylist, flashed onto the screen.

Shelia's already fragile disposition weakened when she saw pictures of the two men whom she had just befriended a couple days earlier. Thomas had a daughter that he was sending to private school. And Jacob supported his elderly mother. She felt sorrowful for their family's loss. Steamed with anger, Shelia imagined the biggest lawsuit ever filed against the airport. Now there were two potential lawsuits, because she was definitely suing the fool who had caused her to lose her baby. Anticipating revenge, she was able to get through a few worry-free minutes. But then the anxiety re-emerged.

She was barely holding on to her last semblance of composure when the door to her room opened and Troy walked in. She sensed that the smile on his face was for the family's benefit only. The doctor in him was struggling with the man. It could be seen on his face.

All eyes turned on Troy, who stood at the foot of the bed. Looking at his parents and Shelia, he took a long breath. "Well, Charles is in recovery. The operation went well. They have removed his spleen and have stopped the internal bleeding. That had been a big concern. He's resting comfortably, but he hasn't regained consciousness. They don't think he's in a coma." His mother gasped. "We're just waiting for him to come out of the anesthesia, Momma. Don't worry. Charles will be all right. He's strong."

He spoke haltingly, so his alert wife went directly to his side. Troy put an arm around her and kept going, "I would suggest that you all go to the hotel and get some rest, but I already know you won't. Maybe after he comes to, we'll head out for a little while. In the meantime, Nathan says they will find a way to make everyone as comfortable as possible in here."

"Shelia, how are you feeling?" a nurse was asking. "Would you like a little more medicine for the pain?"

"No, thank you, I don't want anything." Her leg was killing her, but the painkiller might make her drowsier than she already was. For the last three hours, she had been fighting a losing battle with fatigue. "Where is everybody?" she asked, panicking. "Where did they go?"

The nurse put a hand on Shelia's shoulder, gently pushing her back against the pillow. "It's all right. They just went to the cafeteria to get something to eat. Your food is right here. Would you like to eat now?"

Shelia was about to decline, but her stomach rumbled in protest. As she picked at her food and waited for the families to return, Shelia idly switched from one television station to another. Several stations were still showing shots of the crash scene. However, one station was showing Charles in a different light—leaving or entering several entertainment events. There was pictures from the award show she attended with him. A flood of memories from that weekend came into focus. She didn't recognize the other events. Her demanding school schedule made it difficult for her to attend them with him.

She smiled to herself, recalling their conversation before one event. When Shelia couldn't accompany him, his agent, Everett, had been adamant about Charles showing up with a beauty on his arm. Charles had called to get her permission. It was so cute. He had sounded like a little boy afraid to ask for a cookie right before dinnertime. Shelia had told him that she trusted his judgment. She laughed hard when she saw him on TV entering the event with his cousin Emily, Chauncey's youngest sister, on his arm. He then set a pattern of taking only female relatives to these events— either one of his cousins or his sister Devin.

But her smile soon soured, and tears once again came to the surface. She silently thanked the Lord for not taking Charles away from her, vowing that she wouldn't take this second chance lightly.

She felt that she had always planned to make Charles hers. Why else would she have waited so long for him? When she discovered that her feelings for him were reciprocated, she jumped at the opportunity to develop a relationship. She had taken it for granted that he would be there when she needed him and when she didn't.

They had gone into this relationship not fully appreciating what they had. They loved each other completely, but they had never given thanks for that love. They had never looked at the spiritual side of it, had never dealt with it on a higher level. It was just something that was there. Now she could see that love by itself did not necessarily guarantee forever. They had to start truly cherishing their love and their time together.

As she drifted off again, a nurse came into the room to give Shelia more medicine. No, she wanted to say, but the words wouldn't come. The medicine took instant effect and she descended into a peaceful darkness.

Low voices bought Shelia to consciousness. Her eyes half open, she listened to them.

"Finally," Tia said, hugging her husband, Jeff. Everybody was hugging somebody.

"So, when can we see our son?" John Sr. asked, looking Dr. Adams straight in the eye, almost daring the man to make him wait a minute longer.

"Soon, Mr. Avery, but before you do, let me make it clear to you all that Charles is not fully awake. He's still struggling to get his bearings. I only want two people in the room at a time, and each visit cannot last more than two or three minutes. He still needs plenty of rest. Troy, because of your medical status, you will be able to visit as often as you like to keep your family abreast of his condition."

Nathan slowly looked around the room. "Two other things. First, I have a room full of reporters awaiting word on Charles' condition."

"His agent, Everett Sampson, is on his way," Troy spoke up. "He just called again to say he's having a hard time getting here. With the airport closed down, he had to take a train. Needless to say, that's not going so well either."

"That's not really the problem. It's customary for the next of kin to give approval for such a news conference when the patient is indisposed. In this case, that would normally be the parents, Mr. and Mrs. Avery." He took a deep breath. "However, for the past half hour, Charles has been asking very specifically for his wife."

"What?!" A few people in the room cried out in unison. Jaws dropped.

Troy stepped forward. "Nathan, you've got to be kidding. My brother isn't married."

"All I know, Troy, is that he's been asking for his wife. I heard him myself. 'My wife…my wife…I need her.' "

"That's impossible. He's been going with Shelia for the last eight or nine months."

"Maybe it's something he didn't tell you about," Dr. Adams suggested.

They all looked at each other, dumbfounded.

"Married to who? Maybe it's that super-model woman?" Edward suggested.

Tia refused to believe it, "Charles would have told us, even if they were divorcing, or if it had been a mistake. He would have told us." Everybody agreed with her.

"My God," Brenda began. "If he's married and he didn't tell us, it must have been very important—the reason that he wouldn't or couldn't tell us." She looked over at the bed. "And what about poor Shelia? We can't let her find out this way."

Elizabeth was standing by her friend's side and saw the muscles in Shelia's face twitching. Shelia must have heard what was said and was fighting against it. The idea of Charles being married had left them all befuddled. Imagine what her baby was going through.

Shelia had heard what they were saying, and she was fighting, fighting like the devil against this crazy medicine they had given her. If only she could wake up and tell them. In her mind, she was screaming, *It's me...it's me. I'm Charles' wife. Charles needs me. Oh, God, please help me. Please.* She prayed and prayed that she would regain consciousness. It was a nightmare.

As Charles' mother and father followed Nathan and Troy out of the room, Sylvia moved to the other side of the bed and wiped her sedated daughter's tears. Her heart kept sinking further and further. All of her life Shelia had wanted this man. Now she would have to deal with yet another crisis—another woman.

Two by two, they took turns visiting Charles. They were not prepared for what they saw. Tia was so shocked, she left the room immediately. The nurse kept assuring them that he looked a lot worse than he actually was. But her words didn't help any.

A cast covered the upper left half of his body and arm, with his arm set apart from his torso by a thick metal rod. His bed was raised at the top to help him rest better. Bandages were wrapped tightly around his midsection. The bandages and tape were fairly easy to look at, but his family had a hard time looking at areas that couldn't be easily covered. Charles had deep purple and blue bruises all over his body. It was too easy to imagine how he must have been tossed around during the crash. The cuts had been cleaned, but they were very visible. Several deeper wounds had been sewn and covered with tape. He looked as if he was in terrible pain.

Mr. and Mrs. Avery went in to see their son again after everyone else had gone. Brenda sat down and talked to him. He moaned a little but didn't seem to hear her. She heard him call for his wife, but not by name. If only he would wake and talk to them. That was all she really wanted. It didn't matter to her if he was married or not, or if he had kept it from them or not. She just wanted her baby to wake up.

Everyone rejoined Elizabeth back in Shelia's room. When she came to again, they were in the middle of a prayer, so she stayed quiet. They weren't acting as if anything terrible had happened to Charles, so she didn't worry. After they finished, she turned to her mother.

"Have you heard anything about Charles?"

Surprised that she was awake and not knowing exactly what to say to her, Sylvia, for once, stumbled over her words.

"Shelia, dear…you, you, should just relax."

Now, she was worried. The look on her mother's face told her to worry.

"What's wrong?" Trying to sit up, she asked again, "Mom, what is it? Jeff, help me."

He was right by her side, "Calm down, squirt. I'll raise the head of the bed for you."

She grabbed his hand tightly. "Tell me, Jeff." Looking into his eyes, she pleaded, "Tell me."

"Okay, listen, promise to stay calm."

"Okay…okay…what?"

"Charles hasn't come all the way to yet. He's been mumbling in his sleep a lot. Shelia, he keeps asking for his wife."

Shelia inhaled in stunned relief. She was so choked up and happy that he was asking for her she could barely control of herself.

"Shelia, are you all right? Did you know he was married?" Jeff was trying to console her. Their parents' gathered around the bed as Elizabeth moved away to let them closer and watched silently as she broke down. Or what they thought was her breaking down.

Shelia pushed the sheet away from her body and asked Troy to get her a wheelchair.

"Um…Shelia, I know you must be upset, but now is not the time," stopping when he saw the determination in her face.

"Troy, go get me a wheelchair, or I will hop down to Charles' room. He needs me."

Seeing that she was serious, he called to a nurse from the doorway.

They looked at her as if she was crazy. But she wasn't crazy; she was determined, determined to get to her husband. If he was asking for her, then he was fighting to come to her. And she was going to be there when he came back.

When the wheelchair was pushed into the room, she was already halfway off the bed. She would have fallen if Jeff hadn't been there to grab her.

"Easy, squirt," he said, placing her back on the bed.

"Thanks, Jeff." She lifted a hand to his cheek.

"You're welcome, but Shelia…" He stopped thinking the same thing everyone else was probably thinking; she must be in denial. "Did you hear me? Charles keeps asking for his wife."

"I heard you." A big smile on her face, she said, "He's asking for me. I'm Charles' wife." The gasps were long but short-lived. Actually, she heard some relieved laughter and saw smiles on Elizabeth and Tia's faces. "Open that drawer, please, and hand me my rings." Jeff hesitated a bit, but did as she asked.

"Shelia," her Dad began, but she wouldn't let him finish. She held up a hand to silence him. She had to get if off her chest and make them understand. Shelia refused to go another minute with the lies still hanging over her head. Charles needed her.

"Mom, Dad, I know you wanted me to wait, and I'm sure you're disappointed in me." Shelia looked her parents in the face. She had already decided that it was past time for the truth. She should have never kept her marriage a secret. It saddened her to think he had almost died without anyone knowing about them. "I'm sorry if I hurt you, but I had to do what was right for me, and at the time marrying Charles was right. It's still right, and I won't apologize for it."

She reached a hand out her mother. "Please, don't cry, Mom. Charles wanted to tell you, all of you. He wanted to ask Daddy for my hand, but I stopped him. Dad, I knew you would have one of your fits, and I didn't want to deal with it. Even after Charles told me that you and he talked during Christmas break, I couldn't tell you. I guess I was too scared."

Turning to his family, she said, "If you're going to be mad at anybody, be mad at me. He only stayed quiet because I asked him to. I made him promise not to tell even Troy because, no offense, Troy, but you would have told Stephanie, and so on, and so forth."

"But, Shelia, how, where?" Her mother was happy, but shocked. Shelia had never been impulsive about anything. She went after what she wanted, but she always had a plan.

"We were married the same week I returned to school. That Wednesday afternoon, Charles came to Washington and picked me up in a limousine. Oh, it was so romantic. We rode to Elkton, got married, and drove back." She told them about the airplane banner and the roses. She looked at her rings. "I love him so much. I could have lost him today, and no one would have known that we were married. He only kept this a secret because I asked him to. I feel so awful."

The room was quiet for a long while. Then Jeff spoke up, "I knew it. I knew something was up. So when that story broke about him kissing a married woman at the airport in California, it was true? I knew it was you in the picture, but I thought they had painted the ring on or something."

"No, it was true. Charles didn't want me to take off my rings except when I was around the family. We didn't think that someone would be at the airport taking snapshots. We were going to come clean then if we had to, but nobody asked any questions, so we just kept quiet. Anyway—time is a-wasting. Troy, take me to Charles, please."

Nathan was standing in the doorway. Before he could say anything, Shelia started in on him as well. "I don't want to hear it, Dr. Adams. I'm not getting back in that bed until I see Charles. So, whatever you have to say, just save your breath." She was still very sore and more than a little under the influence of her drugs, but Shelia knew what she was saying and was completely motivated to see her husband.

"Touchy. Actually, that's not why I'm here. Although I do wish you would calm down and take it easy. Now that our little mystery is cleared up, I need your permission to release information on Charles' condition. And Mr. Sampson is on the phone; he is in the city and will be here within the hour. He wants to speak to you, Troy."

"Oh, well, I guess his fans should know that he is alive and getting better, right?" She glanced at her in-laws, who nodded their approval. "Okay, as soon as Everett gets here, you can release the information, but I want Troy there to show that the family is present, and I also want him to answer any personal questions that might pop up." She took his hand, "Is that okay with you, Troy?"

"Of course, Sheila." He kissed her cheek. "Whatever you say."

"Good. Now, take me to my husband. It's time to wake him up. He's been asleep long enough."

He felt her presence as soon as they wheeled her into the room. Charles had been floating in a comfortable gray haze. Once or twice, his mother's voice had made him try to pull himself to the surface, but the pain was too excruciating. Slowly, he would move away from the pain and return to the gloomy depths of unconsciousness.

This was much different; Shelia needed him. He could feel her grief and sadness. She needed him. Charles fought his way to the surface. He struggled with the pain until he felt a warmth slowly move through his body. It started in his hands, flowed across his chest, then spread throughout his limbs.

Shelia was tired; her energy had quickly dissipated after the earlier excitement. It seemed as if she had been in his room for days instead of only a few hours.

The doctors and nurses had tried to convince her to go back to her room to rest, but she wouldn't hear of it. So, they tried to make her as comfortable as possible in his room. The wheelchair was replaced by a full-back lounge recliner that electrically lifted off the ground like a barber's chair so that she was more parallel with Charles. She didn't have to lean over to hold his hand. All she had to do was lie back and keep still. They brought her pillows to prop her leg on. She was actually more at peace like this than she had been in her own room. And it was all because she was with her husband.

News traveled fast around the hospital, and soon, many of the hospital staffers, as well as patients, were sending messages of hope and encouragement to the room.

The families kept vigil in the waiting room. Everyone agreed to let Shelia stay in the room with Charles alone for as long as possible, then they would again start taking turns going in. When he did wake up, she would be the first person he would want to see.

Shelia was dozing when she felt the muscles contract around her hand. Startled, she opened her eyes and sat up. He was looking at her. Those beautiful hazel eyes that she was afraid she might never see again were staring at her.

"Hey…" Charles managed to squeeze out huskily.

"Hey, yourself." Her tears flowed freely. "Don't try to talk. Let me call the doctors," she said, already pressing the call button. "I love you, Charles," she said through a wet smile.

EPILOGUE

Shelia and Charles were having their first year anniversary party at their newly finished home in the grove. A house full of guests was there to help them celebrate. Besides their combined large families, there were actors and singers, models and agents, club owners and school-teachers, nurses and waitresses—all friends of theirs, old and new.

"Liz, I thank you so much for helping me get all of this organized. I couldn't have done it without you."

"Yes, you could have. But I'm glad I could help. It was fun. This house is absolutely beautiful. Charles knows you so well. It was designed with you in mind. You can just tell."

Shelia smiled, "Well, in a couple of months, we'll be at your wedding. I can't wait to be your matron of honor. Greg looks happy; he has barely let you out of his sight since he got here."

"Will you still be able to fit in your dress in a couple of months?" Liz looked at her curiously, taking in the glow of her skin and the sparkle in her eye. "You haven't told him yet, have you?"

"How did you know?" she asked. "What are you, psychic or something?" She had only found out herself last week.

"I can tell by looking at you. You are glowing, Shelia. It's truly breathtaking to see."

"Thank you. I'm going to tell him as his anniversary gift. It's the only thing that I could give him that he doesn't already have." Just then a waiter rang the bell and announced that dinner was served.

Their guests filed into the lavish ballroom—decorated in royal blue, silver, and white—and found their place names on the table. A large dance floor was in the center of the room. There would be dancing and partying later. They dined on chicken and pork roast with mixed vegetables and salad. Toasts were made with bottles of champagne as everyone cheered the happy couple.

Troy rose and emotionally toasted to his brother and sister-in-law. He nearly broke down when he talked briefly about the accident, the memory of which was still very painful for him. He did break down when Charles got up and hugged his big brother, thanking him for his love and support over the years.

After dinner, Charles rose to unveil his wife's anniversary present. Going to the ceiling-to-floor windows that opened to the backyard, he flicked on the floodlights outside, and there stood a brand-new, fully loaded silver Mercedes 325si sedan wrapped in royal blue, white, and silver ribbons.

Her hand covering her mouth, Shelia moved closer for a better look. She loved it. Then it dawned on her why Charles had been pressuring her for months to get rid of her faithful Ford Escort. She had resisted the idea.

"I guess I don't need Betty Ann anymore."

"That's what I've been trying to tell you," he replied, returning her thank-you kiss.

"Charles, I love it, but it's too much."

"Shelia, do you have to be so stubborn? Why can't you just enjoy it?"

"It's too much."

"Just enjoy it," he said firmly, pushing the keys into her hands and kissing her to loud applause.

"It is lovely. Now, it's your turn," she said, mischief in her eyes.

"Okay."

"I had a really hard time trying to figure out what to get you. I wanted it to be something that you couldn't get yourself with just a snap of your fingers. So, I searched high and low, racking my brain for just the right thing. And I think I got the perfect gift."

Charles opened the small rectangular box Shelia handed him. One eyebrow raised, he began reading the attached card aloud:

ONE OF THESE DAYS

Our love has blossomed over the years; You fill my heart with hope and cheers
Promise me more years of love; don't falter
And pray for...
(Open gift)
Doing as directed, Charles pulled out a silver baby rattle. The tag read 'a son or daughter'. He dropped it, stunned. Everyone jumped up and cheered as he pulled Shelia into his arms.

"Oh, baby, for real? I love you," he said, kissing her in gratitude.

"I love you, too." Their guests were all but forgotten as she fell in love with her husband all over again. She knew she would.

ABOUT THE AUTHOR

Michele Sudler lives in the small, East Coast town of Smyrna, Delaware. Busy raising her three children, Gregory, Takira, and Kanika Lambert, she finds time for her second passion, writing, in the evenings and on week-ends. After attending Delaware State College, majoring in Business Administration, she began and continues to work in the corporate banking industry.

One of These Days is her second novel. Her first, *Intentional Mistakes*, was released by Genesis Press in April 2005. She is currently working on her next novel in the Avery family tree.

Besides spending time with her children and writing, Michele enjoys playing and watching basketball, traveling, and reading.

ONE OF THESE DAYS

2007 Publication Schedule

January

Corporate Seduction
A.C. Arthur
ISBN-13: 978-1-58571-238-0
ISBN-10: 1-58571-238-8
$9.95

A Taste of Temptation
Reneé Alexis
ISBN-13: 978-1-58571-207-6
ISBN-10: 1-58571-207-8
$9.95

February

The Perfect Frame
Beverly Clark
ISBN-13: 978-1-58571-240-3
ISBN-10: 1-58571-240-X
$9.95

Ebony Angel
Deatri King-Bey
ISBN-13: 978-1-58571-239-7
ISBN-10: 1-58571-239-6
$9.95

March

Sweet Sensations
Gwendolyn Bolton
ISBN-13: 978-1-58571-206-9
ISBN-10: 1-58571-206-X
$9.95

Crush
Crystal Hubbard
ISBN-13: 978-1-58571-243-4
ISBN-10: 1-58571-243-4
$9.95

April

Secret Thunder
Annetta P. Lee
ISBN-13: 978-1-58571-204-5
ISBN-10: 1-58571-204-3
$9.95

Blood Seduction
J.M. Jeffries
ISBN-13: 978-1-58571-237-3
ISBN-10: 1-58571-237-X
$9.95

May

Lies Too Long
Pamela Ridley
ISBN-13: 978-1-58571-246-5
ISBN-10: 1-58571-246-9
$13.95

Two Sides to Every Story
Dyanne Davis
ISBN-13: 978-1-58571-248-9
ISBN-10: 1-58571-248-5
$9.95

June

One of These Days
Michele Sudler
ISBN-13: 978-1-58571-249-6
ISBN-10: 1-58571-249-3
$9.95

Who's That Lady
Andrea Jackson
ISBN-13: 978-1-58571-190-1
ISBN-10: 1-58571-190-X
$9.95

2007 Publication Schedule (continued)

July

Heart of the Phoenix
A.C. Arthur
ISBN-13: 978-1-58571-242-7
ISBN-10: 1-58571-242-6
$9.95

Do Over
Jaci Kenney
ISBN-13: 978-1-58571-241-0
ISBN-10: 1-58571-241-8
$9.95

It's Not Over Yet
J.J. Michael
ISBN-13: 978-1-58571-245-8
ISBN-10: 1-58571-245-0
$9.95

August

The Fires Within
Beverly Clark
ISBN-13: 978-1-58571-244-1
ISBN-10: 1-58571-244-2
$9.95

Stolen Kisses
Dominiqua Douglas
ISBN-13: 978-1-58571-247-2
ISBN-10: 1-58571-247-7
$9.95

September

Small Whispers
Annetta P. Lee
ISBN-13: 978-158571-251-9
ISBN-10: 1-58571-251-5
$6.99

Always You
Crystal Hubbard
ISBN-13: 978-158571-252-6
ISBN-10: 1-58571-252-3
$6.99

October

Not His Type
Chamein Canton
ISBN-13: 978-158571 253 3
ISBN-10: 1-58571-253-1
$6.99

Many Shades of Gray
Dyanne Davis
ISBN-13: 978-158571-254-0
ISBN-10: 1-58571-254-X
$6.99

November

When I'm With You
LaConnie Taylor-Jones
ISBN-13: 978-158571-250-2
ISBN-10: 1-58571-250-7
$6.99

The Mission
Pamela Leigh Starr
ISBN-13: 978-158571-255-7
ISBN-10: 1-58571-255-8
$6.99

December

One in A Million
Barbara Keaton
ISBN-13: 978-158571-257-1
ISBN-10: 1-58571-257-4
$6.99

The Foursome
Celya Bowers
ISBN-13: 978-158571-256-4
ISBN-10: 1-58571-256-6
$6.99

Other Genesis Press, Inc. Titles

A Dangerous Deception	J.M. Jeffries	$8.95
A Dangerous Love	J.M. Jeffries	$8.95
A Dangerous Obsession	J.M. Jeffries	$8.95
A Dangerous Woman	J.M. Jeffries	$9.95
A Dead Man Speaks	Lisa Jones Johnson	$12.95
A Drummer's Beat to Mend	Kei Swanson	$9.95
A Happy Life	Charlotte Harris	$9.95
A Heart's Awakening	Veronica Parker	$9.95
A Lark on the Wing	Phyliss Hamilton	$9.95
A Love of Her Own	Cheris F. Hodges	$9.95
A Love to Cherish	Beverly Clark	$8.95
A Lover's Legacy	Veronica Parker	$9.95
A Pefect Place to Pray	I.L. Goodwin	$12.95
A Risk of Rain	Dar Tomlinson	$8.95
A Twist of Fate	Beverly Clark	$8.95
A Will to Love	Angie Daniels	$9.95
Acquisitions	Kimberley White	$8.95
Across	Carol Payne	$12.95
After the Vows	Leslie Esdaile	$10.95
(Summer Anthology)	T.T. Henderson	
	Jacqueline Thomas	
Again My Love	Kayla Perrin	$10.95
Against the Wind	Gwynne Forster	$8.95
All I Ask	Barbara Keaton	$8.95
Ambrosia	T.T. Henderson	$8.95
An Unfinished Love Affair	Barbara Keaton	$8.95
And Then Came You	Dorothy Elizabeth Love	$8.95
Angel's Paradise	Janice Angelique	$9.95
At Last	Lisa G. Riley	$8.95
Best of Friends	Natalie Dunbar	$8.95
Between Tears	Pamela Ridley	$12.95
Beyond the Rapture	Beverly Clark	$9.95
Blaze	Barbara Keaton	$9.95

Other Genesis Press, Inc. Titles (continued)

Blood Lust	J. M. Jeffries	$9.95
Bodyguard	Andrea Jackson	$9.95
Boss of Me	Diana Nyad	$8.95
Bound by Love	Beverly Clark	$8.95
Breeze	Robin Hampton Allen	$10.95
Broken	Dar Tomlinson	$24.95
The Business of Love	Cheris Hodges	$9.95
By Design	Barbara Keaton	$8.95
Cajun Heat	Charlene Berry	$8.95
Careless Whispers	Rochelle Alers	$8.95
Cats & Other Tales	Marilyn Wagner	$8.95
Caught in a Trap	Andre Michelle	$8.95
Caught Up In the Rapture	Lisa G. Riley	$9.95
Cautious Heart	Cheris F Hodges	$8.95
Caught Up	Deatri King Bey	$12.95
Chances	Pamela Leigh Starr	$8.95
Cherish the Flame	Beverly Clark	$8.95
Class Reunion	Irma Jenkins/John Brown	$12.95
Code Name: Diva	J.M. Jeffries	$9.95
Conquering Dr. Wexler's Heart	Kimberley White	$9.95
Cricket's Serenade	Carolita Blythe	$12.95
Crossing Paths, Tempting Memories	Dorothy Elizabeth Love	$9.95
Cupid	Barbara Keaton	$9.95
Cypress Whisperings	Phyllis Hamilton	$8.95
Dark Embrace	Crystal Wilson Harris	$8.95
Dark Storm Rising	Chinelu Moore	$10.95
Daughter of the Wind	Joan Xian	$8.95
Deadly Sacrifice	Jack Kean	$22.95
Designer Passion	Dar Tomlinson	$8.95
Dreamtective	Liz Swados	$5.95
Ebony Butterfly II	Delilah Dawson	$14.95
Ebony Eyes	Kei Swanson	$9.95

ONE OF THESE DAYS

Other Genesis Press, Inc. Titles (continued)

Echoes of Yesterday	Beverly Clark	$9.95
Eden's Garden	Elizabeth Rose	$8.95
Enchanted Desire	Wanda Y. Thomas	$9.95
Everlastin' Love	Gay G. Gunn	$8.95
Everlasting Moments	Dorothy Elizabeth Love	$8.95
Everything and More	Sinclair Lebeau	$8.95
Everything but Love	Natalie Dunbar	$8.95
Eve's Prescription	Edwina Martin Arnold	$8.95
Falling	Natalie Dunbar	$9.95
Fate	Pamela Leigh Starr	$8.95
Finding Isabella	A.J. Garrotto	$8.95
Forbidden Quest	Dar Tomlinson	$10.95
Forever Love	Wanda Thomas	$8.95
From the Ashes	Kathleen Suzanne	$8.95
	Jeanne Sumerix	
Gentle Yearning	Rochelle Alers	$10.95
Glory of Love	Sinclair LeBeau	$10.95
Go Gentle into that Good Night	Malcom Boyd	$12.95
Goldengroove	Mary Beth Craft	$16.95
Groove, Bang, and Jive	Steve Cannon	$8.99
Hand in Glove	Andrea Jackson	$9.95
Hard to Love	Kimberley White	$9.95
Hart & Soul	Angie Daniels	$8.95
Havana Sunrise	Kymberly Hunt	$9.95
Heartbeat	Stephanie Bedwell-Grime	$8.95
Hearts Remember	M. Loui Quezada	$8.95
Hidden Memories	Robin Allen	$10.95
Higher Ground	Leah Latimer	$19.95
Hitler, the War, and the Pope	Ronald Rychiak	$26.95
How to Write a Romance	Kathryn Falk	$18.95
I Married a Reclining Chair	Lisa M. Fuhs	$8.95
I'm Gonna Make You Love Me	Gwyneth Bolton	$9.95
Indigo After Dark Vol. I	Nia Dixon/Angelique	$10.95

Other Genesis Press, Inc. Titles (continued)

Indigo After Dark Vol. II	Dolores Bundy/Cole Riley	$10.95
Indigo After Dark Vol. III	Montana Blue/Coco Morena	$10.95
Indigo After Dark Vol. IV	Cassandra Colt/	$14.95
	Diana Richeaux	
Indigo After Dark Vol. V	Delilah Dawson	$14.95
Icie	Pamela Leigh Starr	$8.95
I'll Be Your Shelter	Giselle Carmichael	$8.95
I'll Paint a Sun	A.J. Garrotto	$9.95
Illusions	Pamela Leigh Starr	$8.95
Indiscretions	Donna Hill	$8.95
Intentional Mistakes	Michele Sudler	$9.95
Interlude	Donna Hill	$8.95
Intimate Intentions	Angie Daniels	$8.95
Ironic	Pamela Leigh Starr	$9.95
Jolie's Surrender	Edwina Martin-Arnold	$8.95
Kiss or Keep	Debra Phillips	$8.95
Lace	Giselle Carmichael	$9.95
Last Train to Memphis	Elsa Cook	$12.95
Lasting Valor	Ken Olsen	$24.95
Let's Get It On	Dyanne Davis	$9.95
Let Us Prey	Hunter Lundy	$25.95
Life Is Never As It Seems	J.J. Michael	$12.95
Lighter Shade of Brown	Vicki Andrews	$8.95
Love Always	Mildred E. Riley	$10.95
Love Doesn't Come Easy	Charlyne Dickerson	$8.95
Love in High Gear	Charlotte Roy	$9.95
Love Lasts Forever	Dominiqua Douglas	$9.95
Love Me Carefully	A.C. Arthur	$9.95
Love Unveiled	Gloria Greene	$10.95
Love's Deception	Charlene Berry	$10.95
Love's Destiny	M. Loui Quezada	$8.95
Mae's Promise	Melody Walcott	$8.95
Magnolia Sunset	Giselle Carmichael	$8.95

Other Genesis Press, Inc. Titles (continued)

Matters of Life and Death	Lesego Malepe, Ph.D.	$15.95
Meant to Be	Jeanne Sumerix	$8.95
Midnight Clear	Leslie Esdaile	$10.95
(Anthology)	Gwynne Forster	
	Carmen Green	
	Monica Jackson	
Midnight Magic	Gwynne Forster	$8.95
Midnight Peril	Vicki Andrews	$10.95
Misconceptions	Pamela Leigh Starr	$9.95
Misty Blue	Dyanne Davis	$9.95
Montgomery's Children	Richard Perry	$14.95
My Buffalo Soldier	Barbara B. K. Reeves	$8.95
Naked Soul	Gwynne Forster	$8.95
Next to Last Chance	Louisa Dixon	$24.95
Nights Over Egypt	Barbara Keaton	$9.95
No Apologies	Seressia Glass	$8.95
No Commitment Required	Seressia Glass	$8.95
No Ordinary Love	Angela Weaver	$9.95
No Regrets	Mildred E. Riley	$8.95
Notes When Summer Ends	Beverly Lauderdale	$12.95
Nowhere to Run	Gay G. Gunn	$10.95
O Bed! O Breakfast!	Rob Kuehnle	$14.95
Object of His Desire	A. C. Arthur	$8.95
Office Policy	A. C. Arthur	$9.95
Once in a Blue Moon	Dorianne Cole	$9.95
One Day at a Time	Bella McFarland	$8.95
Only You	Crystal Hubbard	$9.95
Outside Chance	Louisa Dixon	$24.95
Passion	T.T. Henderson	$10.95
Passion's Blood	Cherif Fortin	$22.95
Passion's Journey	Wanda Thomas	$8.95
Past Promises	Jahmel West	$8.95
Path of Fire	T.T. Henderson	$8.95

Other Genesis Press, Inc. Titles (continued)

Path of Thorns	Annetta P. Lee	$9.95
Peace Be Still	Colette Haywood	$12.95
Picture Perfect	Reon Carter	$8.95
Playing for Keeps	Stephanie Salinas	$8.95
Pride & Joi	Gay G. Gunn	$8.95
Promises to Keep	Alicia Wiggins	$8.95
Quiet Storm	Donna Hill	$10.95
Reckless Surrender	Rochelle Alers	$6.95
Red Polka Dot in a World of Plaid	Varian Johnson	$12.95
Rehoboth Road	Anita Ballard-Jones	$12.95
Reluctant Captive	Joyce Jackson	$8.95
Rendezvous with Fate	Jeanne Sumerix	$8.95
Revelations	Cheris F. Hodges	$8.95
Rise of the Phoenix	Kenneth Whetstone	$12.95
Rivers of the Soul	Leslie Esdaile	$8.95
Rock Star	Rosyln Hardy Holcomb	$9.95
Rocky Mountain Romance	Kathleen Suzanne	$8.95
Rooms of the Heart	Donna Hill	$8.95
Rough on Rats and Tough on Cats	Chris Parker	$12.95
Scent of Rain	Annetta P. Lee	$9.95
Second Chances at Love	Cheris Hodges	$9.95
Secret Library Vol. 1	Nina Sheridan	$18.95
Secret Library Vol. 2	Cassandra Colt	$8.95
Shades of Brown	Denise Becker	$8.95
Shades of Desire	Monica White	$8.95
Shadows in the Moonlight	Jeanne Sumerix	$8.95
Sin	Crystal Rhodes	$8.95
Sin and Surrender	J.M. Jeffries	$9.95
Sinful Intentions	Crystal Rhodes	$12.95
So Amazing	Sinclair LeBeau	$8.95
Somebody's Someone	Sinclair LeBeau	$8.95

Other Genesis Press, Inc. Titles (continued)

Someone to Love	Alicia Wiggins	$8.95
Song in the Park	Martin Brant	$15.95
Soul Eyes	Wayne L. Wilson	$12.95
Soul to Soul	Donna Hill	$8.95
Southern Comfort	J.M. Jeffries	$8.95
Still the Storm	Sharon Robinson	$8.95
Still Waters Run Deep	Leslie Esdaile	$8.95
Stories to Excite You	Anna Forrest/Divine	$14.95
Subtle Secrets	Wanda Y. Thomas	$8.95
Suddenly You	Crystal Hubbard	$9.95
Sweet Repercussions	Kimberley White	$9.95
Sweet Tomorrows	Kimberly White	$8.95
Taken by You	Dorothy Elizabeth Love	$9.95
Tattooed Tears	T. T. Henderson	$8.95
The Color Line	Lizzette Grayson Carter	$9.95
The Color of Trouble	Dyanne Davis	$8.95
The Disappearance of Allison Jones	Kayla Perrin	$5.95
The Honey Dipper's Legacy	Pannell-Allen	$14.95
The Joker's Love Tune	Sidney Rickman	$15.95
The Little Pretender	Barbara Cartland	$10.95
The Love We Had	Natalie Dunbar	$8.95
The Man Who Could Fly	Bob & Milana Beamon	$18.95
The Missing Link	Charlyne Dickerson	$8.95
The Price of Love	Sinclair LeBeau	$8.95
The Smoking Life	Ilene Barth	$29.95
The Words of the Pitcher	Kei Swanson	$8.95
Three Wishes	Seressia Glass	$8.95
Through the Fire	Seressia Glass	$9.95
Ties That Bind	Kathleen Suzanne	$8.95
Tiger Woods	Libby Hughes	$5.95
Time is of the Essence	Angie Daniels	$9.95
Timeless Devotion	Bella McFarland	$9.95
Tomorrow's Promise	Leslie Esdaile	$8.95

Truly Inseparable	Wanda Y. Thomas	$8.95
Unbreak My Heart	Dar Tomlinson	$8.95
Uncommon Prayer	Kenneth Swanson	$9.95
Unconditional	A.C. Arthur	$9.95
Unconditional Love	Alicia Wiggins	$8.95
Under the Cherry Moon	Christal Jordan-Mims	$12.95
Unearthing Passions	Elaine Sims	$9.95
Until Death Do Us Part	Susan Paul	$8.95
Vows of Passion	Bella McFarland	$9.95
Wedding Gown	Dyanne Davis	$8.95
What's Under Benjamin's Bed	Sandra Schaffer	$8.95
When Dreams Float	Dorothy Elizabeth Love	$8.95
Whispers in the Night	Dorothy Elizabeth Love	$8.95
Whispers in the Sand	LaFlorya Gauthier	$10.95
Wild Ravens	Altonya Washington	$9.95
Yesterday Is Gone	Beverly Clark	$10.95
Yesterday's Dreams, Tomorrow's Promises	Reon Laudat	$8.95
Your Precious Love	Sinclair LeBeau	$8.95

Order Form

Mail to: Genesis Press, Inc.
P.O. Box 101
Columbus, MS 39703

Name _____

Address _____

City/State _____ Zip _____

Telephone _____

Ship to (if different from above)

Name _____

Address _____

City/State _____ Zip _____

Telephone _____

Credit Card Information

Credit Card # _____ ☐ Visa ☐ Mastercard

Expiration Date (mm/yy) _____ ☐ AmEx ☐ Discover

Qty.	Author	Title	Price	Total

Use this order

form, or call

1-888-INDIGO-1

Total for books _____

Shipping and handling:
$5 first two books,
$1 each additional book _____

Total S & H _____

Total amount enclosed _____

Mississippi residents add 7% sales tax